I0735994

RONAN
SVESTI FATED MATES   BOOK 4
WAVY MARTIN

OTHER BOOKS BY
Wavy Martin

SVESTI FATED MATES SERIES
Vared

Devik

Ash'n

Table of Contents

Prologue

YES, REALLY THIS time. Now that the characters from previous books have released their stranglehold on my keyboard, I can get back to my outline and all of us can spend some time that's not on the space cruiser.

For those who've read the first three books in this series—*<fist pump> Yeah! You came back. <happy dance>*—consider this a refresher. You can skip this part if you want, but you know you won't. *Never know what'll come out of Wavy's keyboard. Gotta read on, just in case.*

For those who've just stumbled upon this book, I'll give you enough background without giving away any significant spoilers from the previous books. But you really should go read them. I'm not just saying that because I'm the author. *<cough> Bullshit. <cough>* Of course, I'm saying that because I'm the author. I love my characters, even when they make me want to smack them over the head with said keyboard. I want everyone else to love them, too.

Let's get to the prologue then. All dates mentioned are using Earth's calendar.

Unbeknownst to humans, since the early 1900s an alien warrior race called the Svesti have been guarding Earth's region of space, as well as others, from another warrior race called the Zuvgran. Not because they see great things in humans, but because the Zuvgran are that bad.

How bad, you wonder? Well, the Zuvgran like to invade worlds, kill the elderly and the very young and some of the males. Then they take the rest as slaves or subjects for their experiments. Ruled by an Emperor, they like to strip conquered worlds of all their natural resources and move on. They're not that picky, really. They'll attack anyone they feel is weaker, so ships or colonies are unsafe as well. The species as a whole just doesn't give anyone the warm fuzzies.

The Svesti home world, Costonia, is ruled by a King and a Council representing their twelve Houses. They worship a deity they refer to as the Goddess. For those wanting to know about the goodies, they have claws, fangs, and a tail. Oh, and nodes, three head nodes and one base node on their, shall we say, equipment. *Gotta love those nodes.* <sigh> They would look at home in gladiator pits with their toned bodies, tight black pants, and leather. *<fanning self> Seriously, just look at the book covers.* But their technology is much more advanced than anything on Earth.

The Svesti also call each other by their last names, unless they are family or close friends, who use first names. If there is more than one present of the same last name, they use titles as well. Titles are also used in formal situations or when the situation calls for additional respect or gravitas. Females are called by their first name preceded by Lady.

In the early 2000s, the Zuvgran released a virus on Costonia killing eighty percent of the Svesti females, including all female young, and rendering the remainder infertile. It's now 2037 and for thirty years, Svesti scientists have been searching for ways to keep their race from dying out. No other race has been biologically compatible, until—you guessed it—they discover human females.

Now like all large groups of beings, they're not all bad or all good, although as a whole, the Svesti check most of the boxes in the good column. *They can check my box any time. <wink> <wink>* The Svesti Council is divided. Some want to invade Earth and take whatever females they want, while others believe any young born of a Svesti-human couple would no longer be Svesti. *Racial purity, aisle two.* The current ruler, King Traxen Sovex, is much more level-headed and wants to open up negotiations with Earth to receive willing human females for breeding or troth contracts.

King Sovex sends Commander Vared Durek of the *Invictus*, a space cruiser holding 3,000 warriors, to Earth to initiate first contact. Durek's long-time best friends serve on the *Invictus* as well—Lieutenant Karid Wurvez, head tactical officer; Lieutenant Devik Tolvex, head security officer; and Healer Ash'n Rivezt, head healer. The *Invictus* gathers information about Earth, copies their internet to their own computers, and hacks into the various genealogical databases. It seems humans with a particular DNA strand have the ability to interact and learn some of the Svesti technology faster.

After their research of Earth, Durek initiates first contact with six countries based on the size of their territory or influence. It should be no big surprise to any of us that humans still haven't figured out how to become one planetary entity. Each country convinces, or orders, one woman to take the two-month trip to Costonia, live there and gather information for fourteen months, then return to Earth. Of course being human, Earth's leaders are especially interested in Svesti military capabilities, weaponry, and technology.

Unbeknownst to the six women, Earth's leaders allow the Svesti to believe the women have volunteered to be part of a Choosing at the King's Court, where they are to choose a male for a breeding or troth contract. Needless to say, when this information becomes known to the women, they don't take it well. *Can you say seriously pissed off women?*

A troth contract is similar to a short-term marriage. A breeding contract, now called a birthing contract, is specifically for the bearing of Svesti young. The Svesti also have true mates, where they have the biological urge to bite the other and mate for life. True mating supersedes both contracts. The Svesti used to have fated mate bonds where it was believed the Goddess blessed a couple by gifting them the one being in the universe who is their other half. However, there hasn't been a fated mate bond recorded on Costonia in over a century.

The American woman, Talia Sullivan, was appointed as an Ambassador by the President and works with the Svesti on a fair treaty. About a month and a half into the trip, Durek receives word from the *Defiant*, the ship they left to protect the space near Earth, that Earth's leaders are publicly saying the Svesti kidnapped the six women. Earth's leaders are calling for increased military funding and giving the appearance of gearing up for war. Humans can't help but demonstrate their political stupidity to the universe.

Talia comes up with an idea to get the correct information to Earth. King Sovex approves the plan and allocates resources to ensure it happens. When all is said and done, King Sovex names Durek and Talia Co-Ambassadors to Earth.

During their travel to Costonia, Commander Durek, his trusted friends, and the women become aware that there is at least one Svesti traitor onboard the *Invictus* who is communicating with a Svesti noble on the home world. These traitors are attempting to kill human fertility via another virus with the help of the Zuvgran. What the traitors don't know is the virus also kills Svesti male fertility. Fortunately, the Svesti, with the help of the human physician and botanist/biochemist, Natasha Petrov and Lin Chang respectively, develop a vaccine to protect humans and Svesti before the virus is spread.

So far, the loyal Svesti have not been able to identify the traitors. Based on information they do know, Durek has sent Wurvez and another warrior, Grulen Jevax, on a secret mission. However, they missed four daily check-ins and Durek sends another team of five to find them.

Ten days from Costonia, the *Invictus* receives a distress call from Talonka Six, where a mining collapse at the junction of three tunnels has trapped 281 beings, most of the Ermipa race. The *Invictus* has rerouted to Talonka Six and the crew has been making preparations to assist.

Still with me? Then, on to the story....

Chapter 1

Over thirty years ago
September 12, 2005 (Earth calendar)
d'Olorg Estate, Praxis (Zuvgran-controlled planet)

U NDER THE BRANCHES of an old shade tree, the soft blanket protected five-year-old Ronan d'Olorg's bare stomach as he played with his younger sister. Her chubby little legs churned the air and her giggles made him smile when he tickled her. Taking care to keep his claws retracted and the short horns on his head from her body, he lifted the hem of her shirt and blew a raspberry on her soft gray belly. Patting her stomach, he reached for her favorite rattle and handed it to her. She shook it happily, then stuck it in her mouth, gnawing and drooling. Wide silver eyes that mirrored his own followed his every move.

"Ugh, Marris. You're making a mess. I know Mother says some of your teeth are coming in, but it's gross," he complained as he grabbed a cloth to wipe her wet face. He indulgently shook his head at her still-toothless grin when she waved the rattle in his face. *She's adorable. I can't wait until she's old enough to play real youngling games with me.*

He sat up and placed the soles of his bare feet together, making a diamond with his long thin legs. Carefully, he lifted Marris to sit with her back against his stomach, his legs supporting her.

"Try not to tip over, *picana*. No bumps or bruises for you or Mother won't let me watch you anymore." Ronan leaned forward, the loose strands of his brown hair that escaped his braid brushing her head. He pointed.

"Look, Marris. See the green grass?" Swaying softly with her, he said, "Mother says on her home world, Costonia, the grass is blue, even some of the leaves on the flowers and trees. Not pale blue like our sky, but dark rich colors. Can you imagine?"

Marris babbled. Ronan grinned.

"She says she's going to take us there someday so we can see it ourselves. That means we'll get to fly on a spaceship high in the sky, like Father sometimes does." Ronan gently hugged her. "But don't worry if you're scared, I'll take care of you. That's what males and big brothers are supposed to do. Mother says that's what the Goddess wants." He looked around furtively and whispered, "Oh, but we're not supposed to talk about the Goddess except in our safe space. You won't tell on me, will you?" He kissed her fuzzy scalp.

"I'm so glad you're getting bigger, Marris. I love Mother and Father, but sometimes it gets lonely without other younglings to play with, especially when I have to stay in the safe space for days if someone visits Father. And since there's no one else like you and me." His thin face saddened. "Father says we're medical marvels, but Mother says we're her miracles sent by the Goddess." He looked down at Marris tugging at the hem of his shorts.

"Should I tell you more? Or wait until you're older, *picana*?" Ronan grinned at his sister bobbing her head and shaking her toy enthusiastically. "Looks like you want to hear more."

Ronan glanced around ensuring they were still alone. "Well, Mother said she was on Himita Prime studying the Wrestikan's folklore. She was visiting a friend who worked at the medical center for midday meal when the Zuvgran attacked. They were able to hide in an old laboratory."

Marris blew a bubble. Ronan gently stroked the tiny fingers on her free hand. His tail rubbed light circles on her tummy.

"Father is a jen...eckitest—scientist—tasked with downloading information on tests and stuff." Ronan huddled close and confided, "I don't really understand what Father does, *picana*."

"Anyway, after a few days, Father realized there were people hiding close to where he was working. Every day he brought food and left it behind. When he got told he was being sent home soon, he spoke loudly, letting them know the building would be destroyed when the Zuvgran had no more use for it. Mother showed herself. He said he could get her off Himita Prime, but only as far as Praxis. But she would have to remain hidden on his shuttle in a small space for two days because it would be docked on the Zuvgran warship."

Ronan picked up his sister and turned her around so she was facing him. He rubbed noses with her, loving her laughter.

"Mother agreed, although her friend stayed on Himita Prime. Mother doesn't know what happened to her. Somehow, Mother and Father fell in love and they wanted young. Father figured out how to allow Mother to have us, which shouldn't be possible between Zuvgran and Svesti. I guess it's because of his job that he could do it. He's so good at it, the Emperor won't let him leave Praxis alone. He always has to be with warriors. Which is why we haven't visited Costonia yet."

"They don't know that sometimes I can hear things through a vent in the safe space. You'll keep my secret, won't you?" He grinned at her showing her his small fangs. "I know Mother has to act like a slave when Father has visitors, which I'm glad isn't often. I don't like having to stay alone in the safe space, and I hate how sad Mother and Father look afterwards." He tickled her tummy with a finger. "But it will be better when you're older and can be with me."

Marris scrunched up her face and a loud sound came from her bottom, then she smiled.

"Eww, Marris. Did you just fill that diaper?" Ronan waved his hand in front of his face and wrinkled his nose. His sister giggled. "You couldn't wait until Mother got back?"

Despite his sister's wriggling, Ronan managed to clean her and change her diaper. "There, all better." He wagged a finger at her. "You know it would go faster if you stayed still." Marris waved her rattle. Ronan looked up to see their mother walking toward them. *She's so beautiful. Her skin looks like gold in the sunlight.*

His mother sat on the blanket next to them and picked up Marris for a hug and a kiss. Holding Marris in one arm, she wrapped her other arm around Ronan and squeezed him.

"Thank you, my sweet male, for watching over your sister so I could finish baking. You are very helpful."

"I like spending time with Marris, Mother."

She smiled down at him, then kissed the top of his head. "You are a good big brother, Ronan. Marris is very lucky." She looked up at the orange sun. "We don't have time today, but maybe tomorrow we can walk to the river and look for the pretty rocks you like."

"Okay. That will be fun." Ronan happily helped his mother gather everything and fold the blanket. He was glad his mother carried the dirty diaper. She also had Marris. Ronan carried everything else in a leather satchel. He walked close to his mother, soaking in the sunshine and her scent while she pointed things out to him. *Mother is so smart. She knows everything. I wonder if Marris will grow up to be like her.*

Ronan's father returned home visibly upset. He said, "It is time." Then he went into his lab. Ronan's mother told Ronan to play on his tablet and picked up Marris to follow his father. After a short while, Ronan realized no one had returned so he went to his father's lab and peeked in. His father looked busy, dumping vials out.

"Jorn, what are you doing?" said Ronan's mother.

"We're leaving, Saletta. Rumor has it I'm under suspicion. An underground for hybrids is willing to help us leave Praxis and take us to a neutral colony. I'm destroying my work. I already have the computer deleting files. You need to pack small bags for everyone. We'll leave as soon as I'm finished."

Saletta gasped. "Are you sure this is the right thing to do?"

Jorn nodded decisively. "Yes. I need to ensure you and the younglings are safe. We're in danger, my love."

Ronan saw tears on his mother's face. *I don't understand.*

"Go. Hurry and pack. Wait in the safe space and I'll get you when I'm done."

"But Jorn—" Saletta's words faltered when a red light started flashing. *That's the signal to get to the safe space.*

Ronan felt torn. He wanted to pull his mother and sister with him, but he had been taught from the time he could walk that the red light meant go to the safe space no matter what. He ran silently down to the basement and pressed the hidden button. He dropped onto the bed as the door closed behind him.

Through the vent, he heard his mother scream for only a moment before it abruptly cut off.

His father yelled, "Stop. You're hurting her."

A commanding voice said, "You, get the files from the computer. And you, find whatever biological samples you can."

A chorus of "Yes, sirs" sounded loud.

Ronan hugged his knees to his chest and silent tears ran down his face.

"Jorn d'Olorg, you and your slaves are coming with us."

"Why?"

"The Emperor knows of your research on Svesti reproduction and has plans for it. Oh, what do we have here?"

"No, don't touch her," Ronan's mother cried. *Marris!*

"A Svesti-Zuvgran hybrid. Proof of your research. This youngling should be impossible. The Emperor will be pleased." Marris started crying. Tears ran down Ronan's face.

Ronan's father said, "Leave them alone. I'll come with you, but you don't need them."

The commanding voice laughed menacingly. "Oh, I don't think so. The slaves will be perfect as test subjects for your research. It's not easy to obtain Svesti females. Shut up that abomination." He spoke to the others, "Take them and search the property for more slaves. I want everyone."

Ronan's father said in a defeated voice, "There is no one else here."

Ronan heard scuffling, cries, and shouts. He tucked his head close to his knees and rocked silently. He warred with himself. He wanted to go to his parents, but they taught him to remain in the safe space especially if bad things ever happened. *Bad things are happening now.* Eventually the voices and noises stopped, and Ronan cried himself to sleep.

Ronan made himself a meal with the synthesizer. Sucking on his trembling lower lip, he debated what he should do. *I haven't heard anything in a long time. I'm supposed to wait until someone comes to get me, but I don't think they can.*

He missed his family terribly. Worried, he ate without paying attention to his food. He dumped the remains of his meal into the recycler, then went to the sanitary facilities to clean up and brush his teeth, just like his mother had taught him. *What do I do?*

When he came out, a Zuvgran warrior stood there. Ronan froze. *He's bigger than Father.* His eyes darted to the door, but the male's huge body blocked it.

"Ronan d'Olorg?" the male said.

Ronan remained silent.

The huge male sighed. "I am Largon d'Ayen. Did your father not tell you about me?"

Ronan shook his head, his brown hair brushing his shoulders.

"Your father asked me to take care of Saletta, Marris, and you if anything happened to him. I just found out someone took him or I would have been here sooner. Is your mother not here?"

"Bad people took all of them." Ronan's voice shook.

Largon shoulders and tail drooped. "Your mother and sister, too?"

Ronan nodded, trying not to cry.

"How long have you been down here?"

"Five days."

"You are a brave youngling. You've taken care of yourself all this time?" Largon's brown eyes were kind.

"Yes."

"May I sit?"

Ronan wasn't sure what to do, but eventually said, "Yes. How did you know where I was?"

Largon smiled, his fangs bright. "I helped your father build this safe space when your mother was pregnant with you."

"Really?"

"Yes." Largon sat in a chair. "Your father and I became friends long ago when we realized we both felt the same."

Curious despite his fear, Ronan asked, "About what?"

"About how our race treats others. Your father wanted to use his skills to help others, not hurt them. Whereas I wanted to use mine to protect those weaker than me rather than prey on them. Neither of those beliefs fit in with the Zuvgran ways." Largon snorted. "Unfortunately, young Ronan, your days of blissful ignorance ended five days ago. I know your father hoped you would be much older before you had to learn the ugly truth of your Zuvgran heritage."

"What do you mean?"

"Where I have to take you, you will see the results of Zuvgran cruelty more often than not."

"Will my family be there?"

Largon's brown eyes were compassionate. "Ronan, it is unlikely you will ever see your family again. I hope I'm wrong, but I doubt I am."

Ronan sniffled. "Are they dead?"

"Probably not yet. But they most likely won't live long after the Emperor has what he wants from your father." Largon shifted uncomfortably on his chair. "I hate telling you this, I truly do. But I will never lie to you, youngling of my friend."

Ronan stared at Largon through watery eyes for a long time. Then he straightened his thin shoulders. "Can you teach me how to be a warrior like you?"

"I can if that's what you want."

"I do. I want to kill the Emperor one day like he's going to kill my family." Ronan's young voice hardened.

Largon shook his head. "That's a goal you may never achieve, Ronan. I would hate for you to die for vengeance. There are better ways to use such skills."

"Teach me those as well, then."

"As you wish." Largon stood and looked around. "Gather what you need so we can leave here and go someplace safer. You probably won't be coming back."

Ronan thought for a moment, then grabbed a leather satchel. He packed a holo of his family taken after Marris was born, a couple rocks, and some clothes.

Largon said, "Is that everything?"

"No, there's one thing I want from upstairs, then we can go."

"Lead on, young warrior." Largon gestured to the door.

Silently they left the safe space. *The last place I saw it was the kitchen.* Quickly, Ronan went there and picked up Marris' rattle. He wrapped it in a clean hand towel and placed it in his satchel carefully.

"I'm ready."

"We need something else." Largon led the way to his parents' bedroom. He pressed a hidden button and a safe slid out from the wall. He punched in a code, opened the safe, and pulled out a couple items before closing it away again. "Your inheritance, Ronan. Your father had some accounts set up for you, just in case."

Ronan nodded. They left the house and got into Largon's flitter.

"You'll have to hide in back, Ronan. The code is the same as your father's flitter."

Ronan took one last look at his home, memorizing it, before turning to press the hidden buttons under the back seat in the correct sequence. The bench seat rose and he placed the satchel near where his feet would end up. He climbed in and laid down before tapping the inside button. The seat closed over him. *This is it. Goddess, I hope I'm doing the right thing by trusting Largon.*

Chapter 2

Present day
May 25, 2037 (Earth calendar)
Invictus (Svesti space cruiser)

THE ALARM CHIME from her comm woke Natasha Petrov from her short nap. Years of medical internships and working in a Moscow emergency room had her ready to go in a matter of minutes. *Honestly, I spend more time French braiding my hair than I do on anything else.* She synthesized a light snack and headed to the med bay.

While she walked, she quickly reviewed the facts from the upload she received hours ago on Ermipa physiology. They were a bipedal species who grew to about four feet tall as adults, covered in fur—mostly brown, round heads, and large oval eyes. They had whiskers, broad noses, short stubby tails, incredibly strong arms, six fingers, and legs ending in paw-like feet that tended to be long for their height. Two hearts and four lungs combined with another organ called a *ristern,* which filtered out dangerous gases such as methane and carbon dioxide, allowed them to breathe in a number of different planetary atmospheres and in mines, such as the arbixium mine on Talonka Six.

Two months ago, I dealt with gunshot wounds, kidney stones, strokes, and heart attacks. Today, I'm going to be treating alien survivors of a mine collapse on a planet I didn't know existed until twelve hours ago. And I learned the most important information about this species from a direct upload into my brain. Who would've guessed?

Entering the med bay, it was full of Svesti warriors. Natasha recognized some of them from when she helped give the medical uploads about Ermipas to the trained medics on the *Invictus.* She looked around at the seven-foot males and noted the medics wore matching armbands over black shirts, while the healers had on white lab coats. *It's strange—even in space, medical personnel wear white lab coats.*

She saw Lin Chang, the Chinese botanist, standing by Ash'n Rivezt, who was the head healer on the space cruiser. At five feet tall, Lin looked dwarfed by everyone in the room—even Natasha was eight inches taller. Lieutenant Devik Tolvex, the head security officer, was also nearby with Emmy Norton who was an Australian computer geek. *Hacker, really, but she's done some great work here on the Invictus. If it hadn't been for her programming a failsafe into the porting technology, all of us would've been infected by the Zuvgran virus that kills the fertility of human females and Svesti males when the traitor tried to port all of us to the Intrepid where Talia and Vared quarantined.*

Lin and Emmy laughed. They both pointed and nodded at each other. *That's weird. Wonder what that's all about.*

Natasha made her way through the crush of males to join the human women.

"What's going on, ladies?" asked Natasha.

Lin giggled. "We were just talking about our clan markings."

Natasha's brow wrinkled. "What clan markings? Only Svesti have them."

Emmy leaned forward and whispered, "Unless you're a fated mate, then you get one, too."

"What are you talking about?"

Lin explained. "You know about breeding, uh, birthing and troth contracts, right? Well, the Svesti can also true mate."

Emmy nodded. "True mating is a biological urge toward a life mate for the Svesti."

Natasha said, "I know that from my medical uploads."

"The Svesti used to have fated mates—one being in the universe meant to be yours. Like soulmates. But they haven't recorded any fated mate bonds in a century."

Natasha felt some knowledge from her uploads coming forward in her brain. "Okay, fated mates had gold clan markings to identify them."

"Yes," said Emmy. "But when I true mated with Devik, his clan marking turned gold and I got one that didn't exist before." She tugged down the collar of her V-neck T-shirt to show Natasha. "So we're fated mates." Her grin grew wide and white against her butterscotch skin.

Natasha's jaw fell and she stared open-mouthed at them. "Okay, I get Emmy and Tolvex, but Lin, who is your fated mate? I didn't even know you were seeing anyone."

Ash'n came up and put an arm around Lin's shoulders. "I am." He looked down at Lin whose cheeks turned pink. *I've been working next to Ash'n since I got on the space cruiser and friends with Lin the whole time. How did I miss this?*

Lin said, "My marking is the same as Emmy's."

"How did I not know you were together?" Natasha was thunderstruck.

"We were careful," said Ash'n. "When we informed Vared earlier, we found out he and Lady Talia are also fated mates."

"That Talia and Commander Durek bonded doesn't surprise me at all," said Natasha. "Were fated mates this common in the past?"

Tolvex shook his head, his braids swaying. "No. I think only twenty percent or so of couples before the bonds no longer sparked."

"But half of the human women now?" Natasha's eyes narrowed. "I wonder why. Do you think it's because of the DNA strand we all have?"

"I don't know. We're curious, too," said Ash'n. "But it will have to wait. We have a distress call to answer."

"Right," said Tolvex. "We need to brief everyone on Emmy's program to track patients."

"Okay." Ash'n raised his voice. "Everyone, we have a briefing for you."

The rumble of conversation quieted.

"Lady Emmy updated our previous tracking program. She added triage columns for the healers, as well as a number of generic columns we can use to identify a patient's location. Once we have an idea of the set-up for the med tents, we'll identify and mark all the tents and give those columns corresponding titles. If, for some reason, we have to move a patient somewhere not already listed, we can title another column with that location to show the move," Tolvex said.

Emmy spoke. "There is also a column to enter date and time if you release someone from medical treatment, so you have a record of it. The data forwards to a main computer which will then periodically update all your tablets. Does anyone have any questions?"

The Svesti nodded their heads and looked down at their tablets to check out the program.

Healer Rexus Markham said, "The triage columns. What goes there? I only see colors."

"The healers and medics need to decide what each color will mean," said Emmy. "I was unsure how many you required or how you break down triage needs."

"On Earth, we use four or five colors, depending on location or incident. Red means the patient requires immediate care. Yellow means observation—currently stable but will require hospital, uh, med bay care. Green indicates the injuries can wait until more critical patients are treated. White isn't always used but means minor injuries that do not require a healer, while black means dead or will not survive much longer given the resources we have on hand," said Natasha. "I do not know if you use a similar system." Emmy tapped on her tablet the entire time Natasha talked.

Ash'n said, "I think the system Lady Natasha explained would work well for us." He looked around. "Does anyone have any input or questions?"

Healer Nerob Sinoaz asked, "Will we be using four or five colors?"

Emmy finished on her tablet. "I just coded the program for those five colors and put a letter identifier in the color to remind everyone. I for immediate; O for observation; W for wait; M for minor; and D for death."

One of the medics spoke up. "I'd like to see a column where we can put a short synopsis of injuries so we can prioritize within the color bands."

Ash'n looked at Emmy. "Is that something you can easily do?"

Emmy nodded. "Sure, it's easy enough to add a free text column. But if you give me some guidance on what types of things you'd find useful, I could create a list where you can check off the most pertinent items to make the entries consistent and save you time in evaluating."

The medic said, "I could help the female."

Ash'n nodded, his ponytail brushing his shoulders. "That would be good, Vepiv. Thank you."

Vepiv came forward and began talking quietly with Emmy. Emmy continued tapping on her tablet.

Ash'n spoke to the room. "Lady Lin also created a *yuffa* solution to use with bandages for interim treatment of injuries that need to wait. I've already sent it to the shuttles and we'll distribute it at the main triage areas. We all will triage, but the healers may leave to attend those who require immediate care."

"Do we have anything else we need to do to get ready?" asked Natasha.

"No," said Ash'n. "We'll wait until Lady Emmy and Vepiv are finished and review the changes. Then we'll head to the shuttle when the Commander orders it. We will be on one of the first shuttles so we can begin triaging."

Natasha let the buzz of conversation flow over her as they waited. *Fated mates? Wow.* She looked at the two couples in the room. *Who would've thought when we ported onto the Invictus two months ago some of us would find love? Especially after we learned our governments lied to us and told the Svesti we volunteered for breeding or troth contracts. Now we're like members of the crew with me working in med bay, Emmy with Tolvex, Ava in the kitchen, Lin in aquiponics, Rachel in the training area, and Talia as our de facto leader.*

If it weren't for the damned traitor causing problems, I'd say this has been a wonderful experience. We're treated with respect here. And the medical equipment and technology is fantastic. We never would've found a vaccine for a virus in just two weeks on Earth.

Natasha paid attention when Emmy briefed everyone on the changes to the tracking program. There were a lot of pleased faces when they saw the upgrades. Emmy looked shy at all the praise for how fast she was able to incorporate their suggestions. *She deserves to feel good about herself. She's had a rough life.*

Chapter 3

A S HE LEFT his ship, Ronan tugged the hood of his gray cloak to hide his face. Locking it and setting the alarm to alert his comm, he strode away without a second glance. The once-vibrant capital city of Pellotia was just a shell of its former self. The tall, brilliantly white buildings were now dingy and brown and the streets filled with refuse.

Glancing up briefly at the yellow sky, he wished he could have seen the world before the Zuvgran invaded twenty solars ago. The Pellotians, a peaceful avian race with jewel-tone green skin and colorful wings, no longer flew because invaders mutilated their wings. They left them enslaved, some with pain collars, living on the streets downtrodden, their colors muted. The multitude of large balconies on the tall buildings fell into disrepair with no one departing to soar the skies in freedom and joy.

So many beings destroyed by Zuvgran expansionists. So many lives lost and families broken. Ronan tamped down his anger and avoided the Zuvgran with their slaves. He walked through what passed for a marketplace without sparing a glance at the pitiful wares on display. He continued on until he came to a row of decrepit warehouses. Finding the one he was looking for, he knocked in the agreed-upon pattern.

The door cracked open and a large flat yellow eye peered at him. Ronan held still and waited.

"Are you the one?" said the Pellotian.

"I am one of many," replied Ronan.

The opening widened to let in Ronan's large body. He stepped in quickly and his eyes adjusted to the lower lighting in the building. The door closed behind him.

"Come, wanderer," said the Pellotian. He hurried ahead of Ronan with his four-toed feet making scratching noises on the floor. "My name is Talos."

Despite his large size, Ronan followed noiselessly. He observed Talos, noting his dullish green skin and the scars on his back at the base of his wings. The wings hung at odd angles and looked painful and lackluster. He stood a head shorter than Ronan, an average height for a Pellotian.

His musings were interrupted when Talos spoke again. "I received a message that you were to call Herrah before leaving Pellotia. She said it was urgent."

Ronan said, "I thank you for the message, Talos. How many?"

Talos turned his yellow eyes to Ronan. "Seven. And myself, if you can manage it."

Surprised, Ronan said, "You wish to leave as well?"

Talos stopped and Ronan halted. "As a teacher, I've done what I can for the past twenty *annums*, but it's getting too dangerous. These seven have been with me for two *annums* with no one new discovered. It's time."

"Did you wish to stay with the seven? Or go elsewhere?" Ronan's mind sorted through what options he could offer the Pellotian.

Talos clicked his tongue twice against his beak. Ronan knew the sound was the Pellotian version of a smile. "I prefer to go with the seven, but I would understand if you will not allow it."

Leading him down rickety stairs, Talos motioned for Ronan to be careful. Ronan stepped on the outside edges of the stairs where beams offered slightly more support. *I hope it holds my weight. Despite Talos' height, his smaller and lighter bone structure make him much less hefty than me.*

"What are their ages?" Ronan asked.

"Ranging from three to eleven solars."

Ronan grunted as they reached the lower level and continued down a dark hall. Talos opened a door to a large room where most of the younglings played a game of some sort on the floor, while the oldest sat reading a book to the youngest in her lap. All were Pellotian-Zuvgran hybrids. Their skin was gray instead of green—a similar shade to Ronan's—but with patterns that reflected in the light. Their wings looked too small for their bodies. Ronan wouldn't be surprised if they all had scars on their backs like Talos.

The younglings froze at Ronan's appearance. Their flat yellow eyes looked to Talos for reassurance. Talos made the double-click noise with his beak and they relaxed a little.

Talos turned to him. "I did not catch your name, wanderer."

"Ronan."

Facing the younglings, Talos said, "This is Ronan. He is here to take you somewhere safer."

The oldest youngling gently moved the one from her lap to the floor and stood. "We do not wish to leave you, Talos."

"Annika, it is no longer safe here. You must go."

Annika shook her head, her ruff fluffing around her neck in agitation. "It has never been safe here."

Ronan slowly moved his hands to remove his hood. The younglings gasped. Ronan knew that he looked Zuvgran with the exception of his skin texture, shorter horns, and hair. He squatted to lower himself closer to them.

"I am a hybrid as you are. My mother was Svesti. Where we are going, there are more hybrids of different races. Most are younglings like you." Ronan kept his gestures and speech measured.

"Where?" Annika demanded. *She is strong and protective. She'll grow up to be a leader, Goddess willing.*

"I cannot tell you yet. I must keep them safe, too." Ronan smiled, keeping his fangs hidden for now. Slowly he stood and spoke to Talos. "Perhaps I should give you some privacy to discuss this. I must return the message you gave me. I will remain on this level and be back shortly."

Talos nodded, his plumage waving. "Thank you, Ronan."

Ronan left the room and walked further down the hall. Opening a door, he found a dining area and chose a seat in the back. Tapping his comm, he patched through his ship to boost the signal.

When he saw the Wrestikan-Zuvgran face, he smiled. "Herrah, you wanted me to comm?"

Herrah frowned, her blue eyes concerned. "We have a serious problem, Ronan."

"Speak." *What now?*

"There is an illness we don't understand spreading throughout the cavern. I contacted Largon and he's dropping off some medical equipment, but you cannot bring anyone new to us. You should not come either without protective gear."

"What type of illness?"

"It started like a simple cold—coughing, sneezing, runny noses, inflamed eyes. High fevers, diarrhea, and ear infections with most of the sick younglings."

"How many have this disease?"

"About a quarter so far, Ronan, have it to some degree. It is highly infectious. I think it may be airborne." Herrah coughed, one of her four arms covering her mouth. "*Grak.* I may be getting it as well."

"Can you show me?" Ronan watched as Herrah stood and walked to where many of the younglings bedded on cots. He heard them coughing, sneezing, and complaining about difficulties breathing. Herrah showed him Zela, a Crestillian-Zuvgran female of two solars. Zela's long snout and arms had a red rash and bandages covered the youngling's hands.

Herrah said, "Zela was the first to show symptoms about six days ago. She also had white spots within her mouth before the rash began on her head yesterday. The rash covers the entire body."

Ronan's teeth clenched. "What happened to her hands?"

Herrah said, "Nothing. The rash causes itching and we were afraid to let her scratch with her claws. She might hurt herself worse or cause an infection."

"I can take the new ones to the backup location. The Pellotian who cares for them may be familiar enough with youngling diseases to point us in the right direction."

"Have you seen or heard of anything like this, Ronan? I'm concerned at how fast it's spreading. We have no idea what to expect or how to treat it."

Ronan shook his head. "No. I don't know if I can get protective gear here, but we can make a stop elsewhere before returning."

"Okay." Herrah's eyes filled with tears. "It's hard, Ronan, to see so many little ones ill and not know what to do."

Ronan smiled encouragingly. "It looks like you're doing your best, Herrah. Keep them comfortable and safe. Lots of fluids will probably help. I'll see if I can find something that will help the itch at least."

"Thanks, Ronan. We'll see you soon."

Ronan disconnected his comm, concerned about Herrah and the other hybrids. He strode back to the room with Talos and the younglings and found them packing. He tilted his head at Talos and stepped back out of the room. Talos followed.

"What is it?"

Ronan quickly told Talos what he knew and replayed the portion of the comm showing the rash.

"You were a teacher. Do you know of this disease?"

Talos clicked his tongue against his beak once. "No. I've never seen or heard of anything quite like it. Will this affect whether you can take my younglings?"

Shaking his head, Ronan said, "I have an alternate location where we can go in the interim. Can we obtain protective gear, antibiotics, fever reducers, or something for itch relief here or will I need to stop along the way?"

Talos looked thoughtful. "I doubt we can get protective gear on Pellotia without endangering ourselves. The rest is also difficult to obtain unless you wish to pay a very high black market price."

"I thought as much. We'll have to stop at Nulorn for the supplies."

"It is best we arrive at your ship before twilight," said Talos. "Our group will be more noticeable after dark."

"Whenever you are ready. I'm parked on the other side of the market."

When they gathered the younglings together, Ronan was pleased to see only four packs of items to take with them.

Annika approached. "There is one toy or book and change of clothing for all of us, except Rina and Brenos. I packed three each for them as they're the littlest." She looked at Talos. "One pack has your teaching books and tablet. I wasn't sure you if you would want to take those."

"That's good, Annika. Hopefully, there will be more resources when we arrive." Talos double clicked his tongue.

"Younglings. It's time." Annika took the youngest, Rina, by the hand, while the rest paired off. Annika and two males hoisted a pack onto their shoulders. Talos put on the last pack and held the hand of a male youngling a little older than Rina. *That must be Brenos.* All of them put on cloaks.

"Ronan's ship is past the south side of the market. Make your way there swiftly and wait for us. You know what to do."

"Are you ready?" said Ronan. Talos nodded.

They made their way out of the building and Talos led Ronan and Brenos via back alleys and streets. Coming out near Ronan's ship, Ronan scanned the area. *This is the most dangerous part, getting everyone onto the ship without being seen.* Seeing no one, not even the younglings, he strode to his ship. He tapped his comm and the ramp silently opened.

He stood on the ramp facing out. After another look around the area, he nodded. He kept a hand on his blaster as younglings quietly entered the ship. Talos and Brenos walked on last. He closed the ramp.

"Talos, take the younglings to the back and strap everyone in. I need to get us airborne quickly."

Ronan went the opposite direction of the others. In the cockpit, he removed his outer garment before sitting and putting on the safety restraint. He powered up the ship and lifted off. Once they cleared the atmosphere, he turned on the ship's cloaking and navigated toward Nulorn. His shoulders relaxed. *That went easier than I expected.*

He made up a list and comm'd Kito Dresine on Nulorn whom he dealt with in the past. Kito survived the same Zuvgran attack as Ronan's mother by virtue of being off planet at the time.

"Ronan, it is good to hear from you." Kito's grin glowed white against his red skin.

"Kito, my friend. How are you?"

"Good. And you?"

"Healthy, but some friends of mine aren't. Could I send you a list of medical supplies to obtain for me? I will be on Nulorn in six hours."

"I will do what I can." Kito looked at the list Ronan sent to his comm and frowned. He looked back at Ronan. "Tell me, are your friends experiencing a rash?"

Ronan leaned forward. "Yes. We've never seen it before. Do you know of it or how best to treat it?"

"Rumors tell me a highly contagious disease is sweeping over Crestillia. Many become very ill. Younglings under five solars and mature beings over twenty make up the majority of deaths. No one appears to be immune. Many survive, but in some cases, there are seizures and pneumonia, even blindness. I have not heard of a specific treatment."

Ronan's tail flicked rapidly. "Some of my friends were recently on Crestillia."

"That is not good, Ronan. Do you have a healer available to you?"

"Unfortunately, no." Ronan's shoulders tensed. "If I have to, I'll find one."

"I think it would be best," Kito said. "I'll have all that you ask for ready when you arrive."

"Many thanks, Kito. Should you be concerned, I have not been near my friends in over a lunar. I've been traveling."

"Thank you for alleviating my worries. I will see you when you arrive." Kito disconnected his comm.

Ronan sat back and blew out a breath. *Grak. This is worse than I thought. Where do I get a healer?*

He checked the ship's course and stood. *I'll figure it out. Right now, I need to give Talos and the younglings a tour and feed them. They look like they could use a good meal.*

Chapter 4

O N THE SHUTTLE, Natasha found herself seated between Healer Nerob Sinoaz and Lin. Looking around, she noted the Svesti with their gladiator-like bodies, fangs, tails, and retractable claws. Their differing shades of bronze skin, be it golden, reddish, or caramel, looked like short-haired fur, but wasn't. From her time working in the med bay, she knew their skin had a suede-like feel, like the softest leather. Their body temperatures ran a couple degrees warmer than humans.

Despite all those differences, she couldn't help but note their similarities to humans beyond having two arms, two legs, two eyes, two ears, a single nose, and a mouth. All were dealing with the anticipation and concern of what they may find on the surface of Talonka Six in different ways. Some had their eyes closed, shutting out the rest of them. Others flicked their tails, tapped their feet, or drummed their long fingers. Some quietly spoke with their fellow warriors, while others were boisterous—joking and laughing. Natasha saw a few double check their bags to ensure they had everything they needed. Some looked at their tablets, whether to review Ermipa physiology or their messages, she had no idea.

Natasha turned to Sinoaz and said, "Do we know where they are in their recovery efforts?"

Sinoaz said, "At the last update I heard was their engineers had worked out a way to send a communication device, food, and water, as well as some medical supplies, down from the surface to the trapped miners. Because the collapse happened at the junction of three tunnels, they did not want to make a larger hole to attempt to lift anyone out from that point. They are concerned about the stability of the area, so they will enter through the tunnel that is the shortest and shore up as they go. They started excavating a little while ago and are removing the debris. It's going to take some time to get to them. We'll be able to set up our temporary medical facilities before the miners are freed. Svesti warriors will help them dig when we arrive."

"Any word on casualties and injuries so far?"

"About a third of the Ermipas are unaccounted for." Sinoaz frowned. "No one knows if they are buried under debris or trapped in pockets. They'll retrieve the large group first before looking for the others."

"So between ninety to one hundred missing out of the 281 we were told." Natasha chewed on her lower lip. "That will probably be where we'll see the worst injuries or deaths."

Brown eyes serious, Sinoaz nodded. "I think you are correct."

Natasha's eyes widened. "I just had a thought. Are the original tunnels even tall enough for Svesti? I mean, if Ermipas built and work in the mine, would they have taken the time to make it larger than what they require for their shorter statures?"

"That's a good question." He raised his voice. "Lieutenant Tolvex, a word please?"

Tolvex approached them, then squatted so they didn't have to look up at him. "What is it, Healer Sinoaz?"

"Lady Natasha has a pertinent question." Sinoaz gestured at her to ask Tolvex.

Natasha repeated her thought and Tolvex's teal eyes narrowed. "I don't know the answer, but I will find out. It could slow recovery efforts considerably."

"It's already been half a day or more since the collapse. We certainly want to get to the trapped miners as quickly as we can," Natasha said.

Tolvex comm'd Durek, who contacted Overseer Roho, the Ermipa in charge on the surface. While they waited for a response, Natasha said with a smile, "I hear congratulations are in order, Tolvex."

Tolvex grinned widely, his fangs bright against his caramel bronze skin. "Thank you, Lady Natasha."

Sinoaz looked at them curiously. "Have I missed something?"

Natasha's face fell. "Oh, I'm sorry. I didn't even think to ask if it was okay to speak about it yet."

Waving a hand, Tolvex said, "Don't worry about it. It would've been noticed the next time I trained without a shirt." He pulled the collar of his black shirt down to show Sinoaz his clan marking.

"Sweet Goddess, is that what I think it is?" Sinoaz whispered excitedly.

Tolvex's braids fell forward as he nodded his head. "Yes. Lady Emmy and myself."

"This is incredible!" Sinoaz tilted his head at Ash'n. "Does he know it's a possibility with Lady Lin?"

"You knew about them?" Natasha asked incredulously. *Was I the only one who didn't know?*

"I have a nose, Lady Natasha. Their scents are constantly mixed."

"Ash'n and Lady Lin share the same bond, as do the Commander and Lady Talia," Tolvex said.

"The Goddess has blessed us. Knowing that Svesti can potentially find their fated mates offers so much more hope than just continuing our lines. We could have real families." Sinoaz's eyes looked watery.

Natasha's eyes teared up at Sinoaz's emotional reaction. *We women have been so focused on how meeting the Svesti affected us. I'm not sure I really internalized how much it means to the Svesti. Most of their females died thirty years ago.*

Their conversation was interrupted when the pilot advised they entered the atmosphere of Talonka Six. Tolvex went back to his seat next to Emmy. A little while later, the ramp to the transport shuttle opened. Natasha squinted at the bright sunlight as she walked onto her first alien planet. *Theron didn't count. It was a space station.*

She moved away from the ramp so others could disembark and looked around curiously. The air felt cool and crisp with a scent she couldn't identify and there was a light breeze. The sun glowed orange in a pale pink sky.

They were at the foot of a mountain range, with several miles of grassy area abutting a desert of gray sand. Off in the distance, she could see more mountaintops. Turning her body, she looked up at the mountains, her neck stretching. *I can't see the peaks from here.* Thin, straggly trees with sparse green leaves grew out of the rocky surface of the mountain. She saw what looked like a stream running down the mountain much further away from their position.

Continuing her turn, she realized that grassy areas surrounded the desert before being enclosed by mountains on all sides. *I wonder if the whole planet looks like this. I never even thought to check the topography.*

She saw Tolvex and Ash'n talking to an Ermipa. *Oh, Ermipas look adorable. I hope their personalities match.* The Ermipa pointed to a place behind him, then waved his hand toward the grass. Both Svesti nodded. Tolvex walked away with the Ermipa to continue their discussion as Ash'n came towards her.

Their shuttle took off and another landed. Warriors disembarked and Ash'n pointed to a spot close to Tolvex and the Ermipa. Awed, she watched as the warriors lined up from the shuttle to the designated spot and unloaded the supplies, passing items along their line. At the end of the line, other warriors used the various items and assembled a large tent. At some point the line of warriors shifted and another tent quickly went up. When the shuttle ran out of supplies, the warriors remained on the ground as it took off and another landed.

Natasha walked towards the first tent, watching in amazement as the warriors from the new shuttle formed another line to the first tent. Cots, sheets, pillows, and medical supplies passed between the two lines. Staying out of the way, she peeked into the tent to see warriors setting up the cots along three outside edges of the tent with a gap across from where she stood. *Must be another entrance.*

She saw two warriors setting up a center island with counters, shelves, drawers, and arranging the boxes of medical supplies on the counters. They left a large area open near the tent entrance where Natasha watched raptly.

"The open area is for triage, as we expect many will be on stretchers," Ash'n said from behind her. "One of the last shuttles will bring in seating."

Startled, Natasha jumped. "Shit, Ash'n, you should wear a bell."

Ash'n grinned. "Sorry." Lin giggled at his side.

"You guys have obviously done this before. What an efficient system for setting up," Natasha said.

"Yes. The healers and medics will stock the center area with the supplies so we know where everything is," Ash'n said, his tail wrapped around Lin's waist.

"How many tents will we have?"

"Eight for medical care, then another four for the warriors to rest as needed. Their cots will be set up dormitory-style," Ash'n said. "We'll have another tent for meals and beverages with some tables and seating."

Natasha looked around. "Will we have a surgical tent?"

Ash'n shook his head. "No. The last two shuttles will have full med beds and supplies on them. We'll use one as a surgical area, and the other to transport back to the *Invictus* as we can." His lips turned down. "We'll also have some stasis pods for those who we can't spend as much time on right away. We will be able to place some in stasis, then take care of them on the ship."

"Is that a viable option? Stasis?" asked Natasha.

"It depends on the injuries. Some continue to worsen even in stasis, while in others injury progression remains stable. It's a judgment call on when to use it," Ash'n said. "If we can avoid it, we do."

"Okay," said Natasha. She looked to see the first two shuttles' warriors head to where Tolvex was, before moving out of her sight. *They must be going to help with excavation and retrieval.* She turned back and saw more tents being erected and filled by Svesti who arrived as they spoke.

"Let's go stock the center island here. Markham and Sinoaz are in the second tent taking care of that one." Ash'n gestured for the women to enter the tent before him. Natasha followed Lin and got to work. *I wonder how long it will be before we have patients.*

Chapter 5

AFTER RONAN FED his passengers, he showed them where they may have to hide in the cargo bay. There was a narrow opening between stacks of crates which led to an area with cots, a food synthesizer, and a small sanitary facility.

"Why?" asked Flitos, the oldest male youngling.

"Because you are Zuvgran hybrids, others expect you to be slaves. If we come across any Zuvgran, it would not be good for them to find you. If anyone boards the ship or if we land on a planet or space station, you'll need to hide," Ronan explained.

"But you're a hybrid, too," said Annika.

"Yes, I spent many years in and out of spaces like this one. Now, I use technology to hide in plain sight." He pressed on a bracelet and he transformed into pure Svesti with no horns. The younglings murmured in awe. He tapped again and he appeared as himself. "It's called a portable appearance cloak. It's expensive and not widely used."

"I want one," said Flitos.

Ronan shook his head. "I have no extras, youngling. You'll have to hide the old-fashioned way if we need it. If you see a

yellow light, you must make your way here swiftly and quietly."
Talos and the younglings nodded.

After they left the cargo bay, Ronan led them to guest quarters and showed them how to use the sonic shower and clothes refresher. Annika's eyes lit up when she saw the facilities. Annika took Rina and the other two female younglings with her to get clean. Ronan suppressed a chuckle when she told the others the males could wait.

"This can be where the females stay. The males can sleep next door," said Ronan with a smile. "You do not have to wait. Your quarters also have the same amenities."

Pulling Talos aside, Ronan updated him on the illness and told him they would be on Nulorn in several hours.

"Will we need to hide while on Nulorn?"

"I don't think so. However, I will have an alarm set when I leave to obtain the supplies. It will flash the yellow light for you to hide if someone attempts to breach the ship without authorization. If the light is red, there is a problem with equipment on the ship."

"I understand."

An hour from Nulorn, Ronan uncloaked the ship and comm'd Kito with his expected arrival time. In an effort to save time and possible exposure to the hybrids onboard, Ronan asked if Kito could deliver the supplies to the dock and Kito agreed.

After receiving approval to land on the planet, Ronan sent the coordinates to Kito. When the ship touched down, Kito waited with a large maglev full of boxes. Reminding everyone to remain in their quarters until after the transfer, Ronan opened the cargo bay ramp and Kito brought the maglev onto the ship.

Ronan walked quickly to the rear of the ship and closed the ramp behind Kito.

"Well met, Kito," Ronan said with a smile.

Kito returned his greeting. "Where would you like these?"

Ronan gestured toward a spot. "We can put everything here."

"I purchased more protective gear than you requested. I don't want you to run out, especially if this illness is spreading amongst planets. I also added some extra fun items for your friends." Kito smiled.

"Thank you." Ronan's muscles bulged as he lifted boxes from the maglev to stack them. "What extras do you mean?" Out of the corner of his eye, he saw Kito lift twice as much. *Well, if I had four arms, I'd be able to unload faster, too.*

"Coloring sheets, stuffed animals, puzzles—things like that for those who have to stay in bed."

"That was very thoughtful of you, Kito." Ronan smiled. "Are you sure you don't wish to join us?"

Kito shook his head. "I can aid the cause better where I am."

"We appreciate the help."

"It is a good thing you're doing, Ronan. Saving younglings from slavery or death."

"I wish we were able to retrieve more of their mothers, but many are motherless." Ronan frowned. *Just like me.*

"All you can do is what you can, my friend. Even if you save only one life, it is worth it." Kito clapped one of his hands on Ronan's shoulder.

"I also brought the implants you asked for last lunar. Eight different species."

Smiling, Ronan said, "Good. Several females asked for a way to avoid conception altogether. Locations are being set up for females to receive the implants covertly. Fortunately, not all Zuvgran agree with the Emperor. It takes time, but we have found some who are sympathetic to the plight of the conquered species and help as they can."

"I checked my sources again about the illness. Two high-ranking Zuvgran officers on Crestillia have succumbed to it and died. I hope they weren't sympathizers."

"We have no high-ranking officers in our group." Ronan looked thoughtful. "So the Zuvgran aren't immune either."

"It appears not."

"I may need to find a healer to help." Ronan's tail swayed faster.

"There may be a way," said Kito.

"How do you mean?"

"My sources also told me a mine collapsed on Talonka Six and a Svesti space cruiser responded to their distress call. It's less than a day from here. You could divert and find a Svesti healer to help you before you continue to your destination." Ronan tensed at Kito's words, but realized the male did not know about the cavern.

"I'll have to consider that. Thank you for the information." Stacking the last box, Ronan asked, "How much do I owe you?"

Kito named an amount much too low for all the boxes in the cargo bay. When Ronan protested, Kito refused to take more. Sighing, Ronan transferred the credits to Kito's account. *He's a good male, but he still has expenses.*

After Kito left with his empty maglev and the ship was airborne once more, Ronan thought about how to find a healer to help. *Svesti on Talonka Six. I wouldn't have expected that. Would they be more or less willing to help because of my heritage?* Grunting, he reengaged the ship's cloaking. *I have fourteen hours to figure out a plan.*

"Sir, we will arrive at Millus in two hours," the Svesti warrior said.

The nobleman looked up from his tablet. "Thank you for the update." The warrior remained silent. "Was there something else?"

"May I speak frankly, sir?"

The noble waved his hand. "Yes, go ahead."

"Are you certain this is the best course of action? Meeting with the Zuvgran, especially so close to Costonia?"

"Do you doubt me?"

"No, sir. However, I do not trust the Zuvgran. I wonder if the risk is too great. Without you, the cause would falter."

The noble smiled, his fangs gleaming against his caramel bronze skin. "The Zuvgran emperor wishes the Sovex rule to end, just as much as we do. Our interests are aligned for now." With false modesty, he continued, "The cause would continue without me, because Svesti purity is paramount."

The male bowed his head. "I would feel more comfortable with additional warriors guarding you."

"I will be fine. Have faith in the Goddess, as I do. She will protect us as we are following her will."

"As you command, sir."

"I thank you for your concern and honesty. You will be rewarded when our objectives are met."

"The cause is just which is its own reward, sir."

"That is why you are one of my trusted guards—your commitment to our race." The noble paused. "Was there anything else?"

"No, sir. I will notify you when we begin our descent."

The noble dipped his chin imperiously. "Always Svesti."

"Always Svesti." The warrior returned to the cockpit of the luxury speedster.

Naroon. So easily led. How dare he doubt my decisions. The noble clenched his fist under his plush robe. *I will be king. Then I will defeat the Zuvgran and take their empire.*

Chapter 6

NATASHA WAS BONE-TIRED. In the past thirty-six hours, she only had a restless two-hour nap on a cot in the corner. Looking around the tent, she let out a sigh. Ermipas filled the space. She and the other healers and medics treated broken limbs, concussions, and even some burn injuries. Lin's *yuffa* solution helped with the burns. Those with internal injuries went to a shuttle med bed where Markham watched over them. *And these are just the ones we've been able to rescue so far. Still so many unaccounted for.*

She warred with her instinct to use her own eyes instead of the scanner to find bruises and breaks. It was easier to diagnose some things with the technology since the Ermipas' long fur made viewing their skin difficult, if not impossible, at times. *At least with Svesti, their skin may look like short-haired fur, but it isn't.*

Natasha was impressed at the Ermipas' attitude. Even hurting, they tried to maintain a positive outlook and they were certainly hardy beings. *I think they have denser bones. They're definitely heavier than they look. Lifting or rolling them over when they're unconscious proved difficult without help.*

Svesti warriors still dug with the Ermipas to find the remainder of the missing miners. Fortunately, most of the original tunnels were wide and tall due to the nature of arbixium ore.

Talia was the only human to remain onboard the *Invictus* as the Commander did not want her on the planet without him. Neither of them were comfortable being apart after her recent kidnapping on Theron.

Rachel and Emmy opened an information station for families, which alleviated interruptions in the triage and treatment processes. Lin helped Ava and Talen Previv, the ship's cook, at the dining tent, handing out food and beverages to the warriors. Periodically, one of them brought sustenance to the tents as well. *Good thing they did or I wouldn't have had anything to eat or drink during all this.*

Listing a little on her feet, she dropped heavily into a chair at the center island. Her eyes felt dry and scratchy. *Shit. I'm pretty sure we didn't bring artificial tears with us.* Picking up a water pouch and a clean cloth, she wet the soft material and pressed it against her eyes. *Oh, that feels better.* After a minute, she tossed the cloth in the nearby refresher and sipped from the water pouch. She closed her eyes and sighed. *I think I could fall asleep right here.*

Hearing footsteps approach, she opened her eyes and looked up at the Svesti towering over her.

"Natasha, you need rest," Ash'n said, his blue eyes concerned. *He looks tired, too. Hell, even his golden bronze skin looks dull.*

"We all do."

"I'll take over here. All the human females will bunk on the shuttles for their safety. Go. Sleep for at least eight hours. If we need you, we'll comm." Ash'n crossed his arms and pinned her with his stare. "No arguments."

Natasha blew out a breath, stirring some strands of hair that had slipped from her French braid. "Fine. Let me give you a quick briefing." She proceeded to tell him about the patients and their treatment.

"I've got this, Natasha. Besides, there are five medics here that can answer any questions if I have them." He gave her a hand to help her up. "I already had an argument with Lin about getting some sleep. Don't make me argue with you, too."

Natasha's lips turned up slightly. "Did she leave?"

Grunting, he said, "Eventually."

A soft laugh escaped Natasha's mouth. "I'm going. What time is it?"

"Almost sunset."

"Okay. I'll use the back entrance so I can see it on my walk." *I could use the time to wind down.*

"That sounds like a good idea."

Natasha gathered her bag and went out the rear door of the tent. The sun was just setting behind the mountains. She leaned on a support to watch the orange sun turn the pale pink sky shades of red and purple. *The first sunset I've watched on an alien planet and it's absolutely beautiful.* She drew in the crisp, cool air and exhaled slowly.

Movement out of the corner of her eye caught her attention. She turned her head to see a small shuttle skimming over the desert to land further to her left on the grass. A ramp at the rear opened up and a cloaked figure jumped out.

"Female, get me a healer! I have hurt younglings here," the figure yelled in Galactic Standard as he maneuvered a stretcher.

Natasha began running to the shuttle. "I'm a healer. What happened?"

The cloaked figure turned as she arrived beside him. Silver eyes looked into hers as he said, "I apologize for this, healer." Natasha felt the prick in her neck. Her hand slapped at his.

"You bastard. What did you—" Natasha's words trailed off as the drug hit her system. *Why do I smell coffee, almonds, and spearmint?*

The cloaked figure caught her as she began to fall and gently placed her and her belongings on the stretcher. "I truly am sorry about this, but I need help. The effects are temporary. You won't be able to move or speak for a bit, but you will remain aware."

Unwillingly compliant, Natasha wanted to gnash her teeth and yell when he pushed the stretcher into his ship and closed the ramp. After he strapped down the stretcher, she suffered the indignity of him carrying her to the cockpit and carefully buckling her into a seat. *I hope he's telling the truth about the drug, because not being able to move or talk is scary as hell.*

Natasha would have gasped if she could when he removed his cloak and took his place at the console. *A Svesti-Zuvgran hybrid? But their species aren't compatible.* Shoulder-length brown hair with broad hints of red fell forward as he tapped on the console with long fingers. She saw two straight horns sticking up at the front of his scalp. The shuttle lifted off without a sound.

Her body frozen, Natasha cursed silently. *Kidnapped. Really, Natasha? You should've gotten one of the medics to go with you since you didn't recognize the shuttle or the male.* Her eyes drifted shut as the adrenaline left her system. *Can't fall asleep yet. Need to know what's happening.* Her head slipped sideways as exhaustion took over. *He looks a little older than me, but I'm not sure I'm right. It's hard to judge with aliens.*

Brown dust churned under the luxury speedster as it landed on Millus near the center of what had once been a centuries old fighting pit prior before the Zuvgran invaded it. The Svesti joined the fight to remove the Zuvgran and push them back out of the solar system, but the damage had been done. Now Millus was a lifeless world within two days travel of Costonia—a somber reminder of the Zuvgran's lack of regard for the planets they plunder.

Accompanied by two warriors, the Svesti noble descended from the ship. The dust settled quickly in the still air. The only illumination was the yellow moon above, but it was enough for the noble to see the Zuvgran waiting.

He gestured to the warriors to remain behind and he approached the Zuvgran confidently. One Zuvgran stepped forward, his horns gleaming in the moonlight. *They are ugly animals.*

"The Emperor sends his greetings."

"I hoped he would attend this meeting."

"The Emperor is a busy male. This meeting is beneath him."

The noble's eyes narrowed at the deliberate slight.

"Perhaps he should consider maintaining congenial relations with the future king of Costonia."

"I will relay your suggestion, Svesti."

"I was disappointed at the events on Theron. Your people did not perform to my expectations."

The Zuvgran snorted. "Hired help. Perhaps your people should have taken care of it yourselves."

"We agreed I would inform you when the females would be at the space station and you would ensure they were infected with the virus. I kept my end of the agreement. Did you? My understanding is only one human was kidnapped and subsequently rescued." The noble's lips twisted in disgust.

"Our lab was destroyed. The Emperor is not pleased."

"Your lab is not my concern. Whether or not you upheld your agreement is."

"The records were destroyed with the lab. It is unknown whether the female was infected." The Zuvgran's face registered his displeasure at having to admit a possible failure.

"I see. Perhaps I should take care of it myself. Do you have the virus?"

The noble's face hardened when one of the other Zuvgran swiftly approached and spoke quietly to their leader.

"We have an issue," the Zuvgran said.

"Which is?"

"We are not alone here. Did you send others?" Distrust laced his voice.

"Of course not. I do not spy on my allies."

"We will wait together, then."

Several minutes later, three additional Zuvgran dragging a struggling Svesti entered the pit. They forced the reddish bronze male to his knees. The noble's eyes widened when he recognized the Svesti.

"Is he one of yours?"

"No. He's loyal to Sovex."

"You *crekkin'* traitor. The king will have you executed," Karid Wurvez said angrily.

"Who else is with you?" demanded the Zuvgran.

"No one."

"Where is your ship?"

"Hidden."

The Zuvgran nodded and one of the others punched Wurvez in the jaw. Blood droplets arched before falling into the dust.

"Try again. How did you know we would be here?"

"I didn't." Wurvez received a kick to the stomach. He bent over as far as he could and coughed.

"Keep him," said the noble. "Question him as you like. All I ask is you inform me of what you discover and he never returns to Costonia."

"You don't want him?" The Zuvgran sounded surprised.

"Consider him a gift from me to you. The virus?"

"I do not have it."

The noble growled. "Get it to me and I'll ensure it's done."

The Zuvgran studied the noble, then nodded. "I will pass along your request to the Emperor."

"It's not a request. It's the completion of our original agreement."

Wurvez growled low. "I will see you dead, traitor."

The noble crouched in front of Wurvez and drew an extended claw along the prisoner's jawline leaving a trail of blood in its wake.

"It is good that you are already kneeling in front of the future king. Too bad you won't live long enough to do it again."

Wurvez bared his fangs and spit on the noble. "You will never be king."

The noble backhanded him. "Watch how you speak to me." He stood and faced the Zuvgran. "We're done. Contact me when you are ready to uphold your end."

The Zuvgran dipped his chin, then ordered his warriors to take Wurvez.

The noble walked away without looking back. When he rejoined the waiting Svesti warriors, the one who questioned him earlier spoke.

"We are not taking the Svesti, sir?"

"No. It is not the Goddess' will."

"I know you're not a warrior—" The noble grabbed his throat, his claws pricking the male's neck.

"What was that?"

"Currently." The male choked out the word. His breathing calmed when the noble released him. "I only meant that those of us who remain in the warrior ranks have difficulty seeing a Svesti at a Zuvgran's non-existent mercy, regardless of our beliefs."

"It is not easy for me either. I do not wish any of us to have Svesti blood on our hands if there is a way to avoid it. We are brethren. However, we cannot have our brother impeding our plans. The best option is to leave him to the Zuvgran."

The warrior lowered his eyes. "As you command, sir."

"Exactly."

How did Wurvez know I was on Millus? And why is he alone?

When they entered the speedster, the noble ordered, "Scan for nearby Svesti ships. If you find any, contact the Zuvgran and relay its position."

How much does Sovex know?

Chapter 7

ARLIER, RONAN DROPPED off Talos and the seven younglings at a cavern unconnected to the main one. He apologized for having to leave them so soon, but they took it in stride. Fortunately, it was stocked with whatever they would need in the short term while Ronan was gone.

With the ship cloaked, he hovered over the desert to observe the temporary Svesti presence near the Veba Mine. His group routinely monitored the mine's communications to ensure the safety of their refuge, so he listened to some of those while he made a plan. When he saw the white coat indicating a healer, he uncloaked his vessel and hoped his plan worked.

It had, but now Ronan was concerned. The healer was unconscious and he didn't know why. *The drug shouldn't have knocked her out. But I don't know what species she is either. Please, Goddess, don't let her be hurt. That was never my intention.*

He engaged the ship's cloaking and dampener just in case she had a tracker. In the caverns, he wouldn't need to worry about it, since the surrounding rock was a natural dampening field. It was one reason he and Largon chose Talonka Six for a temporary refuge. *Why is she with the Svesti? It must be voluntary or she would not have been unsupervised. Besides, they aren't known to keep slaves.*

He looked at the female. She was a head shorter than him and had long blonde hair in a braid. After he injected her, she looked at him in fury, her brown eyes with hints of green snapping with energy. Long brown eyelashes aided in hiding those flashing eyes from his perusal now. Full pink lips softened the sharpness of her high cheekbones set in a narrow face. She only said a few words, but her voice sounded low and husky.

Her scent captivated him most of all—citrusy with a subtly sweet hint of bitterness underneath—and reminded him of something from his past, but he couldn't pin it down. For some reason, it made him think of morning meals and holidays. The white lab coat she wore covered her assets, but he felt her large breasts soft against his chest when he held her. He shifted uncomfortably in his seat. *Enough of that. She doesn't need you lusting after her. How can I even think of things like that when the younglings are so ill?*

Ronan got up and placed his fingers on the vein pulsing on her neck. *Her skin feels silky and warm.* Her heart beat steadily and he let out a relieved breath. He opened her lab coat. He saw the neckline of a nanosuit peeking through the collar of her plain brown shirt. She wore blue pants made out of a material he didn't recognize. Squatting, he pinched the fabric near her ankle. *Sturdy.* Her footwear seemed unusual, too. White with a pattern on the sides, they looked flexible with their rubbery soles. Long strings crisscrossed across the top ending in a bow. *How curious. I've never seen anything like it.*

He rose and took his seat again. *Now what do I do?* His thoughts crowded his head. Curtly nodding to himself, he adjusted their course to the large cavern holding the sick. *I'll wait until she awakens, explain, and then she can examine the younglings. Hopefully, she'll know what we can do to help them.* Long moments passed in silence.

His comm chimed. When he answered, Herrah's skin looked dull, her nose swollen, and her blue eyes red.

"Yes, Herrah?"

"We're getting worse, Ronan." Her eyes filled with tears. "Gromm died an hour ago. He had convulsions and his little heart quit."

Ronan choked back an angry noise. "No. He was only three solars." *He was such a happy youngling.* A Wrestikan-Zuvgran hybrid like Herrah, Gromm bonded with her like a younger sibling when he arrived two solars ago. *If my heart hurts, Herrah's must be breaking apart.*

"Ronan, more keep getting sick. We don't have enough adults to take care of them properly and we don't know how to cure them." Herrah sniffed.

"Tell me," the healer croaked. Ronan eyes turned to her. "Symptoms, everything." Her voice strengthened. *Thank the Goddess she's awake.*

Ronan turned back to Herrah. "This female is a healer, Herrah. I am bringing her to help."

"Oh, thank you." Herrah sounded relieved. She told the healer everything that happened so far.

"Can I see the rash?"

Herrah moved to where a Durelian-Zuvgran hybrid rested on a cot. A red rash covered his gray skin and his three bulbous black eyes appeared swollen.

The healer sat up straighter and she leaned forward. "How long did you say the cold symptoms lasted before the rash started?"

"Between four and six days. For some, we noticed white spots in their mouths the day before the rash appeared."

The healer brushed her hair from her eyes. "It sounds similar to an Earth disease called measles. I'll have to run some tests."

"Whatever you need, we'll do our best to provide," said Ronan.

She snarled at him. "I'll deal with you later. I'm not happy with you."

Ronan put his hands up in a gesture of peace. "I understand." He spoke to Herrah. "We'll be there soon." Herrah nodded and ended the transmission.

He tapped his console and said without looking at her, "My name is Ronan."

"Ronan, my name is Dr. Natasha Petrov and I'm pissed at you. You drugged me."

He turned his head to see her with her arms crossed. "I was desperate, Dr. Natasha Petrov. So many are ill and we do not know the causes." His tail snapped.

"You could've asked for help," Natasha said.

Ronan shook his head. "I could not risk it. When you see them, you will understand why."

"How many people have been exposed?"

"Almost a hundred. As far as I'm aware, no one has been in or out since I was last there a lunar ago."

"Good. They've effectively been in quarantine. It will help keep the spread down." She pushed her hair from her forehead. "If it is similar to measles, it is highly contagious."

"We suspect it started on Crestillia. The Zuvgran invaded it five solars ago. There are reports of something similar going on there. When I landed here a lunar ago, I dropped off some former residents of Crestillia. At that time, they appeared healthy." Ronan's jaw flexed.

"If it has that long of an incubation period, it's going to be more difficult to stop it." She looked at him. "Do we have protective gear? If it is measles, I'm probably immune. But with that longer incubation period, it might be a different strain, which could leave me susceptible."

"Yes, Dr. Natasha Petrov, we have protective gear onboard. What species are you?"

She waved a hand. "Call me Natasha. I'm human."

"Natasha, then." *I like how her name sounds. It suits her. I've never seen a human before.*

"Have you experienced any symptoms? It sounds like you would've been exposed, too."

"No. Not even a sniffle."

"Good."

"We're here." The ship entered a large cavern on the side of a mountain and touched down. "We'll have to load up the supplies and don the gear before we go the rest of the way on foot. It's not far."

Chapter 8

NATASHA UNBUCKLED HER safety restraints, relieved she could move again. The paralytic Ronan injected her with scared her. If he had dishonorable intentions, there would have been nothing she could do about it.

I can't believe I fell asleep. She didn't know how long she'd been out of it, but it as the voices that woke her. She'd kept her eyes closed while she listened, only opening them when she heard the pain in their voices talking about a child's death. The doctor in her wanted answers. The woman in her wanted to soothe Ronan's pain, even though he kidnapped her. *What's up with that shit? It's a bit early for Stockholm syndrome to kick in, isn't it?*

Grabbing her bag, she followed Ronan to the cargo bay where he opened a box and tossed her a protective suit. She put it on while he loaded boxes onto a maglev. The protective gear self-sealed like her nanosuit, except the facial part—that remained curved and solid. It felt too close to her face, but there was nothing she could do about it.

She turned her attention to the lean, corded muscles of his arms as they bunched and released. His abs flexed under his short-sleeved shirt and when he lifted with his legs, his firm ass strained his black pants. *Oh, my.*

A few beads of sweat broke out on his attractive face which seemed softer than the Svesti faces she'd become accustomed to. She noted his full lower lip and the barely-there, neatly trimmed goatee which ran a little higher on his cheeks than men on Earth wore. *I never liked too much hair on a man's face. His looks simply perfect. Even his mustache isn't bushy.*

He dropped one container near a tunnel and opened it. By the time he finished, a large decontamination unit sat there. Then he put on his gear and she refrained from whimpering at all that maleness being covered. *Damn, I'm getting hot for my kidnapper. I hope he didn't inherit the Svesti sense of smell.* He inhaled sharply and looked at her. *Double damn. Guess he did. How embarrassing.*

Ronan pushed the maglev through a wide tunnel in the rock. He activated a light stick of some sort to illuminate their way.

"These are the remains of arbixium mines that have been played out," he said. "Arbixium ore tends to cluster in very large pockets—room-sized and bigger. The Ermipas start from the highest elevation of arbixium and retrieve it first, so they have a better idea of what supports they need as they go lower. No one has mined in this mountain for at least ten solars."

"Hmm," Natasha said examining her surroundings. The rock seemed to shimmer with small flecks that reminded her of mica.

They walked for fifteen minutes before they began hearing the echoing sounds of coughs bouncing off the walls. *Must be getting close now.*

After another few minutes of passing smaller caves on both sides before they emerged in a cavern larger than the one they started in. Light filtered in from small holes in the high ceiling.

Rows of cots lined the walls. Natasha realized there were only ten adults, who looked to be only in their late teens or early twenties, if she included herself and Ronan. The rest were children of various ages. Every single one of them was a Zuvgran hybrid of some sort.

Herrah walked up to them, her four hands clasping themselves in worry. "I'm so thankful you're here."

Natasha nodded. "Is there any system you have for the layout of the cots?"

"Yes." Herrah pointed. "The ones that first started showing symptoms start there with little Zela. We found it easier to keep track of the progression by arranging them in order of how long they'd been ill."

Ronan said, "I only see about half the younglings. Where is everyone else?"

"Jaliel took the ones who are not yet ill to the lower cavern. It was the best option we had available to us. Once we suspected it might be airborne, we synthesized masks for them to wear."

Natasha smiled at the tired female. "That was good thinking, Herrah."

"Thank you."

Natasha pulled her tablet from her pocket. She perused Emmy's program, copied it as another file, and thought how best to mark the extra columns to help her keep track of what was going on. She walked up to Zela's cot and noticed a small tag hanging. The tag had the child's name, age, and dates with symptoms and vitals. *Oh, this is helpful.*

She looked at Herrah. "Have you had medical training?"

Shaking her head, Herrah said, "No. I just tried to keep track of important details to keep it sorted in my own mind."

"You have good instincts, Herrah. If healing interests you, you should pursue it."

Natasha looked and saw a bottle of sanitizer hanging next to the tag. She cleaned her already-gloved hands, then spoke to Zela. *The poor thing looks miserable.*

"Hi, Zela. I'm Natasha. I'm a healer. I'd like to examine you and see if there's anything I can do to make you feel better."

Zela coughed and nodded, her eyes miserable above her gray snout covered with a flat red rash.

While Natasha checked Zela, she kept up a low stream of questions and chatter to distract the girl. In a confidential tone, she said, "I'm new to space travel, Zela, so I don't know a lot of species yet. I think you're part Zuvgran, but what's the other part?"

"Crest...cres..." Zela tried to say.

Ronan said, "Crestillian."

"Oh, that must be where your lovely eyes come from," said Natasha. She smiled down at Zela.

Zela tried to grin.

"Are you itchy?"

Zela's snout bobbed frantically.

"Oh my, that looks like a definite yes," Natasha said. "Let's see if we can do something about that. We need you to drink lots of fluids, but not just water. I'm going to see if we can come up with something that's a little sweet and salty. It should help. Now you get some rest while I talk with Herrah and Ronan." She patted Zela's bandaged hand, jerked her head at Ronan, and sanitized her hands again, before walking toward the center of the cavern.

"If I knew in advance what species I would be treating, I could've downloaded medical information for them. I'm working with one hand tied behind my back. Hell, I don't even have info on Zuvgran in here." Natasha tapped a finger on her forehead in frustration. "I don't know what's safe to try for them." She tried searching on her tablet. "And I can't reach the Svesti database to research."

"The rock of the cavern is a natural dampening field and blocks most communications," Herrah said. "Even with our comms, we need to boost the signal significantly to talk to each other."

"Well, then I'll have to go outside to do some research."

"No," Ronan said emphatically. "We cannot risk the Svesti tracking you here."

Natasha spit out, "I don't think you understand. If I give any of them the wrong drug or in the incorrect amount, I could kill them. The Svesti will help. They have much better resources available to them."

"Are you willing to bet all our lives on the Svesti helping?" Ronan said in a low, angry voice and waved a hand. "Look at us.

We're part Zuvgran—their sworn enemies." His tail flicked in short, hard movements.

"Are you their enemy? That's not what I see."

"No, those of us here are not, but I cannot risk the younglings. I promised to keep them safe."

"Well, if they're dead, they won't be that safe, will they?" Natasha's face heated with her words.

"Cease, female. I've made my decision." Ronan stalked away, shoulders tense and tail snapping.

Herrah placed a gentle hand on Natasha's forearm. "Let him go, healer. Ronan takes our safety very seriously."

"I swore an oath to do no harm, Herrah. I'm afraid I might harm the patients if I don't have the correct information available to treat them." Natasha's eyes filled. "Before we had a vaccine for measles on my planet, death rates and complications rose as high as thirty percent. Even today we haven't eradicated the disease entirely."

"Do what you can and use your best judgment. That's all we ask." Herrah bit her lower lip. "And if some die, at least they'll die free and among those who care about them."

Well, shit. "I'd rather they live free, Herrah." Natasha blew out a breath.

"As would we, but we'll take what we can get under the circumstances."

After giving Herrah instructions on how to make the fluids she wanted the patients to start drinking, Natasha worked tirelessly to examine each one. The children—younglings—ranged from one to sixteen years old. Natasha made another round to take blood samples, meticulously identifying each one before putting them into storage to be tested later. She started most of the patients on antibiotics and fever reducers. She hesitated to give them Vitamin A doses because she wasn't sure their bodies would assimilate it the same way as humans.

She sat on an empty cot to gather her thoughts. Looking around, she saw Herrah and the other adults spreading some type of salve on the children. *Probably for itch relief.* Ronan gave out the meds. *Makes sense—he's in the protective gear. It'd be hard to rub salve on someone with covered hands.* Yawning, she leaned back. Black tinged the edges of her vision and she slowly slipped sideways.

Chapter 9

EVEN THOUGH HE tried not to watch her, Ronan tracked the healer's movements at all times. He was impressed not only with her efficiency, but also her care and kindness with the younglings. An observer would never see her fear and frustration, but Ronan did. He hated that his actions caused her pain. He might not be able to admit it, but he feared he made the wrong decision. He was responsible for all of them and he desperately wanted them healed. But he was also worried that if they involved the Svesti, they may be forced back into slavery or worse. He wasn't sure what he should do. *Maybe I should comm Largon and get his opinion.*

His thoughts cut off when he saw Natasha fall sideways onto a cot. *Grak. What's wrong with her?* Rushing to her side, he saw her chest rise and fall rhythmically. He tried waking her, but he only got a disgruntled "five minutes" from her. Herrah came up beside him.

"Take her back to the shuttle so she can rest without the suit, Ronan. She seems exhausted."

"We've only been here several hours. What if something is wrong with her?" His tail flicked.

"When was the last time she slept?"

"I would assume last night."

Herrah huffed. "If she's been helping the Ermipas, she may not have slept in days."

Ronan cheeks heated when he realized Herrah was probably right. *I should have realized. That's probably what happened on the shuttle, too.*

"You're right, of course. I'll take her now." Gently, he picked up Natasha and stood.

"Did you want the maglev?"

"No. I've got her." His heart tripped in his chest when Natasha turned her head into his neck and snuggled, her suit's face plate bumping against him.

"You get some rest as well, Ronan. I'll comm you if anything happens." Herrah gave him a tired smile.

"Herrah, please take a nap while we're gone. You've been dealing with this for days."

"I will. Now go." Herrah shooed him off with all four hands.

Holding Natasha close, he strode quickly through the tunnel. He savored her weight and softness against him, wishing the suits were not blocking her scent. He opened the decontamination unit and placed her on the wide seat in the corner. Stripping the protective gear off himself then her, he hung them on hooks and started the decon cycle. The air in the unit held the electric sensation of ionization. Ronan wrinkled his nose at the smell. Sitting beside her, he closed his eyes waiting for the unit to finish.

Once the decon was complete, he carried Natasha to his quarters and laid her on the bed. He squatted and removed her odd shoes. Frowning, he considered that she had no other clothes. *She'll probably want clean clothes when she wakes.*

He removed her socks, marveling at her feet and small toes. Cautiously maneuvering her body, he took off the sturdy blue pants and her shirt, leaving her in the nanosuit. The suit outlined the feminine lines of her body, highlighting the bountiful curves at her hips and chest. Unbinding her braid, he rubbed some strands of her hair through his fingers enjoying the silky feel as her scent wafted up and tickled his nose.

Ronan covered her body with a blanket. He quickly undressed, pulled on some shorts, and tossed their dirty clothes into the refresher. Getting into bed under the covers next to her, he stayed on his side of the bed not touching her. Sleep eluded him as he closed his eyes and silently worried over those in his care. Natasha rolled closer to him and burrowed into his chest. Her arm wrapped over his waist. His tail wrapped around her ankle and he rested a hand on her back. His mind calmed as he fell asleep with a smile on his lips.

Ronan woke to a slap on his chest. Instinctively, he grabbed the hand. Opening his eyes, he saw Natasha glaring down at him with her sparking brown eyes. Her blonde hair was awry and one cheek looked darker than the other.

"You bastard," she snarled at him.

Confused, he said, "Natasha? What's wrong?" He released her hand.

"You undressed me and slept with me." She looked around his quarters. "How did I even get here?"

"You passed out in the cavern, so I carried you here to rest comfortably. I only took off your outer garments to put them in the refresher so you would have clean clothes when you woke."

Abruptly she sat up and patted herself. She brought her knees to her chest and ran her hands through her hair.

"Why did you sleep with me?"

"I was too tired to go elsewhere and this is my bed. I stayed on my side." He smirked at her as he rose to a sitting position. "You were the one who sought me out."

Glaring at him, she said, "And that's all that happened?"

Smugly, he said, "If more had happened, Natasha, I guarantee you would not have to ask. You'd still be feeling it."

Snorting in disbelief, she said, "Yeah, right. Men always think that."

Tunneling a hand into her hair, he brought her face close to his. "I promise you, *caliana*, you would know." His tongue traced her full lips, her breathing quickened, and her eyelids drifted shut. He pulled back and smiled.

"You can use the sanitary facilities first. I'll go make us something to eat." Ronan threw back the covers and strode out of the room. He chuckled when a pillow hit his back.

Ronan went to the cockpit to check whether the Svesti were looking for Natasha yet and how close they might be. While sitting there, he found another tablet and began downloading information onto it. *I should have thought to do this sooner.*

He comm'd Largon. He grinned when he saw the male's face. "Largon."

"Ronan. Are you with our friends?" Largon's eyes were serious.

"I found a healer and arrived yesterday. We'll be heading back after we eat. I left the latest eight in the backup location."

"Where did you find a healer?"

"I kidnapped one helping with the mine collapse."

"Kidnapped? Ronan, what were you thinking?"

"I was thinking the younglings needed help and she was the closest available. Little Gromm died." Ronan shifted in his seat. *Grak. Largon is the only being alive that can make me feel like a misbehaving youngling.*

Largon shook his head. "You'll bring trouble upon us." He frowned. "Gromm died? This is worse than I thought."

"I just checked and the Svesti don't even appear to be searching for her yet."

"Svesti?" Largon growled. "Why would the Svesti be looking for her?"

"Because I'm traveling with them," said Natasha from behind Ronan. "If they're not looking for me yet, it's because they think I'm still resting. That's where I was going when you accosted me."

Largon ran a large hand over his face. "*Grak.* You need to take her back, Ronan."

Natasha crossed her arms. "No. I want to help the sick children here." She turned to Ronan. "I just wish you'd let me contact the Svesti. They would help, too, and they have better resources."

"We can't risk it, Natasha," Ronan said firmly.

She threw her hands up in exasperation. "What can I say to convince you?"

Largon interrupted. "Are you willing to bet your life on their willingness, female? Because you would be risking all of ours."

She bit her lip. "I think I can diagnose this disease, but I don't have access to what I need to be sure. The Svesti can get the information I need from my home planet, and they also have MISI."

"Missy?" Ronan and Largon parroted.

"Medical Information and Simulation Imaging. MISI. It's a device that can help test potential treatments for different species before we administer them. I'm just not familiar enough yet with all the various species to be sure I'm choosing the best treatments."

"You think you know what the disease is?" Largon asked.

"It seems to be remarkably similar to a disease on Earth called measles. We have a vaccine for it. If I could test the blood samples I took yesterday from the patients, I could determine if it's a variant of one of our known strains." She tapped her fingers on her arm. "This one appears to have a longer incubation period than what we've seen—twice as long actually."

"Earth? Are you a human?" Largon said with a frown.

"Yes."

"I've heard rumors about human compatibility with Svesti."

"And?" Natasha's lips firmed.

"If that is the case, your species is in grave danger from the Zuvgran."

Natasha remained silent.

Ronan spoke. "My sources tell me Crestillia is seeing the same disease. I believe the last younglings I brought here carried the infection. Supposedly two high-level Zuvgran have died."

Largon waved a hand. "No great loss, I'm sure. But we have people on Crestillia who need protection."

"If this is a measles variant, it will be highly contagious and difficult, if not impossible, to contain among an unvaccinated population. Those who are malnourished, under five solars, or over twenty solars will be at higher risk of death or serious complications. Blindness, pneumonia, and encephalitis are only a few of the complications." She paused. "If the mothers weren't already vaccinated before or during pregnancy, then babies under one solar are at extremely high risk. On Earth, we recommend inoculating babies at twelve lunars and again between four and five solars."

"So this disease may spread to other worlds?" Largon said with a frown, his fangs showing.

"Depending on how much space traffic Crestillia sees, then I would say it already has." Natasha's brown eyes hardened. "Even more reason to let me contact the Svesti. We need to develop a vaccine quickly, especially if more planets are at risk."

Ronan protested. "No, Natasha." His tail snapped and he clenched his fists.

Her brown eyes flashed at him and her cheeks reddened. "Whatever you two have going on here pales in comparison to this. We have a moral obligation to help. Period." Her breasts heaved. *Grak. She is gorgeous when she's angry.*

"Natasha? Could Ronan and I speak alone?" Largon's calm voice drew Ronan's eyes to him.

"Fine. I'll just go punch something." Natasha whirled about and stomped from the cockpit. Ronan watched her hips sway.

"Ronan, she has a point. If it's as contagious and potentially dangerous as she thinks, we should consider the ramifications of not involving the Svesti." Largon's dark brows drew close.

"What if she's wrong about the Svesti? If it were just me, I'd take the risk. But it's not." Ronan unclenched his fists.

"Talk to her calmly. She seems intelligent. You usually are. Find a way to meet in the middle." Largon sighed. "If it goes well, maybe the Svesti will help with our underground activities. We could do so much more with their support."

"Look at us. A Zuvgran and a Svesti-Zuvgran hybrid. You really think they'd care about what we're doing?" Ronan snorted.

"I do not know why you distrust them so much, Ronan." Largon's eyes narrowed.

"I'm a product of two warring races who hate each other. I fit in nowhere, Largon. I accepted that fact years ago. They certainly aren't going to trust me."

"Then make a place to fit. Maybe the female is the bridge to opening trust."

"I doubt that. Besides, I don't want her to be in the middle."

Largon's eyes widened. "You like her."

"Of course I like her. She's trying to help."

"That's not what I meant and you know it."

"Fine. Yes, I like her. Something about her reminds me of when I was young—before my family died." Ronan's cheeks heated.

Largon's voice softened. "That's not a bad thing, youngling of my friend. One of the differences between you and those we rescue is that you were a product of love. Those experiences and memories are invaluable."

Ronan grunted and crossed his arms. "I do not wish to talk about it."

"As you wish, my friend. I'll try comm'ing our contacts to see if the disease is spreading. Do what you need to with the Svesti. I know you'll find an answer."

"I'll do my best."

Chapter 10

Gritting her teeth, Natasha made her way to what looked like a dining area. Her breath sawed in and out of her lungs. *I can't believe how pissed I am. I want to throw something.*

She gripped her elbows to keep from giving in to her temper, effectively hugging herself. Leaning back on the wall, she closed her eyes and tried to calm down. *Measured breaths, Natasha. Don't let your anger control you. You control it.*

As her breathing evened out, she thought about Ronan's reluctance to contact the Svesti. She wasn't stupid. She knew he and the Zuvgran—*never did get his name*—looked to be running some type of rescue for hybrid children who were most likely motherless and probably born as slaves. In her opinion, it was a noble mission. To be truthful, one she hadn't expected to see a Zuvgran part of given what she knew of the species. *I don't want to endanger what they're doing, but I also don't want anyone to die if I can help it either.*

Waking up in Ronan's arms still had her off-kilter and might be affecting her feelings now. As she slowly became aware of her surroundings this morning, she felt safe and warm and enveloped by the coffee, almond, and spearmint scent. When she realized where she was and had no recollection of how she got there, she panicked and lashed out in anger. *Not my finest moment.*

After a long while, she calmed and opened her eyes to see Ronan watching her quietly. He grabbed some fruit and beverages from a cooling unit and placed them on a table. Programming a food synthesizer, he waited patiently until two plates of food appeared. He gestured to the table.

"Sit, Natasha."

Her stomach rumbled as the smell of the food reminded her she hadn't eaten in a long time. Sighing, she took a place at the table and opened a beverage, which tasted a little like fruit juice.

He slid a tablet towards her.

"What's this?" she asked as she picked it up.

"I downloaded medical information on the various species for you."

Her eyes lit up and she began tapping on the tablet. She looked up at his short laugh.

"What?" Her eyes narrowed.

"Try eating first, *caliana*. I have a feeling you're the type of person who gets so involved in work you forget to eat."

Cheeks pink, she admitted, "You're right. I'm just so happy to be able to have something to work with." *How can he know that about me already?*

"I know you care and I can feel your frustration. I'm doing my best for the younglings." Ronan picked up his fork and began eating something that looked like orange scrambled eggs.

Natasha set aside the tablet and followed his example. "This is good." Suddenly ravenous, she concentrated on her food as they sat in comfortable silence for a few minutes.

When she'd finished, she sipped at her juice.

"Can we start again?" Ronan said.

Her brow wrinkled. "How do you mean?"

He straightened. "Hello. My name is Ronan d'Olorg. Are you a healer?"

Smiling, she said, "I'm Dr. Natasha Petrov. Yes, are you ill?" *He's cute like this.*

"No, but I have close to one hundred beings in my care, the majority are younglings. They have a never seen before illness. I was hoping you might help."

"I'd be happy to."

Ronan grinned, then his silver eyes turned serious. "Do you think we can come up with a way to get the help you'd like from the Svesti without exposing our location?"

"I know you're worried, but I really do believe your secret and the younglings would be safe with them."

Ronan shook his head. "I'm not ready for that much trust yet, Natasha, but I'm trying to work with you. Does it have to be all or nothing?"

She stared into his eyes for a long moment, then sighed. "No. I believe it would be faster doing it my way, but I think we might be able to figure something out."

"I'd like that. I'm also concerned the disease will spread across multiple planets. I just can't risk the younglings." *It's admirable how dedicated he is to the children.*

"Okay. Let's see what we can do." Natasha flashed him a grin.

Natasha took notes on her own tablet as she and Ronan came up with a plan. *It's not perfect, but it will do.* The more they talked, the more Natasha saw his intelligence and his willingness to accommodate as much as she wanted as long as they protected the younglings first. *He's got a sweetness to him under the dedicated warrior.*

They decided to return to the main cavern to check on everyone first, as well as pick up the blood samples. Donning their protective gear, they made good time through the tunnels. Natasha made the rounds, noting changes, and updating medications based on the information Ronan gave her. On the tablet, she found Ronan also included a list of available medical supplies.

Four adults took care of the younglings. They told Natasha and Ronan that two of the adults from the lower cavern had volunteered to come up and help the night before. Natasha nodded in approval when they told her the other five were resting and would take over in a couple hours. Now that they had a treatment plan of sorts, they could manage taking shifts. They smiled tiredly when they said the extra bodies to help prepare, distribute, and clean up made mealtimes easier. There were only three new patients who had fevers and a cough but no other additional symptoms yet.

Ronan helped the other adults with folding clean sheets, refilling beverages for the patients, and then handing out some toys and puzzles to keep the younglings occupied. The youngest among them received stuffed animals. Even the most miserable patients smiled and laughed with him. *They love and trust him. Look how they light up when he's around.*

She was pleased to see some of the younglings had improved a little. Although, Herrah looked miserable in her own cot. Examining the female, Natasha pushed Herrah back down when she attempted to rise.

"Where do you think you're going?" asked Natasha.

"To help." Herrah coughed. Sweat glistened on her face.

"No, you're not. You're going to rest, drink fluids, and take the medications," Natasha said firmly.

"They need me."

"They need you healthy, not overworked. Others can take care of them. I'll bet you've been running on fumes for days and I'm concerned." When Natasha saw Herrah's confused look, she said, "It means you've been pushing yourself too hard."

Herrah frowned and crossed her arms. *Wow. That looks strange to see two sets of arms crossed on one body.*

Natasha leaned forward. "I get it, Herrah. I'm the same way. Which is why I passed out yesterday. Take this time to heal and gather your strength. It will be better for you and the younglings in the long run."

"Fine." Herrah's arms loosened.

"Let me get a blood sample, then you can rest." She finished quickly, then patted Herrah's hand. "You'll be ready to go in no time." Natasha felt Herrah's worried eyes on her as she took samples from the newest ill younglings and put the tubes in the container from the day before.

"Are you almost ready?" asked Ronan.

"Yes." Natasha looked around the cavern again. "I am concerned three patients might be contracting pneumonia, but overall, they're not in bad shape."

Ronan picked up the container. "Then let's go."

They headed back to the decontamination unit. While they sat waiting for the cycle to finish, Ronan told her stories of some of the younglings and their circumstances.

"How long have you been rescuing slaves?"

"Most of my life," said Ronan. He leaned his head back and closed his eyes.

Natasha glanced at his relaxed body. "May I ask about your parents?" She paused. "I learned Zuvgran and Svesti are not supposed to be compatible, but clearly I was misinformed."

Stormy gray eyes opened. "No, you are correct. As far as I'm aware, only two Svesti-Zuvgran hybrids exist—myself and my sister."

"You have a sister?"

Ronan face saddened. "No longer. She died at the same time as my parents when I was five solars. She had not yet reached one solar."

"I'm sorry." Natasha reached for his hand and squeezed it. *His body temperature is closer to human than Svesti.*

"Thank you." Ronan's chest expanded as he drew in a deep breath. "My father worked as a geneticist and after he and my mother fell in love, he found a way to allow them to have children." He grimaced. "It would've been better if he had never done so."

"How can you say that? If he hadn't, you wouldn't be here to save those younglings."

"I suspect many people suffered because of his work."

Natasha thought for a bit, then asked, "So, a Zuvgran and Svesti in love. How did they even meet?"

Ronan told her the same story he told Marris years ago.

"Wow. Your mother was so brave."

Ronan pursed his lips. "I hadn't thought of it that way, but I guess." He smiled fondly. "I remember thinking she was the smartest person ever. Our lives were mostly good up until their death. For whatever reason, the Zuvgran didn't wreak as much havoc on Praxis as they have on other worlds. They destroyed the cities, but the countryside remained mostly intact. A number of Zuvgran had estates there. Probably still do. I've never been back to where we lived."

The cycle finished and they moved to the shuttle. Ronan strapped the container down, then gestured for Natasha to take a seat. She buckled the safety restraints and watched him start up the shuttle, his movements fluid and concise. *I'm going to have learn to fly one of these things someday.*

Continuing the conversation, Natasha asked, "So who raised you after your parents died?"

"Largon," Ronan said as he glanced at her. "The male on the comm yesterday. He and my father were best friends." Lifting off, he cloaked the vessel. "He taught me everything I know about being a warrior." Shaking his head, he said, "I was determined to learn it all so I could assassinate the Emperor for ordering my family's deaths. Largon eventually convinced me a better way to use my skills was to do what we're doing—saving hybrids." His tail snapped. "Although, if the opportunity arose to kill the Emperor, I would probably take it."

"I think what the two of you are doing is admirable," Natasha said. At his sideways glance, she smiled. "Really. If my information is correct, many hybrids are killed outright. If they're not, they have a life of slavery ahead of them. At least this way, they have a chance of happiness."

"I wish I could give them a better life than hiding and moving periodically. They deserve a home where they feel safe and loved." Ronan's chest rumbled.

"From what I've seen, they are safe and loved. The rest is geography."

Ronan's cheeks reddened. *How cute. Blushes show up much better on his gray skin than the Svesti shades.*

"Thank you, Natasha."

Chapter 11

*N**ATASHA'S CORRECT. KNOWING** what I know now, my mother was exceedingly brave. She trusted a Zuvgran, spent two days hidden in his ship while on a Zuvgran war vessel, then made a life in a Zuvgran-controlled world, never seeing her family again. Goddess, I miss her.*

Ronan admitted to himself how much he enjoyed just spending time with Natasha—talking not only about their day but about their pasts. He liked that she understood why he chose to rescue hybrids and protect them. With his unique heritage, he always doubted a female who wasn't also a Zuvgran hybrid could accept him.

He made them evening meal while she talked more about her training as a healer and some of the unusual situations she encountered. While he heard her words and responded appropriately, he spent more time enamored by her enthusiasm and intelligence, not to mention her face. Her expressive brown eyes with their flecks of green, long eyelashes, and full lips framed by wisps of silky blonde hair fascinated him.

She drew him out, asking questions about his time growing up with Largon. Her laughter rolled over him as he shared stories of him as a youngling, struggling to be a warrior like Largon and the amusing mistakes he made imitating his surrogate father.

"There I was, six solars, and Largon gave me a youngling-sized staff. I insisted I could use one like his. When he finally gave me the one I wanted to train with, it stood almost twice as tall as me at the time. The first time I swung it, the weight of it took me to the ground because I was too stubborn to let go." Ronan shrugged with a chuckle.

Laughing, she said, "I can see it. I'll bet you were all scrawny and limbs."

"How'd you guess?"

"Most boys, er, males are at that age." She paused. "What did Largon do?"

"He gave me a hand to help me up. Then he crossed his arms and gave me a hard look." Ronan demonstrated the stance and deepened his voice to imitate his friend. "Young warrior, it is not the size of the weapon that is important, it is how you wield it. Train with ones that suit your size and the weapons will get larger as you do." He grinned. "I've never forgotten that advice."

"Where did you live?"

"All over. Largon and a few friends started an underground organization to relocate sympathizers and hybrids to neutral colonies just before they took my family. I found out later we were supposed to be utilizing it to leave Praxis." His fists clenched. "But the Zuvgran found us before we could leave." *I don't think it matters how many solars pass, I will always be angry about that.*

"How did you escape?"

"I didn't. They didn't find me. My father had built a hidden space under our home. They had trained me from the time I was little that I should go to the safe space when I was told to or when a certain alarm went off. I was hiding there when they caught my parents and Marris." He sucked in a breath. "I heard the whole thing through a vent. Five days later, I met Largon. He knew about the space because he helped Father build it."

"So you never made it to a colony?"

"No. The Zuvgran began attacking small colonies on unprotected worlds. Largon started looking instead for places like the caverns to hide the younglings. For the most part, I went where he did and helped keep the younglings calm during travel. When I was old enough and had developed the proper skills, I started leading the retrievals more often."

"I'm glad you had Largon after your family died. Your life could have turned out very differently and that would have been a shame." Her eyes turned serious. "And now you're there for others—bettering their lives." She squeezed his hand. "It just goes to show that one person's actions can make a huge difference."

Ronan held on when she tried to pull her hand away. He studied the contrast of her lighter skin against his gray tones. Unlike him, she did not have a discernable pattern on her flesh. Her fingers were long, thin, and soft against his callused palm. He rubbed his thumb over her fingertips. Her scent thickened in the air.

Raising his eyes to hers, he said, "I think you see me as more than I am, Natasha. I am only a male."

"Some people on Earth believe in something called karma. In its simplest terms, it means what goes around comes around."

His brow wrinkled. "I'm not sure I understand."

She met his eyes. "It means your intentions and actions cause consequences. If you behave honorably, then good things will come to you—either in this life or the next. The opposite also holds true." Her face lightened. "Or, as Emmy would say— payback's a bitch." She patted his hand. "You're building up some good karma."

"As are you, *caliana*."

"I believe life is hard enough as it is. We should be making it easier for each other, not worse." She ground her teeth. "And I really hate when people prey on those weaker than themselves." *She may not have claws or horns, but she has a warrior's heart.*

"I agree with you." His heart thumped hard in his chest. "Tell me, do you have a mate waiting for you on your planet?"

"Hardly. I haven't met anyone who made me think in terms of forever. I put all my effort into my schooling and work which didn't leave much time for finding someone." Natasha tilted her head. "Humans don't have anything like Svesti troth and birthing contracts. And we certainly don't have true or fated mates. We just muddle along and if a relationship goes badly or isn't meeting our needs, we end it by leaving."

Ronan pursed his lips. "My mother told me about the Svesti, although at the time I did not fully understand breeding and troth contracts."

"What about the Zuvgran? Do they have something like true or fated mates?" Her brown eyes held curiosity.

"Largon told me they used to have ordained mates, which sounded like a bond similar to Svesti fated mates. He said he hadn't heard of anyone in recent memory being bonded mates. I'm not even sure how someone would know it was a possibility." Ronan's forehead wrinkled. "Being a hybrid, I don't know if I would be able to form any of those types of bonds."

Natasha frowned. "I don't know either. The hybrid physiology is new to me. We're all one species on Earth, so we haven't had any publicly known contact with aliens until recently."

"You think there has been contact you didn't know about?"

"Oh, yes. I found out that there are some species who have been abducting people from Earth to sell as slaves out here in the universe. Some women have been out here for years." Natasha's lips thinned. "I just don't understand the appeal of owning slaves. Sentient beings don't deserve such treatment."

"Profit motivates too many. And some, like a lot of Zuvgran, feel more worthy than others." Ronan ground his teeth. "I've heard tales of them culling their own and killing weak younglings because it reflects poorly on its sire."

"We've had events in our history where one group felt superior to others. It always ends badly and innocent people suffer." Natasha's eyes filled with sorrow. His nose wrinkled at the change in her scent.

Ronan squeezed her hand lightly. "Enough sad talk. Let's go enact our plan."

Chapter 12

THE SHUTTLE HOVERED over a grassy area about a mile from the Svesti tents.

"It's time for the first part of the plan," Ronan said.

Natasha watched him stand, then release the container of blood samples from its straps. He lowered the ramp and gently placed the container on the grass. Hustling back into the shuttle, he closed the ramp and took his seat again. He maneuvered the cloaked shuttle to a new location.

"Are you ready?"

She nodded. "Ready when you are."

Ronan fiddled with some controls. "Okay. I've set the camera to show only you in the seat, scrambled our location, and initiated an encrypted comm with the *Invictus* using your name."

Natasha drew in a deep breath. *Here goes. I hope I'm right about the Svesti or this is going to go very badly.* She rubbed her hands on her jeans.

"Lady Natasha? Where are you? Are you all right? We just got word an hour ago that you were missing and haven't been able to track you." Commander Vared Durek's facial scar was white against his golden bronze skin. His lavender eyes narrowed.

"Commander Durek. I'm fine and I'm safe. But there are others that require some assistance. Is there any way we can get Healer Rivezt on this comm so I only have to explain once?" Natasha kept her voice level and calm.

"You need to return to the *Invictus* now," Durek growled. She saw Ronan stiffen out of the corner of her eye. *Great. Pissed off males everywhere. Just what I need.*

"I'm not ready to come back, Commander."

Talia Sullivan spoke up. "Vared, let Natasha explain before you get all grumpy." Talia's face entered the screen next to Durek. "She looks and sounds fine. I'm sure she has an explanation for whatever is going on."

Natasha's eyes met Talia's. "I do. It's important. There are younglings at risk, as well as others."

"Children are involved?" Talia turned to Durek. "Do as she requested, Vared. Get Tolvex involved if it makes you feel better."

"*Kirani,* may I remind you that I command this vessel?" Durek's voice calmed.

"And I consider Natasha under my protection." Talia's voice hardened.

Shaking his head, he said, "Brauvix, get Tolvex and Rivezt on an encrypted comm." He looked fondly at his mate. "We'll talk about chain of command later."

Talia huffed. "Whatever." Natasha suppressed a laugh at how normal their arguing felt. *They just can't help themselves.*

"Natasha. Thank the Goddess you're alright," Ash'n said when he joined the conversation right after Tolvex.

"I'm fine, but I need your assistance and MISI."

Ash'n frowned. "Whatever for?"

Natasha said, "There is a virulent disease spreading that is strikingly similar to Earth's measles. I left blood samples at these coordinates." She rattled the location off. "I need those ported to the sterile med bay and tested. You'll have to go into the database for Earth for information about the strains as well as the vaccine we use. I'll send you a link to a secure site with my login so you can get the best data."

"We would have to have the *Defiant* download the information," said Tolvex. "Our communications relays would not be sufficient."

"That's fine. Just so long as Ash'n receives the data." She looked at the healer. "There are a number of species involved. I'll send you a list. But we need a vaccine for each variation. I also need you to check if Vitamin A would be detrimental to any of those species." She nodded at Ronan and he sent everything she wanted the Svesti to have.

"Why can't I track you?" Tolvex said with a frown.

"Dampening field to protect the younglings."

"Younglings?" asked Ash'n. "What younglings?"

"The ones I'm trying to treat. However, I hear this disease is already spreading on Crestillia and may be spreading to other worlds. We need to develop a vaccine. It's highly contagious and death and complication rates in unvaccinated populations are high."

"Are the human females at risk?" asked Durek.

"If I'm correct, probably not," said Natasha. "It's a fairly routine vaccination on Earth so most people have had it."

Talia nodded. "I know I'm good."

"Depending on what Ash'n finds, we might need a booster of some sort, but I think we'll be fine. I don't know about the Svesti, though." Natasha blew out a breath. "It seems to have a longer incubation period than Earth strains, so that's a major concern. It may be impossible to contain the spread."

Ash'n glanced up from his tablet, his blue eyes staring at her. "Natasha, looking at your list of species, I want to ask again—are you alright?"

She smiled at him. "Yes, Ash'n, I really am okay. I am in no danger from the people I'm with." Her lips turned down. "How are the rescue efforts with the Ermipas?"

Tolvex said, "We found another large pocket of survivors, but the search continues for another twenty beings."

"All the rescued have been treated. We know of five Ermipas who died during the initial collapse and another three from their injuries before we could get to them," Durek said with a frown.

"Then I'm not leaving you shorthanded?"

Ponytail swirling over his shoulders, Ash'n said, "No, we have enough personnel here. In fact, with your permission, Commander, I'd like to port Lin and myself to the *Invictus* and begin testing the samples Natasha mentioned."

"Tolvex, port the samples to the sterile med bay, then arrange to port Rivezt and Lady Lin," Durek ordered. "How do we get in touch with you, Lady Natasha? I dislike not knowing where you are." Natasha's attention shifted to Ronan pointing at the container disappearing in a whitish-blue light. *Oh, good. They have them.*

"You can comm me, but I may not receive it right away."

"I want you to check in with us at a minimum twice daily—before morning meal and after evening meal," Durek said.

"That may be difficult."

"It is non-negotiable, Lady Natasha. We need assurances of your safety and you need to communicate with Rivezt about his findings."

Natasha sighed. "Okay, I'll do my best."

Durek's growled loudly. Talia laid a hand on his arm and said, "Natasha, do as he says. It's a reasonable request." Talia stressed the word 'request.' "You know how difficult this is for the Svesti, having you outside their protection. And they're willing to help."

Natasha nodded. "You're correct. I apologize, Commander. I'm not used to having to account for my presence. I will check in as you requested."

Durek said, "Thank you."

Smiling, Natasha said, "I appreciate your assistance in helping these younglings."

"Of course. Do you require anything else at this time?"

"No, that's it for now."

"Then I expect to hear from you later this evening."

"Yes, sir."

Ronan disconnected the comm. She turned to him. "I told you they would be willing to help."

"Yes, you did. I appreciate you keeping the cavern's location secret."

"Well, I guess we can head back and check on our patients again."

Ronan turned the shuttle and headed back across the desert.

"Regardless of how this all turns out, I want to thank you for all your help. You are a dedicated healer and advocate."

Natasha was surprised at how much Ronan's appreciation meant to her. She mumbled, "Thank you."

Chapter 13

O N THE RETURN to the cavern, Ronan adjusted the camera to show him rather than Natasha and comm'd Talos. He reassured him that they weren't experiencing symptoms and didn't need anything at this time. Recalling Annika's statement about what they packed, he made a mental note to obtain more clothing for the Pellotian-Zuvgran hybrids.

"Who are they?" Natasha asked.

"I brought them from Pellotia just before we met. I set them up in another location because I didn't want them exposed to the disease. Unfortunately, I can't integrate them into our community yet." *I feel bad about that. The younglings adjust better when they are surrounded by other younglings.*

"You made the right decision to keep them separate."

Ronan landed the shuttle and they went through the same process as earlier in the day. Natasha started her rounds with Zela while he checked on Herrah. The sick female was sitting up, coughing, and generally looking miserable.

"Hello, my friend," he said as he drew up a chair.

"Ronan," she said in a hoarse voice.

"Are you feeling any better?"

"I don't have a fever, so that's progress. This *grakkin'* cough hurts though."

"Mention it to Natasha when she comes by. Maybe she can give you something for it." Ronan clasped one of her hands. "I'm sorry I wasn't here to help you when this all started."

Herrah shook her head. "It turned out better this way. You found Natasha because you were away. Speaking of which, how are our new friends from Pellotia?" *That's so like her to worry about others before herself.*

"I spoke to them a little while ago. Talos says they're fine. No one's ill and they don't need anything." He smiled. "The oldest, a female named Annika, reminds me of you."

"How so?"

"She's confident, protective, and takes charge."

Herrah's face brightened. "How old is she?"

"Eleven solars."

"About the same age I was when you rescued me." There was a faraway look in her eyes. "That seems so long ago."

"It also seems like yesterday to me, Herrah, even though it's been what? Ten solars?"

"Twelve."

"Already?" *Where does the time go? I remember when she was scrawny and all limbs.*

She nodded. "Best twelve years of my life so far."

"I hope you have even better ones." Ronan paused. "Natasha asked the Svesti for aid in testing and developing a vaccine."

Herrah's body stilled. "Do they know we're here?"

"Not our specific location. I would never endanger all of you."

"Once we get through this disease, do you think they would be willing to help us find somewhere else? Maybe our own colony somewhere?" she asked.

Brows creasing, Ronan said, "Why?"

"I worry the younglings aren't able to play outside in the sun or even the rain, Ronan. We're free, but we're not because we have to stay hidden. They should be able to climb trees, pick flowers, and have a roof over their heads instead of rock." She gestured around them. "I want more for them."

Sitting back, he said, "How long has this been on your mind?"

"A while now. We've been in these caverns eight solars. Some of our younglings don't remember anything else. I feel it's time for better." She crossed both sets of arms.

"I'll talk with Largon and see what he thinks." *Where could we go and be safe? None of our other locations can handle an influx of over a hundred beings. We have over six hundred hidden overall. Although, it would be nice to bring them all together.*

As Ronan and Natasha walked through the tunnels, he said, "I'm curious. Why are you with the Svesti?"

Natasha glanced sideways at him. "Well, you're trusting me with your secrets, I guess I can trust you with mine." She took a deep breath. "About two months ago, the Svesti made first contact with my planet, Earth. Because of human compatibility with Svesti, they were hoping human females would consider troth and birthing contracts with them. As I'm sure you know, the Zuvgran virus thirty solars ago killed most of the Svesti female population and rendered the remainder infertile."

Ronan's tail tried to whip inside his protective gear. "You plan to bear Svesti young?"

"No. I came to learn about alien biology and medicine. The leaders of my country told me to gather information, learn, and report back hoping alien advanced technology would also benefit humans."

They entered the decontamination unit and took off their suits. Sitting on the bench seat, she leaned back with her eyes closed.

"Anyway, that's what my government said, but we women found out that they told the Svesti differently. They said we were volunteers for those types of contracts."

Ronan's tail flicked. "Do the Svesti know the truth? Will they be forcing you to honor your government's agreements?" *I won't take you back if that's the case.*

Shaking her head tiredly, she said, "No, they're not making us do anything." A half-smile graced her plump lips. "We had some bumpy moments in the beginning, but since then, they've been accommodating and treated us very well."

"I'm glad they've treated you with respect." Ronan's tail slowed.

"Anyway, there are five other human women with me. I just found out a few days ago three of them have formed fated mate bonds with Svesti."

Ronan's brows came together. "If I remember correctly, they haven't had fated mate bonds in a very long time."

"They said it's been over a hundred years. The Svesti are hoping for a treaty with Earth in the near future."

"Will you be going back to Earth?" Ronan's heart froze.

"Not for at least another solar. I don't know what my future holds." She opened her eyes to look at him. "Out here in space, I'm feeling challenged in a way I didn't feel on Earth. I'm enjoying all the new species, medicine, and technology. I would miss it." She smiled. "Maybe I'll stay on Costonia. They'll need doctors for the human women and any children they bear."

"Do you have family on Earth?"

"No. My parents died in a car accident just after I finished medical school. Drunk driver. And my *Babushka*—grandmother—died a solar ago. I have no siblings. Most of my friends are married and have children, so I don't see them as often anymore either." Natasha bit her lip. "I just realized no one would really miss me all that much if I never went back."

"I just met you and I will miss you when you leave." *What the grak am I saying?*

She sighed. "I feel the same."

After evening meal, Ronan flew Natasha in the cloaked shuttle to a new location on Talonka Six while she comm'd the *Invictus*. In the event the Svesti were able to track the communication, he wanted to ensure the hybrids remained hidden.

"Commander. Checking in as requested," Natasha said.

"Lady Natasha. Give me a moment while I add Tolvex and Rivezt to our conversation," Durek said.

Once the others were present and exchanged greetings, Rivezt said, "Natasha, I got the information you requested from Earth. We haven't had time to test all of the samples, but we've completed most of them. You are correct. It is measles. There's a slight variation from one of Earth's known strains, which might account for the longer incubation period."

"I thought that might be the case. You received the vaccine info with its components?" Natasha leaned forward.

The healer nodded. "Yes. I have MISI running simulations now. It appears Svesti may be naturally immune. Using the list of species you gave me, all show the same level of susceptibility as humans with the exception of the Zuvgran. They seem more likely to contract the disease. It's still early, but using Earth's vaccine, we may be able to adjust it to adequately protect all species except the Zuvgran. It would give them some protection, but not immunity. I still have to run simulations for the hybrid combinations you sent me."

"Why would we wish to protect the Zuvgran?" Durek said, his face hard.

"Not all Zuvgran are bad, just as not all Svesti are good," said Natasha. "Right now, I'm trying to protect the children I'm treating and prevent others from getting the disease. Some of those children are half-Zuvgran. They had no choice in who their parents were." Her lips thinned.

Durek dipped his head. "I have no issues with helping younglings whatever their species, Lady Natasha. But developing a vaccine for our enemies requires more discussion."

"These younglings are alive and free from slavery because of some Zuvgran who disagree with their Emperor." Natasha's face reddened and her eyes sparked. "Are you saying we should just ignore that?" *Grak. She's beautiful.*

Tolvex said, "I can see both sides of the issue. Assuming we do develop a vaccine that protects Zuvgran as well, what do you see us doing with it? Are we supposed to set up clinics on Zuvgran worlds?"

Natasha impatiently pushed the loose strands of her hair behind her ear. "No, but we can distribute some through the sympathetic Zuvgran. Even send a message to their Emperor with the information so they can synthesize and inoculate their own people."

"You think they would believe us?" Durek said incredulously.

"They have lots of scientists who can check it. They can choose to use the information or not. If they don't protect their own people, that's on them." Natasha frowned. "I see not sharing as supporting biological warfare."

"That's what they did to us," said Durek, his scar white on his face.

"Yes, it is. It wasn't morally right then and it isn't morally right now, even if you didn't start the spread of the disease,"

Natasha said with crossed arms. "We can't control what they do, but we can act with integrity."

Rivezt cut in. "We can discuss this later. For now, Natasha, do you need anything for the younglings? Food, clothing, things like that?"

Ronan shook his head when she glanced at him.

"No. Oh, did you check about the Vitamin A like I asked?"

"Yes. It would not be harmful for any of the species. Whether or not it will help, I do not know," Rivezt said.

"Okay, I'll add it to their treatment plans and see if it makes any difference." Natasha sighed. "I do appreciate all the assistance with this situation."

"Now that most of the Ermipas have been rescued and treated, we can spare a healer and some medics to help you," Rivezt said.

Natasha shook her head, her long braid brushing her shoulder. "We're not at that degree of trust here yet, Ash'n, but if that changes, I will ask for the help."

"As you wish."

"If there's nothing else, I'll talk to you in the morning." Natasha smiled.

Ronan disconnected the comm when the Svesti finished. He rose from his seat to kneel in front of Natasha. Resting his hands on the armrests, he inhaled her scent.

"I am in awe of you, Natasha—standing up for what you believe. Too many beings don't," he said.

Her cheeks turned pink. "I'm nothing special, Ronan."

"That's where you're wrong, *caliana*. You are very special." He bent toward her. "I would like to kiss you."

Her lips turned up in a delightful manner. "Are you asking me or telling me?"

"Which would you prefer?" Nuzzling her ear with his nose, he smiled when she turned her head to give him better access. Softly, he trailed a slow path with his lips along her jawline.

"I prefer action over talk," she moaned. *As do I.*

Hovering over her lips, he said, "As you wish." He lightly pressed his mouth to hers, marveling at the softness under him. Tracing the seam of her lips with his tongue, he invited her to open for him. When her tongue touched his, his entire body heated with ardor. He let her lead the kiss, opening wider for her exploration. His tongue licked at her blunt teeth before deepening the kiss. *She tastes like a holiday celebration.*

His hands gripped the armrests to keep from pulling her closer before she was ready. Her fingers caressed his face, stroking his beard and bare cheek. Groaning, his mouth left hers and turned to kiss the center of her palm. Her soft gasp melted something inside him. Taking care to keep his horns from scraping her, he rested his forehead on hers and shared ragged breaths.

After long moments, he drew back and unclenched his stiff hands from her seat.

"We should return to the cavern while it's still light," he said.

She opened passion-glazed eyes and nodded. "Yes."

Returning to his seat, he strapped in and guided the shuttle. Inhaling the scent of her arousal, he suppressed a groan. *Grak. I want her, and not just for a single rutting. She'll go back to the Svesti and leave me behind. Do I risk it?*

Glancing sideways at her, her flushed face made him want to thump his chest like a primal beast. *She looks like that because of me from a single kiss.*

Chapter 14

DAMN, THE MAN can kiss.

Even though she wanted to squirm to relieve the ache between her thighs, Natasha sat quietly as Ronan flew them back. For the past two months she lived among three thousand warriors on the *Invictus*—all with hot bodies—and not one of them drew her feminine interest for more than a passing glance. Yet, Ronan with his kind eyes and sweet nature, combined with a keen intelligence and scorching body, reminded her she was a woman with needs that hadn't been met in a long time.

Peeking sideways at him, she admired his profile and easy competence flying the ship. His facial hair looked like it would scratch, but it was just soft enough to cause shivers down her spine when it touched her skin. When he leaned over her, instead of feeling trapped, she felt surrounded and protected. And the coffee, almond, and spearmint scent she kept smelling was definitely coming from him.

While her government told the Svesti she was a volunteer for a Choosing to enter a troth or breeding contract, everyone now knew the truth. Her status when she reached Costonia was uncertain. After living with the Svesti on the space cruiser, she didn't believe they would force her into anything, but what if the situation soured. She would fight against it, of course. But if things went wrong, then she might be spending a year with someone as an arrangement. Ronan could be her only chance in the near future to be with someone who actually excited her.

But is it fair to him? Our time together is finite and he's a good man. I've only known him a couple of days. She suppressed a snort. *Yeah, Natasha, be honest with yourself. It's not like you haven't hooked up with a guy in less time.*

She still hadn't made a decision by the time they returned to their cavern. *I'll just play it by ear and see where it goes.*

"Do you have something I can wear?" Natasha asked as she tugged at her shirt. "I want to put everything in the refresher. My nanosuit is going to get up and walk away on its own soon." *Not to mention my underwear and bra.*

Ronan put down his tablet and stood. "Let me see what I can find."

She followed him into his quarters. He pressed the wall and a drawer slid out. Rummaging, he pulled out a silky shirt and tossed it to her. He grabbed some shorts for himself.

"Thanks." She paused. "Should I use the facilities in one of the other quarters?"

"No. You're welcome to stay here. I'll be out in the dining area," Ronan said as he left the room.

Hair unbraided and her body stripped down, Natasha stepped into the sonic shower. When she finished, her hair and body felt clean. *I still prefer water showers. I could use the hot water on my aching muscles.* She pulled on the silky dark green shirt Ronan had given her. *Damn, this feels good against my skin.* It had a V-neck collar which rested low on her cleavage, short sleeves that ended at her elbows, and the length fell just above knees. There was a long slit, though, just below her ass. She stared, confused for a moment, then realized it must be to accommodate his tail. *I'll just have to remember not to bend over.*

She picked up all her dirty items and tossed them into the refresher. She swore she could feel her breasts sigh in relief at her lack of bra. *I've been wearing it for almost five days straight. That's just cruel and unusual punishment.* She sniggered at herself. She left her hair down after brushing it with a hairbrush she found in the bathroom. *Damn, it feels good to be clean and comfortable.*

Padding on bare feet to the dining area, she noticed the transport floors weren't freezing. The shirt shifted on her skin, making her aware of her nakedness underneath. *I really like this material. Maybe I can get some and sew some nightgowns for myself.*

She stood for a moment just admiring Ronan. He also cleaned up and changed into the shorts. Just shorts. Currently, he was bent over getting drinks from the cooling unit. *Look at that ass and legs.* Her eyes traveled along his corded muscles. He straightened and turned. She held her breath for a moment, admiring the view of his smooth pecs, taut abs, and defined arms.

When she raised her eyes, he smiled. *His fangs look shorter than most Svesti.*

"Snack?" he asked.

"That would be great. Thanks." She sat and tucked one leg under her with the other bent, foot on the seat. She tugged the shirt to make sure she wasn't flashing him. *Stupid seats are too high on this ship, too.*

Along with the beverages, Ronan brought over a plate of bite-size cheeses, fruits, and green crackers. Natasha took a small bite of a cracker, then added some cheese to it before taking another bite.

Shaking his head, he said, "Weren't sure you'd like the cracker?"

"It's green. Where I come from crackers are not green."

They ate silently for a bit. Taking a sip of his drink, Ronan said, "You haven't spoken of the other human women. Do you like them?"

"Oh, we've been so busy, we haven't had much time just to talk about normal things but yes, the women who came with me from Earth are amazing." She tilted her head, her long hair brushing her arm. "What should I tell you about them?"

"Anything you wish to share. I want to know everything about you and how you feel about the beings around you." A light tinge of pink rose on his cheeks. "There hasn't been a female who's drawn my interest like you...ever."

She ducked her head as her own cheeks heated. "Well, you saw Talia on the comm with the Commander. She's American and was secretly made an ambassador by her government. Before this trip, she worked as an author, writing paranormal romances." She smirked. "Talia and Durek's tempers have caused arguments in some fashion since the first day. I wouldn't necessarily enjoy a relationship like that, but it works for them. She's very intelligent, and she has an adult son and sister back on Earth. We women let her be our spokesperson for matters that concern all of us. But, truthfully, we usually discuss it all first."

"You sound like you admire her."

"She's passionate and cares. She's been through some shit and come out stronger. So, yes, I guess you can say I admire her."

"What is...American?"

"Earth doesn't have a central planetary government, so we have countries with individual rulers in different parts of the world. I'm Russian."

Ronan leaned forward, his chin resting on the knuckles of one fist. "Who else?"

"There's Lin, a super smart, petite Chinese botanist who is so gentle and kind you just want to shield her from life's ugliness. Surprisingly, she and Ash'n, the healer on the comm, are fated mates." Natasha shook her head in bewilderment. "I'm still not sure how that all happened without me knowing."

Ronan frowned. "I'm assuming you spend lots of time with the healers. Did you want him for yourself?"

"Oh, no. Ash'n and I are just work colleagues bordering on friends." She paused. "Emmy is an Australian hacker." At his confused look, she said, "She gets into computer systems she doesn't have access to. She's also very smart, pretty closed off, but has been opening up. Underneath all her attitude, she's got a caring heart. She's Tolvex's fated mate. He was the other Svesti on the comm and the head security officer on the *Invictus*."

"That's three. Four counting you. So two more females?"

"Yes. Rachel is British, a total badass, and our self-defense teacher." Natasha laughed. "Our first training session, she taught us about our center of gravity and how not to be where an attacker expected us to be. Some big warrior walked up trash talking how he could easily catch her. She made him look like a bumbling idiot before she tossed his arrogant ass to the mat."

"I think I'd like her." Ronan grinned.

"Yeah, I think you would. She's a good person. Last, there's Ava, a Canadian chef who loves experimenting with Svesti foods. She looks like the girl next door, so sweet and innocent, but gets fiery when something is important to her." Natasha pouted. "I miss her cooking."

"You sound like you enjoy their company."

"I do. They can be a lot of fun and they're genuine, you know?"

"I understand."

"How about you? Do you spend most of your time here? Who's important to you?"

"We have several locations where our hybrids live. I rotate between them all. Largon or I usually pick up new rescues and help them settle in. We also bring in supplies when needed. Sometimes I take short-term mercenary jobs to help finance our efforts."

"Sounds like you keep busy. Given your unique heritage, how do you pass unnoticed on the different planets or on those jobs?"

"Mostly by wearing a cloak like the one you've seen me in. But I also have a portable appearance cloaking device that makes me look Svesti."

"No way. Can you show me?"

"Let me go get it." Ronan bounded up and went to his quarters. Natasha watched his ass flex and his tail sway as he left. *He looks as good from the back as he does from the front.* She sighed. He returned with a bracelet and put it on. He pressed a button.

"Holy shit!" Natasha stared in awe at Ronan as pure Svesti. The device changed his skin tone and hair color, and his horns were no longer visible. "Are your horns still there?"

"Of course." He squatted next to her. "You can still feel them. Try, but use caution not to hurt yourself."

Natasha held up a hand and tilted her head as she decided the best way to find his horns. She placed her fingers on his temple and slowly followed his scalp before bumping into a horn. She grasped it, trying to reconcile what her hand felt and what her eyes didn't see. *Oh, his horn is warm with barely perceptible grooves in it. I expected it to be cold and smooth.* She explored his horn as it widened near his head.

His body tensed and he drew in a breath.

She let go immediately. "Am I hurting you?"

"No. My horns are very sensitive at the base. It feels exceptionally good when you touch them." *Horns as an erogenous zone. I wouldn't have thought of that.*

"Turn it off," she said. "I like you better as yourself."

Heavy-lidded eyes rose to meet hers. "I'm glad." He pressed the bracelet. Slowly, his hand reached for her hair. He fingered it. "Your hair is like satiny sunshine. I like it unbound. You look more relaxed." His scent sat heavy in the air. His nostrils flared. *Uh, guess he smells me, too.*

She felt her blush rising and her cheeks heating. "Thanks."

Standing, he clasped her hand and drew her to her feet. His body heat warmed her through her shirt and her nipples pebbled as his scent surrounded her. Tenderly, his other hand cupped her face.

"You are a beautiful female, Natasha."

"That's what *caliana* means in Svesti, doesn't it?"

"Yes." His hand fell from her face. "Come. Let's rest."

He led her to his quarters. She stopped in the doorway.

"I'm not sure I'm ready for more, Ronan."

Ronan turned back to her. Staring into his silver eyes, she noted blue flecks dotting the irises, reminding her of the ocean.

"Nothing more than sleep, *caliana*. Maybe conversation if we're not tired enough yet. I enjoy your company and I'll rest easier if you're near."

She searched his earnest eyes. *He really means it.*

"You're very protective, aren't you?"

"I am." He grinned. "Maybe it's the Svesti genes. Mother taught me from a very young age that males must protect females and younglings." His expression turned serious and his tail drooped. "I only wish I had been able to protect her and Marris."

Natasha let go of his hand and got under the covers.

"You were too young, Ronan."

He laid on top of the blanket facing her, his head resting on his hand. She mirrored his position.

"In my head, I know that, but in my heart—" He paused. "I adored both of them so much. I loved my father, but it felt different." His eyelids closed and his face tensed. "I'm not even sure when, where, or how they died. I never got to say goodbye."

Her fingers traced the strong lines of his face. *He could have grown up angry and bitter, but instead, he's caring and thoughtful.*

"They would be proud of the male you've grown up to be, Ronan."

Opening his eyes to gaze at her, he said, "I hope so." He turned his head to kiss her palm. "Thank you."

"Tell me more about them, please. I want to be able to picture them."

Ronan told her stories of his family, his love for them in his voice. As the night grew longer, she also shared stories of her parents, but especially her beloved *Babushka*. She fell asleep enveloped by his scent with his chest rumbling low under her ear.

Chapter 15

WAKING UP SLOWLY, Ronan inhaled Natasha's unique scent. Her warm body slept entwined with his. His hand wrapped around her hip, but he refrained from stroking and squeezing her. *I haven't slept so well in solars.*

Cautiously slipping from her hold, he stood up from the bed. In the sanitary facilities, he performed his usual morning routine, leaving the shower for last. His cock demanded attention. Thoughts of Natasha filled his head as he grabbed his member. Her hard nipples hard under the silky shirt, her long blonde hair swaying above her ass, her scent filling his nostrils, the light in her eyes when she got excited or angry, and the smile on her face as she talked about her *Babushka* were all fodder for his fertile imagination as he stroked himself. In his mind's eye, he envisioned circling those nubs with his fingers gently before tugging and sucking on them with her hair shining against his pillows. His fantasy had her scent ripening, her eyes darkening with arousal, and her face a rictus of pleasure as he licked at her core. His body bowed with the force of his pleasure as his cum streaked the wall of the shower. He grunted as he held back from calling her name.

Breathing heavily with his eyes closed, he rested the tips of his horns on the wall as his body calmed. *Grak. I want her even though I have nothing to offer but pleasure and a life of danger and hiding.*

Ronan finished making the morning meal as Natasha walked into the dining area, dressed and ready for the day. They chatted easily as they ate.

Afterwards, he flew the cloaked shuttle to another location so she could comm the *Invictus*. His mind wandered slightly as Natasha and the Svesti healer spoke in medical terms, but her excitement at his words lit her face and her elegant hands gestured wildly. *I should pay attention to what they're saying instead of imagining her with her hair down.*

Out of the corner of his eye, he saw a flashing emergency code on his console.

"What is it?" Natasha said with a concerned look.

"You'll have to call the *Invictus* back. I have an urgent comm." Ronan frowned.

As soon as Natasha disconnected, Ronan answered the incoming comm.

"Ronan, we need you," Crutaw, a Romittel-Zuvgran youngling of fifteen solars said quietly, his breathing rapid. "They found us." *Grak.*

Ronan leaned forward. "Are you safe?"

Crutaw shook his bald head, his brown skin damp with sweat trailing off his high, narrow forehead.

"I counted twelve of them. They attacked during morning meal. We're still in the dining area—locked in." Crutaw's oval eyes watered and his fat lower lip trembled. "They took Teeka. We could hear her screaming." *No!* Ronan's tail swung in hard, short flicks, banging on his seat.

"Where is Largon? This is his comm." Ronan's claws extended and he clenched his fists, the bite of pain in his palms keeping him centered.

"He handed me his comm to hide when they first broke in. He tried to fight them when they grabbed Teeka. He killed four of them before they subdued him and took him away. I don't know where he is." Crutaw's breath sawed in and out.

"Breathe evenly, young warrior. Do you know what their timetable is?" *I'm three hours away.*

"Yostal heard them say they were ordered to keep us here until some scientist showed up tomorrow which gives them time for 'some fun' in their words." Crutaw lowered his voice even further. "What should we do? Should we use the—"

"No. Don't say the word, even amongst yourselves. Do nothing yet. Help everyone stay calm and try to stay together if you can." Ronan pierced the youngling with a hard stare. "When we are done with this comm, you are to power it down and hide it on your person. Do not use it again unless they move you to a new location and you think they'll keep you there for a while. Then just turn it on so I can track you. They cannot know you have it. Understood?"

Crutaw squared his shoulders. "Understood, sir."

Ronan nodded. "You've done well, Crutaw. I'll be there as soon as I can."

"We'll be waiting, Ronan."

Ronan disconnected the comm and stood. He punched the shuttle wall, roaring with rage. Blood dripped from his hands and his tail whipped wildly.

"Are you done so I can heal you? Or do you need to punish the ship some more?" Natasha said drily from behind him.

Breathing heavily, he slumped and turned to her with his head lowered. He retracted his claws. "I apologize for my temper, *caliana*."

She pointed at his seat. "Sit. Show me your hands."

He followed her instructions. Gently she cleaned his hands and ran a healing wand over them.

"How many?" she asked with concern.

"Twenty-three. Teeka is the oldest at sixteen solars. Crutaw is a solar younger." Closing his eyes against the welling tears, he said, "They're probably raping her as we speak." His jaw tight, he clenched his teeth and opened his eyes when he felt under better control. "I hope they haven't killed her or Largon."

Natasha's face hardened, although her hands remained gentle as she treated him.

"Where are they?"

"On Straxis, about three hours from here. It's the sixth planet in the Lestanus system."

"Will you allow me to ask the Svesti to help rescue them? We can't take on eight Zuvgran warriors alone."

Ronan straightened. "We? There is no we. You're staying here."

Natasha stood from where she had been squatting. "Oh, no, I'm not. I'm going with you. I'll be needed to treat injuries—especially if that young female has been sexually assaulted."

"It's not safe for you," he bit out. *I can't let them have you.*

"It's not safe for you either," she countered. "You didn't answer my question. Can I ask the Svesti for help?"

He looked at her crossed arms and set face, her brown eyes flashing with temper and worry. *Grak. She's so stubborn. But she's right. I need help and the closest warriors I know are too far away.*

"Yes, Natasha. Let's contact the *Invictus*." He sent the comm request.

"Lady Natasha. Is everything all right? You disconnected quickly earlier." Durek said with his lavender eyes full of concern.

"Commander, this is Ronan d'Olorg." She gestured at Ronan. "I would like to request your help. One of the other refuge locations was invaded on Straxis. There are twenty-three younglings and a Zuvgran who require rescue before tomorrow. Ronan and I can be there in three hours, but the communication we received indicated eight Zuvgran warriors holding them."

"d'Olorg. Well met." Durek dipped his chin. "Lady Natasha, I will be happy to send warriors with d'Olorg, but I cannot allow you to go to Straxis. You need to return to the

Invictus for your safety." I already tried that. Let's see if you have better luck.

"No. I'm going with Ronan. One of the younglings is a female taken from the group who is probably being assaulted as we debate. She will require a female healer." *Look at her facing off with a Svesti commander with absolutely no fear. My grakkin' cock loves it.*

The facial scar on Durek's face whitened. He closed his eyes and blew out a harsh breath. Ronan heard a number of growls from the *Invictus* at Natasha's words.

Durek opened his eyes and glared at her. "Do none of you Earth females listen to reason?"

"We do, but our reasoning may differ from yours, so we come to different conclusions." *Grak. He's going to lose the argument, too.*

Sighing heavily, Durek looked to his side. "Tolvex, how close is Security Team Alpha to Straxis?"

Tolvex said, "About two hours away."

"Add them to this encrypted comm."

A moment later, another Svesti with short dark hair and brown eyes joined them. "Commander." He turned to them and said, "Lady Natasha." Ronan noticed the male's eyes flicker once when he took in Ronan's appearance, but nothing else. *He's good. He barely registered surprise at a Svesti-Zuvgran hybrid.*

"Tesix," said Durek. "I need the *Rectitude* to divert to Straxis to meet with Lady Natasha and Ronan d'Olorg for a mission."

"What is the mission, Sir?"

"d'Olorg," Durek said, waving a hand.

"There are twenty-three Zuvgran hybrid younglings and one Zuvgran male that have been captured by the Zuvgran. Last intel suggested there are eight Zuvgran holding them awaiting a scientist who is to arrive tomorrow at an unknown time," Ronan said.

Tesix said to someone in the Rectitude's cockpit, "Change course to Straxis, Xoriv." He returned his attention to Ronan. "How old are the younglings?"

"From four to sixteen solars. I anticipate the oldest and the Zuvgran male to require medical attention. They may not be able to move under their own power." Ronan entered a course for Straxis himself and his shuttle zoomed forth. "Lady Natasha and I will be there in three hours."

"Lady Natasha will be there?" Tesix queried.

"Is that a problem, Tesix?" Natasha said with a bite in her tone.

"No. I'm assuming you've already had the discussion with d'Olorg and the Commander. I have no desire to argue with you." Tesix's lips turned up at the corners. *Smart male.*

Ronan tapped his console. "I'm sending you two sets of coordinates. The first is where to land. Do you have cloaking ability?"

Tesix nodded.

"Obviously, you'll need to remain hidden. The second set is the exact location of the refuge. Since you'll be there before us, it would be helpful if you monitor to ensure the enemy numbers are correct and they don't move the younglings."

"We can extract them before you arrive," Tesix said.

Ronan shook his head. "No. I have a plan that minimizes the risk to the younglings. However, I need to be there to coordinate with you and to ensure the younglings don't run from you. They know me."

"Acknowledged. We'll meet you at the landing coordinates," Tesix said. "Is there anything else we need to know before you arrive?"

"No."

"Commander, is there anything else from you?"

"No, Tesix. Remember *Invictus'* primary mission and keep everyone safe. d'Olorg will be in charge unless his plans include something exceptionally dangerous. Use your best judgment," Durek said.

"As you command. *Rectitude* out," Tesix said.

"How many warriors are on the *Rectitude*?" Ronan asked.

"Five," said Durek. "Do you require more?"

"No, that's perfect."

"Comm me when the mission is complete. If necessary, we can take the younglings onboard the *Invictus*." *Natasha was right. They are willing to help.*

Ronan's chin dipped. "I appreciate your assistance, Commander."

Durek grunted. "*Invictus* out."

"Strap in, Natasha. We'll be leaving the atmosphere soon," Ronan said.

Natasha sat and buckled the safety restraints. She smiled. "My second planet in three days."

Chuckling, he said, "It's going to get crowded in here with all the younglings."

"Maybe the *Rectitude* has more room."

"The younglings will want me nearby."

"We'll worry about that once we rescue them, Ronan." She leaned over and squeezed his hand. "We will rescue them."

"You'll be staying on the shuttle or the *Rectitude*, Natasha." Raising a palm, he continued over her protest, "That's non-negotiable. You're not a warrior. You're a healer. The warriors will get the younglings and Largon and you will heal them as soon as we have them safe. I cannot do what I need to do if I'm worried about you, too."

She blew a strand of hair out of her eyes. "Well, fuck. I hate that you're right. I won't participate in the rescue portion unless there's something I can do from one of the ships."

He laughed. "You couldn't help but put a caveat on your agreement, could you?"

Grinning, she said, "I guess not."

Chapter 16

A S MUCH AS it irked her, Natasha silently agreed she would be a hindrance to the actual rescue. *I'm still surprised Ronan and Durek didn't fight me more about going to Straxis at all. I'm glad they relented. We don't have time to waste.*

She paid attention as Ronan flew the shuttle, hoping to learn more about the controls. He set the ship on automatic pilot and stood.

"I'm going to put on my nanosuit and grab my weapons," he said. "I want no delay once we arrive."

"Okay. I'll wait here."

Alone, she marveled at the scene outside the cockpit. Occasional strands of light from the Lestanus sun relieved the inky darkness. One planet in the system appeared blue from a distance, while another looked yellow. *I'm flying in space in a solar system I'd never even heard of. It's fucking amazing.*

I feel so small in such a vast universe. Her thoughts drifted to what she learned in the last two months about the various species and worlds. *In some ways, Earth is a microcosm of what's happening out here. Our messed up relations has a ring of familiarity among the unfamiliar here in space.*

She snorted at herself. *I need a good stiff drink if I'm going to be philosophizing about life and the universe. I should get ready myself.* Efficiently, Natasha checked her pack to ensure she had enough medical supplies.

Natasha turned when she heard Ronan's boots on the metal floor. *Holy shit.* Dressed in a self-sealing, body-hugging nanosuit, his muscles were displayed for her viewing pleasure. Keeping her mouth closed so she wouldn't drool, especially when she saw the bulge at the apex of his thighs, she took in the weapons harness that blocked some of the scrumptious dips and rises of his corded flesh. *He is one fine-looking male.*

Is that a blaster or ray gun of some sort? He opened a compartment she hadn't noticed before and started filling the various empty sleeves in the harness with daggers, knives, and something that looked like grenades. He put on the bracelet controlling his portable appearance cloak. *I hope he doesn't have to use it. I really do prefer him as he is.*

"You look like you're ready for war," she teased.

Solemnly, he said, "I will do what is necessary to free the younglings and Largon."

Ronan took a small dagger with a sheath and handed it to her along with a leather strap.

"Why are you giving me this?" *I don't know if I can stab anyone.*

"Just in case. Please wear it under your lab coat. Upper thigh works well. Easy access."

She huffed. "I don't think I can use this, Ronan. I'm a doctor, not a soldier."

"I would rather you have it and choose not to use it than not have it when you need it. I hope you won't need it, but it would make me feel better to know you are carrying it." He paused for a moment. "Besides, you don't have to try to kill someone. You can stab or slice somewhere to incapacitate, not kill. So long as you keep yourself safe."

She slid the dagger from its covering and waved it back and forth before returning it. Sighing, she threaded the strap through slits in the sheath, then fastened the whole thing to her upper thigh.

"Just so you know—I don't like this."

He dipped his chin. "Thank you for humoring me, *caliana.*"

On Straxis, Natasha caught the cloak Ronan tossed her after he landed the shuttle in a clearing.

"Come," he said. "Let's go meet the Svesti."

She shrugged into the outer garment and pulled the hood over her head. *Thank goodness I braided my hair. It's easier to hide.* She followed him down the ramp. *Damn. My white sneakers don't blend in, though.*

They had only been walking a few minutes in the tree line when Ronan stopped.

"What is it?" she said quietly as she furtively searched the area. She saw only red dirt and brown-barked trees with red leaves.

"I'm waiting for them to let us in." As he spoke, a ramp appeared out of nowhere. She saw Brauvix and Xoriv with blasters standing at the top. "Do you recognize them?"

"Yes."

"Then you may lead, *caliana*." He gestured to the ramp.

Brestov Xoriv nodded his head, shaved except for a single center braid down the middle of his scalp, at them. "Lady Natasha."

Triv'n Brauvix smiled at her. "It's good to see you, Lady Natasha."

"Xoriv. Brauvix. This is my friend, Ronan d'Olorg. Ronan, Xoriv is a pilot; Brauvix is a communications officer."

Both Svesti nodded at Ronan.

"Well met, d'Olorg," said Xoriv as he closed the ramp behind them.

Natasha followed Brauvix to the cockpit. *I wonder how big a ship has to be before they call it a bridge?* Krivez Tesix and Slaiv'n Westov waited for them. Tesix made the introductions and said that Gal'n Kalix would join them shortly. Before he finished speaking, Kalix entered the shuttle.

"Report," said Tesix.

"The intel seems correct. I counted eight Zuvgran in the hour I watched the dwelling. There appeared to be a shift change of those guarding the outside so it's possible there are more inside," said Kalix.

"I would think so. They would have to have some presence to keep their prisoners afraid," said Tesix.

"d'Olorg? Do you have any insights?"

"I would expect four more at a minimum. I know Largon, the Zuvgran male on our side, killed four," Ronan said.

"What is this plan you have?" asked Tesix.

Ronan smiled, his fangs bright against his gray skin. "There are two hidden tunnels." He pulled out his tablet and showed them blueprints of the dwelling. He pointed. "Here and here is where they enter the house. One leads to the office area, while the other opens in the kitchen storeroom—which is right next to where the majority of younglings were being held three hours ago."

"Where do they emerge?" asked Westov.

"The storeroom entrance is less than a shuttle's width from your ramp. The one from the office emerges a quarter mile to the south of us. "The tunnels are long and there's a door to each that requires a code." *Oh, maybe they can get everyone out without the Zuvgran realizing where they went.*

"Where do you think they're keeping the female and the injured Zuvgran?" Tesix asked.

"My best guess is the office for Largon and this bedroom for the female." Ronan pointed at both locations with his teeth clenched. "I don't know what shape either will be in. I propose we split into two groups—one for each tunnel." He blew out a harsh breath. "As much as I want to rescue Teeka and Largon myself, it would be best if I go in the group to the storeroom to keep the majority of the younglings calm. I only require one other warrior to help evacuate them. Unfortunately, they're used to having to run stealthily."

"So, four to the office?" asked Brauvix.

Ronan shook his head. "No. We'll need a male to guard each shuttle and Natasha will remain on one. So only two for the office tunnel."

"You'll have to show us the entrances," Tesix said.

"Of course. We can also set explosives at the coded doors. We can set them off once we know everyone is clear."

Tesix' brown eyes narrowed. "Brauvix and I will take the office tunnel. Westov, you're with d'Olorg. Kalix stays with Lady Natasha on the *Rectitude*, while Xoriv will remain with d'Olorg's ship."

"No offense meant, but perhaps Brauvix should stay with a ship," said Xoriv. Brauvix glared at him.

"No," said Tesix. "Of all of us, Brauvix is the least likely to frighten a young, traumatized female with his looks." The Svesti shared thoughtful glances before all nodding in agreement.

Westov said, "We have a couple stretchers. Is there room to leave them in the office tunnel so we have a more comfortable way to transport the injured?"

"Yes," said Ronan. "That's a good idea."

"I think I should wait on Ronan's ship if that's where the injured are going," said Natasha.

"There are better defenses on the *Rectitude*," said Tesix.

"The worst injuries won't be here." Natasha crossed her arms. *I know what you're doing.*

"Our primary mission—"

"Don't even go there, Tesix." Natasha shut him down.

"Fine. You'll be on d'Olorg's ship." Natasha refrained from smiling at Tesix' quick capitulation. *No need to poke the bear more than necessary.*

Kalix said, "It makes sense for me to fly you to the ship and return here."

Ronan said, "I agree. I can show Tesix where the entrance is and give him the code."

Once the *Rectitude* was in the air, Ronan guided Kalix to a spot in the clearing. Tesix handed Ronan something which he put in his ear. Ronan showed Tesix and Brauvix the entrance hidden underneath a tree. He spoke with them briefly before they disappeared into the tunnel with the stretchers. He returned to their ship to give Xoriv access to the controls.

Natasha walked him to the ramp.

"Be safe, warrior." Her fingers wanted to caress his face.

"You stay safe and listen to Xoriv, *caliana*. Don't endanger yourself." Ronan's eyes seared her.

Oh, fuck it. She reached up and kissed him. His large hands gripped her waist, but he pulled back, breathing heavily.

"We'll finish this later, Natasha." His silver eyes gleamed. "Go."

She watched him enter the *Rectitude* and lost sight of him once the ramp closed. She went to the cockpit and sat in her usual seat.

From the console, she heard Kalix say, "Landing now."

"When did you meet d'Olorg?" Xoriv asked.

"A few days ago. There's another hidden refuge on Talonka Six with a disease spreading. They needed my help," Natasha said.

Xoriv glanced sideways at her and smirked. "You seem close for only having known each other for so short a time."

Natasha's lips pressed together. "What's that supposed to mean?"

"Just an observation." He paused. "I was monitoring the ramp so I knew when to close it." *Damn. He saw the kiss.*

"I like him." *A lot.*

"It seems fast."

She shot him an annoyed look. "Are you going all big brother on me?"

He chuckled. "Hardly, Lady Natasha. Most of us Svesti haven't had relationships with the opposite gender in a long time. I'm mostly curious. I would've thought you would form a partnership with one of the healers."

Surprised, she looked at him closer. "You haven't heard, have you?"

"Heard what?"

"There are three fated mate bonds on the *Invictus*."

His eyes widened. "You jest."

"The Commander and Talia, Tolvex and Emmy, and Rivezt with Lin," she informed him.

"Truth?"

"Yes." She nodded her head emphatically. Teasing, she added, "Looks like Ava and Rachel are still available."

"They're very nice females, but I'm not sure I see the appeal of being accountable to another." Xoriv shuddered with an exaggerated grimace. *Typical bachelor.*

Laughing, she said, "I can't wait until you meet your mate. I bet you'll fall hard."

"I doubt I'll find a mate. Not sure I want one." He grinned. "Now back to your friend—I did not think Svesti and Zuvgran were compatible."

"His father was a geneticist. He and his late sister were the only two of their kind."

"Sounds lonely," said Xoriv.

She tilted her head. "Yes, it does. Ronan was lucky. Largon, the Zuvgran male we're rescuing, raised him after his family was killed."

"And now they take in Zuvgran hybrids?"

"They rescue them, then care for them."

"Admirable. Dangerous, but admirable." Xoriv's fangs flashed.

"I agree."

They ended their conversation when the teams reported reaching the coded doors.

"Good hunting," Xoriv said under his breath. "May the Goddess be with you." Natasha silently added her own prayers to his.

Chapter 17

A T THE CODED door, Ronan met Westov's focused sea green eyes.

"We'll set the charges just before the storeroom. I'll have the younglings follow you out. I'll be the last and close this door behind us," Ronan instructed.

Westov dipped his chin, his braids barely moving.

"How many?"

"Assuming Teeka isn't with them, twenty-two. If there are any guards, we'll have to try to take them out quietly." At Westov's nod, Ronan tapped the code for the door. "Here we go." *Please let them all be there with no guards in the room.*

They traveled silently along the remaining tunnel. Turning off his handheld light, Ronan cautiously opened the hidden door to the dark space beyond. At the wall to his left, he moved two cleaning bots out of the way of the maintenance opening to the dining area. Long, wide strips of rubber hung vertically to hide the storeroom. They peered through the flaps to count the younglings and check for guards.

Westov shook his head. He mouthed. "No one except younglings."

Ronan clicked his tongue three times. The younglings closest to them sat up straight and tapped shoulders of others. A wave of alertness spread through the room.

"Start scooting back slowly in your pairs," Ronan whispered to those closest to him.

A Wrestikan-Zuvgran hybrid male of six solars kicked the female in front of him gently. When she looked at him, he jerked his head toward the maintenance opening. He scooted back with another youngling of four solars.

When they were close enough, Ronan said quietly, "Come."

The younglings hurried into the storeroom and stood.

Ronan pointed to Westov. "Follow him quickly and quietly."

The small males nodded with wide eyes looking up at the tall Svesti. Westov smiled gently at them and led them to the hidden door. As they went into the tunnel, more younglings swiftly entered the storeroom.

Ronan gave each youngling an encouraging smile and pointed at the tunnel before putting his finger to his lips. The last was Crutaw and a female of eight solars. He stopped Crutaw with a hand on his shoulder as he listened to Tesix report they found Largon in the office alone. He said he and Brauvix moved the Zuvgran back into the tunnel onto a stretcher to keep him safe while they looked for Teeka.

Ronan whispered, "Crutaw, close the coded door behind you once you're through. Keep everyone quiet and calm. At the end, there is a Svesti ship. You must all board it. They will keep you safe. Their names are Westov and Kalix."

"Aren't you coming?" the female asked with a quivering lip.

"I'm going to help look for Teeka. I have other warriors helping me."

She nodded, her shoulders trembling. Crutaw led her to the tunnel.

"You can count on me," whispered Crutaw.

Ronan smiled. "I know. Now go." He closed the tunnel entrance behind them and moved the cleaning bots back to their original spots.

Ronan tapped his ear comm. "Dining area evacuated. I'm in the building and will meet up with the other team to find Teeka." He heard the Svesti acknowledge.

Moving stealthily, he kept low as he traversed the edges of the dining area to one of the doorways. Listening intently, he heard nothing. Frowning, he checked around the doorway for wires or traps. *No guard? That doesn't make sense.*

Cautiously, he opened the door and checked the hall. Seeing no one, he rapidly made his way to where he thought Teeka might be. He met up with Tesix and Brauvix as they left the office. Outside the bedroom door, he heard muffled noises.

Brauvix crouched and opened the door slightly. Ronan saw his face harden and his claws extend. Brauvix looked at Ronan and Tesix, nodded, then held up four fingers. Brauvix stepped back suddenly.

Jangling noises became louder. "Now that I've had her mouth, I'm hungry. I'm going to get something to eat and terrorize the other ones. Don't use her up until I've had a chance at her other holes." *I can smell Teeka on him. I'll grakkin' kill him.*

Ronan forced down his growl as a Zuvgran male exited the room looking down at where he was fastening his blaster belt. The door closed behind him. Before Ronan could move, Brauvix shot up, snapped the Zuvgran's neck, and dragged the male down the hall. Tesix nodded in approval, his expression grim.

Ronan and Tesix moved behind Brauvix when he reopened the door. All three Zuvgran were facing away from them with their pants down and tails relaxed. He couldn't see Teeka. Tesix pointed to a Zuvgran, then himself, indicating which one he would take down. Brauvix did the same. Ronan nodded. *I'll get the last one.*

Tesix lifted three fingers, then put one down at a time as a countdown to attack. Ronan extended his claws. *They don't deserve the quick death of a blaster. Don't look at Teeka until you've done what you have to.* When Tesix made a fist, they silently moved up behind the three Zuvgran and grabbed their assigned males. Ronan covered the mouth of his enemy with one hand while clawing deep tracks in the male's throat with his other one.

"Death comes to dishonorable males who assault younglings and females. If I had more time, I would make you suffer longer," Ronan said in a guttural whisper in the male's ear. Gurgling breaths emanated from the slashes in the male's neck before they ceased forever. Ronan slid the dead body to the floor.

Tesix's male was dead. *Grak. It looks like he tried to pull out his heart through his chest.*

Ronan turned to Brauvix and noted that Brauvix had sliced off the male's cock before slashing his throat. *I'm *impressed.* Then he got his first look at the Praxite-Zuvgran youngling and wanted to howl in rage. His tail whipped behind him in short flicks. Air burst around him as the tails of the Svesti males swished just as hard as his.

Naked on her knees, Teeka's blue eyes were vacant. Anger filled him as he saw her shaking body covered in bruises on her lavender skin underneath the sprayed blood of her attackers. All three of her small breasts had bite marks on them and her claws had been ripped out. Ronan couldn't sort out all the male scents on the small female to count them. *They died much too quickly.*

He grabbed a blanket off the bed and sank to his knees in front of her. Gently, he wrapped the cloth around her.

"Teeka? It's Ronan. My friends and I are going to take you to safety where there's a healer." She didn't react to his presence at all. He closed his eyes in sorrow and his tail drooped. *Oh, little one, I'm so sorry they found you. Goddess, help her, please. She doesn't deserve this. I rescue them to prevent tragedies like this.*

"d'Olorg?" Brauvix rested a hand on his shoulder. "I'll carry her to the tunnel."

Ronan looked at the male and felt old and battered in comparison to the Svesti who was probably only a few years younger than he. "I can take her."

"I'll be gentle, d'Olorg. If there are others and we have to take a different route, you're the best one to lead. I'll protect her with my life." Compassion and determination shone from Brauvix's brown eyes.

"He's right," said Tesix quietly.

Ronan nodded and turned back to Teeka.

"Teeka, Brauvix is going to carry you. We're going to get Largon and leave." He stood and sucked in a breath. Brauvix moved slowly to pick her up with one arm under her knees and another behind her back. She sat stiffly and didn't utter a sound. Ronan secured the blanket more firmly around her before tenderly tucking her blood-spattered white hair behind her ear.

Resolute, he turned. "Come."

He led them down the hall, Tesix taking the rear. Brauvix murmured softly to Teeka, but Ronan couldn't make out the words. Opening the office door, he scanned the empty room before waving the others in ahead of him. *Why are there no other Zuvgran? Did they really leave the other younglings unguarded?*

Closing the office door behind him, Ronan's senses prickled at the ease of rescue overall. Quickly, he opened a hidden safe and secured its contents to his body. He followed the others into the tunnel, listening intently and inhaling. When they reached Largon, Brauvix gently laid Teeka on the empty stretcher and placed a single restraint over her waist so she wouldn't fall off.

Ronan checked on an unconscious Largon. As he took in his friend's bloody state, broken bones, and labored breaths, his anger rose again. *You fought well, my friend.* In his ear, he heard Westov report that the other younglings made it onboard the *Rectitude* and they were lifting off.

He leaned over and whispered, "The younglings are safe now, Largon, as are you. We're going to get you healed up, so keep fighting to live."

Tesix led the way through the tunnel with Brauvix pushing Teeka's stretcher in front of Ronan and Largon. Swiftly, they made their way through the darkness into the late afternoon light of the forest. The ramp to Ronan's shuttle opened and Natasha ran down to meet them.

"Get back inside, Lady Natasha," Tesix growled. "We're coming in to you."

"I can start assessing on the run, Tesix." She gently lifted Teeka's blanket and scowled at what she saw.

"Stubborn female," Tesix said as ran up the ramp.

"Take her to the dining area, Brauvix. There's no med bay on this shuttle and I'll need space to work."

"Yes, Lady Natasha." Brauvix rushed to enter the shuttle with his precious burden.

She turned at the bottom of the ramp to wait for Ronan and Largon. Ronan's claws extended when he saw an arm wrap around her neck from behind. Her scream cut off and she pointed frantically behind Ronan. Tesix yelled in warning.

Ronan pushed hard on Largon's stretcher to gain momentum up the ramp while simultaneously growling and spinning. A Zuvgran horn slashed across his shoulder. *Grak! If I hadn't turned, he would've run me through. Where did they come from?*

The Zuvgran stumbled when Ronan moved. Ronan extended his claws and jumped on the male's back. His claws delved deeply into his opponent's chest. The Zuvgran's claws dug into Ronan's arms. He clenched his jaw and yanked hard downward. The Zuvgran's howl tapered off as the male died. Panting, Ronan retracted his claws and let the male drop.

Natasha!

Chapter 18

SOMEONE SAVE ME from overprotective males. Natasha knew Tesix didn't realize that her being able to assess the injuries quickly gave her a better idea of what needed to be done once everyone boarded the ship. The poor youngling looked horrific, but at first glance, nothing appeared life-threatening. After yelling instructions to Brauvix, Natasha turned to meet Ronan as he pushed Largon's stretcher.

She saw a Zuvgran behind Ronan. She pointed to warn him. Her scream was cut off by a thick, gray arm wrapping around her neck from behind. Remembering Rachel's training, she tucked her chin into her chest at the male's elbow, forcing the pressure of his arm onto her jaw. She dug her hands into his elbow, stepped back swinging her legs around and behind the Zuvgran so the front of her legs were at the back of the Zuvgran's legs, and swiveled. The male lost his balance taking her down with him, but he released her neck. She fumbled for the knife on her thigh. Drawing it, she stabbed the Zuvgran in his neck. Blood spurted and she turned her face to avoid the spray as much as she could.

Tesix yelled, "Get back."

She rolled off to the side along the grass. Tesix fired his blaster at the Zuvgran she stabbed in the carotid artery. Rising shakily to her hands and knees, she panted and looked for Ronan, blood dripping in her eyes. He was just finishing off the other Zuvgran.

Both males rushed to her. Ronan reached her first and helped her stand, keeping his arm around her waist and his tail wrapped around her ankle. She looked around.

"Are there any more?" she wheezed.

"No." Tesix looked pissed, his tail whipping behind him. "You should've stayed in the shuttle. Your rush to provide treatment has now delayed care for the injured."

Well, hell. He's right and I've lost this argument without opening my mouth. She pursed her lips and curtly nodded. *I hate eating my words.*

"I'm glad you had the knife, *caliana*. Even happier that you used it," Ronan said between pained breaths. *And another instance I have to eat crow.*

Natasha checked Ronan over as they walked up the ramp supporting each other. *That's a nasty gash, but he'll live.* Tesix remained vigilant behind them and closed the door when they were all inside.

Ronan said to Tesix, "Go ahead and blow it up." Tesix tapped his comm. Muffled explosions could be heard as they lifted off.

Brauvix watched over Largon and the youngling in the dining area. Brauvix's concern at her appearance was written all over his face.

"I'm fine." Natasha waved him back as she hobbled to Largon. "It's not my blood." *I think I bruised my hip.*

Getting her first good look at the Zuvgran focused her. "Is there a med bed, Ronan? Largon needs one as soon as possible." She grabbed a scanner and waved it over Largon to confirm her suspicions. "He's bleeding internally." *I can't be the one to let Ronan's friend die.*

Ronan let go of her so she could work, but his tail moved to the small of her back. Its warmth calmed her anxiety. He shook his head. "No."

"Tesix," she said without glancing away from her patient. "Is there one on the *Rectitude*? He needs to get into one as of ten minutes ago."

Tesix spoke into his ear comm. "Xoriv, how long until we can meet up with the *Rectitude*? We need a med bed for the injured."

Xoriv answered over the ship's speakers. "Fifteen minutes in this slower beast, even if they turn to meet us."

Natasha shook her head. "I'm not sure Largon can make it that long."

Xoriv's cheerful voice continued, "But we can be in the *Invictus* shuttle bay in five minutes. They were coming to meet us and are speeding up at my request since we just broke atmosphere. Kalix will backtrack and join us there."

"He couldn't have led with that?" Natasha grumbled. The males chuckled tiredly.

"Let's move everyone back to the entrance to save time," said Tesix.

They had just arrived at the ramp with the stretchers when it opened. Ash'n, along with Healer Markham, rushed to meet them. Natasha started spitting out vitals and they ran to the med bay.

"Is any of that blood yours, Natasha?"

"No."

"Then go clean up before you report to med bay. We'll take care of everyone."

"I should—"

"You should wash so there is no chance of contamination," Ash'n said firmly. His voice softened. "The youngling will need you, Natasha. But if you try to help her the way you look now, you'll traumatize her even more." *Well, shit. He's right. I'm on a fucking roll.*

"Fine." She touched Ronan's arm. "Go with them. They'll take care of everyone. I'll be there soon." He squeezed her hand and nodded. She broke off from the group to head to her quarters.

In the corridor near her room, she heard, "What the fuck?"

She looked up and saw Emmy leaving the quarters she shared with Tolvex.

"Are you alright, Natasha?" Emmy's brown eyes widened as she took in Natasha's bloody appearance.

"Yes. I just need to get presentable before I head to med bay."

Emmy followed Natasha into her living area. "Are you going to tell me about it?"

"Not right now, Emmy," Natasha said as she stripped on the way to the shower. "I've got to hurry." She dropped everything into the refresher and hoped the blood would come out of her sneakers. Removing her comm, she took elastic from her hair, unraveled her braid, and stepped into the hot shower.

Emmy stood at the door. "You disappear for days, tell Durek you can't tell him your location, call for help, and finally show up like this. I think there's a story there."

"Personal space, Emmy. I'm in the shower," Natasha said in a singsong voice. She vigorously scrubbed her hair to get all the blood and sweat out.

"I don't care. I want the scoop." Emmy crossed her arms and leaned against the doorway, foot tapping. *Damn, she's persistent.*

Natasha soaped up a cloth and smoothed it over her face and body. *Don't care about proper facial care right now. Just cleanliness.*

"If I give you the very short version, will you go away?"

"With the caveat you will give all the details later," Emmy bargained.

Natasha hung her head and sighed, letting the hot water rinse her off.

"Fine. Zuvgran hybrid refuge, mostly children with about half sick. Variant of measles spreading across planets. Another refuge on Straxis invaded by Zuvgran. Needed to rescue those children and their caretaker. Got messy. Got bloody. Go away." Natasha left the shower for the drying tube.

"You know I wasn't asking for a medical report, right?" Emmy smirked.

"Can't hear you," Natasha said loudly over the air in the tube.

"I'll let you get away with it for now." Emmy's expression showed her concern. "Seriously, are you okay?"

Natasha wrapped a towel around her, securing it over her breasts. She stopped and looked her friend in the eyes. "I really am fine. I wasn't hurt until the last few minutes and I used one of Rachel's moves." Her lips turned up and she teased. "Emmy, you know you're giving the appearance of caring, right?"

Emmy snorted and gave her the finger. "Fuck you, bitch." She darted forward and gave Natasha a quick hug. "I'm glad you're back safe and sound." She walked out saying happily, "Full story later. Don't forget."

Natasha shook her head and laughed at Emmy's antics. *She's got so much energy; she makes me tired sometimes.* Foregoing her normal braid, she pulled her hair up into a ponytail and grabbed her comm.

In her bedroom she opened a hidden drawer in the wall and her hand hovered over her usual white underwear before snatching up a pale pink bra and panty set. She dressed hastily in a V-neck shirt and jeans before digging out a comfortable pair of low-heeled boots. When she saw herself in a mirror, she paused and tilted her head. *Did I just choose my clothing and hairstyle to appeal to Ronan?* She stuck her tongue out at her reflection. *I don't have time for this.*

Controlled chaos ruled the med bay when Natasha arrived. She hesitated at the entrance to orientate herself. On one side of the bay, younglings sat two or three to a med bed, chattering. *I guess the Rectitude made it back.* Tesix, Xoriv, Kalix, and Westov were watching over them while a couple medics examined them.

On the other side of the med bay, Brauvix leaned against the wall near a closed-off area. *That must be where Teeka is.* Ash'n and Healer Markham worked on Largon at a med bed with Ronan standing nearby talking to Durek and Tolvex. *Why has no one treated that gash?*

Natasha grabbed a lab coat, scanner, and supplies before stalking over to Ronan. She listened to their conversation as she scanned him to see if there were other injuries.

"What are your plans for the younglings, d'Olorg?" asked Durek.

"Until the illness is contained, I'll have to take them to a secondary location nearby," Ronan said.

"Strip to the waist, Ronan, so I can heal you," Natasha interrupted.

With a wince, he pulled off his weapons harness and a bag before laying both on a cart. He shrugged out of the top half of his nanosuit, letting it fall to his waist.

Durek inhaled sharply. "That is a House Ruxila clan marking. Who was your mother?"

Natasha cleaned Ronan's chest gently. *Oh, my. Concentrate.*

"Saletta Yemez," said Ronan.

"She was my older cousin. We believed she died in the attack on Himita Prime," Durek said, his scar white against his golden bronze skin. *Ronan and Durek are related? Small universe.*

"She hid with her friend during the attack. She escaped Himita Prime with my father's help."

"I would like to speak more later about this," Durek said, his lavender eyes thoughtful.

"Of course."

Natasha ran the healing wand over the diagonal wound.

"Tesix tells me the rescue went as planned until the end," said Tolvex.

Ronan exhaled heavily. "I don't know how they knew where the shuttle was. They surprised us. I take responsibility for the error." *I hope he doesn't keep feeling guilty. It wasn't his fault.*

Tolvex's braids brushed his shoulder as he shook his head. "From what I understand, there is no blame to be had. These things happen."

Durek clapped Ronan's bare shoulder and grinned. "You borrowed five of my warriors and a shuttle, returned them all in good shape, and rescued all beings. I consider that a success."

Ronan dipped his chin. "Thank you."

With Ronan's wound healed, she said quietly, "I'm going to attend to Teeka now."

In a pained voice, Ronan said, "They hurt her badly, *caliana.*"

"I know." She hugged him. "Let me go heal the physical wounds. The mental ones will take much longer."

As she entered the private area where Teeka lay quietly in a med bed, Natasha met Brauvix' sorrowful, watery eyes.

"Brauvix, I'm going to examine and treat Teeka now. You'll need to leave," Natasha softly said.

He sucked in a wobbly breath. "I don't know where to go." He looked away briefly. "I've been in battles before, but this is the first time I've seen—" His words broke off as he gestured at Teeka.

"Extreme cruelty for its own sake?" At his nod, she continued, "You may want to talk with Ronan or even Largon when he's better. They have much more experience dealing with the emotional aftereffects of a rescue like Teeka's. They understand how you're feeling." She smiled sadly. "This is what they try to save the younglings from, Brauvix. It's why they do what they do."

She squeezed his forearm gently. "Talk to someone who understands. If you're not comfortable with Ronan or Largon, I'm sure there are other Svesti who've been in your shoes. Don't try to do it alone."

"Thank you, Lady Natasha." Taking a last look at the youngling, he said, "I know you'll take care of her."

"I will." After he left, she closed the area off completely and moved to the med bed.

"Teeka? My name is Dr. Petrov. You can call me Natasha. I'm a friend of Ronan's and a healer."

Teeka didn't react at all, even when Natasha scanned her. Natasha frowned and loudly called Brauvix back. She cleaned an area on her patient's upper arm, gave her an injection to anesthetize the area, and used a laser scalpel to dig out the foreign item. She dropped it into a specialized container.

Brauvix said, "You called?"

Natasha held out the container. "Please give this to Tolvex. I believe it's a tracker. It was in her arm."

Brauvix' face hardened. "As you wish."

Chapter 19

RONAN SURREPTITIOUSLY INHALED Natasha's unique scent as she healed where the Zuvgran had gouged him. He wanted to clutch her tightly to his chest to reassure himself she was unharmed, burying his face in her neck and hair. Instead, he attempted to have a conversation with Commander Durek and Tolvex.

Unbidden, his mind drifted back to earlier. When he saw Natasha's attacker, he felt heart-stopping fear. He couldn't get to her until he eliminated the risk to his own life. *If she and Tesix had not alerted me to the danger...*

It had been only moments before he was able to rush to her, but she had already escaped the Zuvgran's hold and stabbed him. *Thank the Goddess she used the dagger.* He suppressed a smile at how ferocious she looked. His cock had hardened despite the pain of his injury. He shifted uncomfortably. *Grak. It's still hard.*

Her hips swayed as she walked toward Brauvix. She spoke quietly with the male, before sending him away. When Ronan heard her call Brauvix back, his shoulders tensed and his tail flicked. *Is something wrong with Teeka?* Brauvix came out moments later, walking swiftly towards them.

"Lieutenant Tolvex, Lady Natasha found this in Teeka's arm. She believes it is a tracker."

"Good. She put it in a dampening container." Tolvex turned to Ronan. "This explains how they knew where to find you."

Ronan's forehead wrinkled under his horns. "I didn't check. They normally don't implant trackers right away."

"They don't?" said Durek.

"No. The Zuvgran usually do it when the slaves are to be sold or it's done later by their owner. If the beings are given to the scientists, then it happens at the lab."

They were silent for long moments. Then Durek asked, "How long have you and Largon been rescuing hybrids?"

"Largon has been doing so for over forty solars. As soon as I had enough skills to help, I became more active."

"How many have you rescued?" Tolvex said.

"I don't know the total number. Right now, we have over six hundred in our custody at all our locations. Primarily younglings, but some adults who help us care for them. That does not include anyone who moved to a colony. We've relocated families of some Zuvgran who don't believe in the Emperor's expansionist policy and treatment of other species. Some of the hybrids move to similar colonies when they are of age."

Durek's chest rumbled. "It is possible this was a trap for you and Largon. If the Zuvgran were aware of you and your activities, they may be looking for retribution against you and anyone you've helped or is aiding you."

"If they know who we are, then I believe they would come for us." Ronan's tail whipped behind him. "I need to contact the other locations and tell them to be on high alert. We have escape plans for all, but if they are caught unaware like this group on Straxis—"

"You're welcome to use our comms," said Durek.

"No offense, Commander, but only Largon and I know every location. It's safer that way. It's better if I use the comm on my ship."

"Understood. Tolvex, escort d'Olorg to his ship, then bring him back here," ordered Durek.

Tolvex said, "Grab your stuff."

Ronan dipped his chin to Durek. "Many thanks." *Is he really a cousin? Do I have other family on Costonia?*

"We'll discuss more later."

Ronan checked on the younglings and told them to behave themselves, then walked beside Tolvex back to the hangar bay. He admired the spacious corridor and the cleanliness of the ship. They passed several warriors who growled at Ronan. Tolvex informed each of them there were guests onboard and the males were to behave accordingly.

Ronan said, "If it's easier, I can turn on my portable appearance cloak. I have no desire to create trouble with your warriors."

Grinning, Tolvex said, "You have one? Let me see."

Ronan tapped his bracelet. Tolvex whistled.

"You can turn it off." Tolvex glanced sideways at Ronan. "I want one, but it's well outside my pay grade."

"They are very expensive, but given my heritage, I needed it to blend in at times."

"I see. Well, be yourself here. The warriors will get used to it or they'll have to deal with Durek." Tolvex chuckled. "He likes to reprimand us while sparring—more painful that way."

Amused, Ronan said, "Don't spar with Durek. Got it."

At the shuttle, Tolvex said, "You may want to pack some belongings for several days, just in case. It'll save you from having to keep coming back to the shuttle. I'll wait for you out here to escort you back to the med bay. Take your time."

"Thank you."

Once inside his ship, Ronan comm'd each location with the instructions to be on high alert and the news that Largon had been injured. When he comm'd Herrah, she said another four younglings had the disease, but the treatments Natasha ordered for early onset seemed to be helping. One youngling had pneumonia but was responding well to different medications. With Talos, he apologized again for not checking in, but Talos said the younglings were adjusting well and enjoyed exploring the caverns.

Ronan put away his weapons, noting some of them required cleaning. He may not have used them, but blood spatter was insidious. *I'll take care of that later. I need to get back to the younglings and Largon...and Natasha.*

In his quarters, his shoulders relaxed as he inhaled the remnants of Natasha's scent trapped in the enclosed space. He quickly took a sonic shower and dressed in black pants and shirt and packed a bag with some clothes. Not expecting to need them, but wanting to be cautious, he finally tossed in two knives and a dagger with sheaths. *Natasha left hers on Straxis.*

Finally, he looked in the bag he took from the safe on Straxis. Both he and Largon kept their most precious possessions in it, as well as data disks with their myriad accounts and encrypted information about their rescues. They routinely changed its holding location for safety reasons. He didn't feel safe leaving it just in case they searched his ship. Pulling out a lockbox, he placed the contents inside, secured it, and placed it in his bag. *I'll keep it with me and ask Largon what he wants to do.*

The healers finished their work on Largon by the time Ronan and Tolvex returned to the med bay. Ronan was pleased to see his friend's color seemed healthier and his face no longer stressed from pain.

Healer Rivezt said, "Ronan, it is good to meet you in person. Thank you for keeping Natasha safe. Your friend, Largon, is sedated. We healed the internal bleeding, which was the worst injury, as well as all his broken bones, cuts, and bruises. He took quite a beating, but he will be fine. He's a strong male."

Relieved, Ronan said, "How long before Largon awakes?"

"I want to keep him sedated until the morning to reduce his pain while everything heals fully."

"Thank you all for everything you've done. Not just with Largon, but with the younglings and the disease, too."

"We are happy to assist." Rivezt paused. "We think we have a viable vaccine for the measles variant. At some point, I'd like to draw your blood and run simulations to see if you require it." He glanced at Largon. "When your friend wakes, I would like to ask him if he would allow us to test him as well."

"You can take a sample from me now." Ronan held out his arm.

"Where are the younglings?" asked Tolvex as Rivezt took a blood sample from Ronan.

"Natasha is still with Teeka. Your warriors and Lady Ava took the others to the dining area to eat and relax. Have you decided where to give them quarters?" Rivezt said.

"d'Olorg, how do you suggest we divide them? All the males in one room, females in another? Half and half? By age? You know them best and we want them to be comfortable," Tolvex said. "I want to keep them in the senior officers' residential area for their safety. The rooms have large beds, as well as two big couches. We can fabricate some cots as well."

"Lady Ava suggested Teeka room with her initially. I have to ask Natasha what she thinks would be best for the female," Rivezt said. "Lady Ava also said if it were necessary, Lady Rachel would give up her quarters to stay with Lady Ava."

Ronan said, "I think the younglings would be more comfortable with males together and females together, even in cramped quarters. Their numbers are close to equal and there are a couple older ones of each who are responsible enough to watch over the littler ones. Separating them from each other would make it more difficult for them to adjust."

"The two rooms next to mine would work," said Tolvex. "d'Olorg and Largon can use the one on the other side of them." *I'm hoping to stay with Natasha, if she'll let me.* "Why don't we go look at them now and you can tell me whether we should fabricate cots for them? They'll also need clothes."

"I'm sure they'll be fine with whatever is there," said Ronan. "You don't need to go to any extra trouble."

Tolvex's teal eyes met Ronan's. "They are our guests who have been through a traumatizing experience. We wish to do right by them."

Sighing, Ronan said, "Let me talk to them and determine their mental states. It might be best to show them the rooms and let them decide." He glanced at the area where Teeka and Natasha were. "I'd like to see Teeka before we go, if it's a good time."

Rivezt said, "Let me check."

Keeping an eye on the healer's progress, Ronan said, "Tolvex, thank you for wanting to help the younglings."

"There's no need to thank me, Ronan. It is the right thing to do."

"You'll have to forgive me if I seem overprotective."

"No forgiveness necessary. What you and Largon are doing is the Goddess' work."

With a sad smile, Ronan said, "Before she died, my mother spoke to me of the Goddess, saying a male's role was to protect younglings and females." *I miss her. Being here around Svesti males reminds me of her.*

Tolvex nodded. "Your mother sounds like a great female. It seems she taught you well."

Rivezt returned. "Natasha said Teeka should be ready for a visitor by the time you check on the others and arrange their quarters."

Looking at Tolvex, Ronan said, "Then I guess we should do that first."

As they walked, Tolvex told him more about the ship. He suggested the younglings might like a visit in the aquiponics area, while Ronan was welcome to train with him in the training area.

When they reached the dining area, Ronan stopped in his tracks as he took in the scene. Amazed, he saw the younglings seated at several tables with Svesti warriors, eating, playing games, and laughing. Some of the youngest were sitting on the laps of the males.

A human female with red curly hair approached them with a huge smile.

"You must be Ronan. I'm Ava." She gestured at the scene. "As you can see, the children are fine. Talen and I fed them." She waggled her brows at Tolvex. "And they love cookies."

Tolvex chuckled. "Everyone loves your cookies, Lady Ava."

"Anyway, while they ate, there were warriors finishing up evening meal. Some of them left and returned with games and toys from their quarters and stayed to help occupy the kids." Ava's expression became serious. "One told me it had been so long since having younglings around, he'd forgotten how joyful they are."

Tolvex tilted his head. "It's true. While we visit other planets, our missions rarely include interacting with younglings. And the last Svesti youngling just turned thirty solars."

"Talia and the other women came by, met them, and took measurements, so I imagine there will be clothing for the kids soon," Ava said.

Ronan's heart swelled in his chest at the generosity and acceptance being shared with his rescued hybrids. Instead of residual fear from their experience, the younglings blossomed under the attention. *Herrah is right. They need more.*

Yostal, a Mostiffian-Zuvgran hybrid, led a Svesti to Ronan, one of his four-fingered hands attached to a long, gangly arm gripped the male's pants tightly. The young blue male of four solars grinned, his three oval eyes happy and his short thin tail waved behind him.

"Ronan, this is my new friend, Hozan Crulex. He's a science officer."

Ronan dipped his chin at the Svesti who was smiling indulgently at the youngling. "Crulex."

Squatting, Ronan said, "Well, you two must have much in common since you love science."

Yostal nodded enthusiastically. "We had cookies." The center eye in his forehead closed briefly. "They were so good."

"I'll have to try one. Are you having fun?"

"Oh, yes. Everyone has been really nice and we're learning new games." Yostal turned to Crulex. "Let's go."

All the males chuckled at Yostal's behavior and followed the youngling to the tables. Ronan greeted each youngling and met all their new Svesti friends. They offered him numerous cookies, but he only ate two. *Yostal is correct. The cookies are good.*

With the help of the warriors and Lady Ava, he rounded up the younglings to take them to their quarters. When they got there, he met more human women—the ones Natasha described to him.

Lady Talia, who had a hair color similar to his own brown with red, spoke. "Tolvex. Thanks for giving Emmy access to the rooms. We put the boys, er, males in this one." She gestured to the door nearest her. "And the females in that one."

Tolvex opened the door Lady Talia indicated. The male younglings whooped loudly when they saw the large space and jostled each other to be first in the door. Ronan saw fruit on a counter in the dining area and games and tablets on the table in the living area. In the bedroom, youngling-sized cots with mattresses lined one wall.

"We asked Volax, the supply master, to synthesize the smaller cots and mattresses so everyone could stay in the same room as they slept. The beds are large enough to hold the older ones and we added extra pillows and blankets. We thought they might feel safer with their family around them," Lady Talia said. "We did the same for the other quarters." She tapped to open the hidden closet and a drawer. "There are a couple sets of clothes for each youngling. Fortunately, we found master designs to accommodate more than two arms or legs or tails. And we could synthesize the games the warriors showed them, so we made extras for each set of quarters."

"This was extremely thoughtful, Lady Talia. I do not have the words to express how much I appreciate all you have done,"

Ronan said. He swallowed hard to push down the lump in his throat.

"With your permission and that of the Commander, I volunteer to remain with the male younglings tonight for supervision," Crulex said from behind him. "With your injured and two sets of quarters, you cannot be everywhere at once."

"The other women will be here until the younglings go to bed. Rachel said she'd stay with the females." Talia grinned. "No one will mess with her."

"That would be acceptable," Ronan said.

After the younglings were settled, Tolvex took Ronan back to the med bay. *Natasha was adamant that the Svesti would help the younglings on Talonka Six. She was right.*

Chapter 20

AFTER BRAUVIX LEFT with the tracker, Natasha kept speaking softly—telling Teeka what she was going to do before she did it. When she saw the female's unnaturally clawless hands and the bites on her young breasts, Natasha grit her teeth. *Bastards. I'm glad they died.* Unlike the Svesti, whose claws extended from their fingertips, Teeka's wounds were where her fingers met her hand.

Natasha kept her touch gentle as she cleaned Teeka's breasts and hands. Teeka winced a couple times, but her eyes remained vacant and she didn't utter a sound. Natasha used the healing wand to seal the open wounds.

"I'm going to start washing your face now, Teeka, then we'll move on to the rest of your body. I want to heal any bruises you may have." When Natasha carefully removed the blood from the youngling's face and saw her swollen and split lips, bruised face, and a deep scratch along her distended jaw, she said under her breath, "Oh, *rypka*, they died too quickly."

"Knock, knock," Ava said quietly as she entered.

"We're busy here, Ava." Natasha kept her attention on Teeka.

"I'm just determining which species we need to feed and making sure no one has allergies or anything like that," Ava said cheerfully in Galactic Standard as she stepped closer to the med bed. "Hi, there. I'm Ava. What's your name?"

Natasha noticed Teeka's eyes dart to Ava before becoming vacant again. *Interesting. I wonder if it's Ava's curly red hair or something else.*

"Oh, honey, I hope the assholes who did this to you got what they deserved." Ava's green eyes flashed in fury. "You're safe with us and Natasha's the best." She grabbed another cloth and started to wash one of Teeka's arms gently. "What lovely lavender skin. Better than my boring pale color. Does your skin burn easily like mine? Probably not." Ava sighed. "I don't know what the plan is once you're healed, but if you stick around long enough, you'll get to meet Rachel." Ava lowered her voice conspiratorially. "She looks like butter wouldn't melt in her mouth, but she can put a huge Svesti right on his ass. It's kind of fun to watch."

Ava continued chattering about the other women and some of the people onboard. Natasha watched Teeka's head turn slightly towards Ava, then her blue eyes began tracking Ava's movements. *I underestimated Ava. She's helping bring Teeka back.*

"Six elegant toes. Guess no pointy shoes for you. They'd just pinch like hell. Humans like me and Natasha only have five toes. I'm a little jealous. I think my toes are ugly." Ava kept up her running monologue.

"Oh, when Natasha says you can leave the med bay, you can come by my quarters and soak in my bathtub. It's so big, I bet you could swim in it." Ava winked. "I have, but don't tell anyone."

Teeka snorted. Natasha kept her eyes on where she was cleaning Teeka's calf and said, "Teeka, Ava is a great chef and she makes cookies that are so good, you'll want to keep them all to yourself."

"What's a cookie?" Teeka asked so softly they barely heard her.

"Just about the best snack you ever tasted. There are so many different kinds, you're bound to find some that you really like. I'll bring you several types and you can tell me what appeals to you. Are there any particular flavors that are your favorites?" Ava answered her with no visible emotional response to Teeka speaking.

Natasha glanced up with a grin. "That's one of the reasons we keep Ava around. Her cooking—especially her treats."

Ava stuck her tongue out at Natasha and tossed her cloth down. "Well, I need to get back to the kitchen before the other younglings riot and take down Talen." She looked at Teeka. "Talen Previv is the head cook on our ship and a great guy."

Natasha spoke to Ava. "I think Teeka can have soft foods—nothing larger than bite-sized—and slushy, cold drinks for now." She checked her tablet. "I don't see anything listed here as harmful foods for Praxites or Zuvgran, so no other restrictions."

"Got it. Fruit smoothies and gentle on the jaw." Ava gave Natasha a mock salute. "I'll be back with it." She turned to Teeka. "It was nice to meet you. I hope you feel better soon." Her curls bounced as she left the area.

"Is she always like that?" Teeka asked quietly.

"Funny, yes. As talkative, no. I think she was showing off for you." Natasha grinned. "She likes you."

"I like her." Teeka's eyes filled with tears. "Thank you."

"*Rypka*, it is my honor to heal you." Natasha gently squeezed her hand.

"What's *rypka*?"

"Oh, it's a term of endearment in Russian, my country's language. It means sweetie." Natasha sighed. "I know you don't want to talk about it, but I need to ask you some personal questions about what happened so you don't have bigger issues later. We can take as long as you need to get through it."

Teeka's lips quivered. "It was awful."

After Natasha asked her uncomfortable questions, she treated Teeka based on better information of what the youngling endured. She sat on the bed, holding Teeka in a gentle embrace as Teeka cried.

Ash'n knocked and poked his head in the door. "Natasha, could I speak with you for a moment?"

She ran a hand down Teeka's back before standing. "I'll be right back, *rypka*."

When Natasha reached the door, Ash'n said, "Ronan would like to visit with Teeka if she is ready for a visitor."

"She needs to shower and put on a gown first. It's going to take a little while."

"Okay. There's something he can do with the other younglings first. That should be plenty of time." Ash'n switched gears and lowered his voice. "How's she doing? Is she still non-responsive?"

Natasha let her fury show on her face as she whispered, "Teeka told me what she endured. They only had her for four hours, Ash'n, but they hurt her badly. I want to kill all of them again—slowly and painfully. She's not going to feel safe for some time." She paused. "Ava's visit brought Teeka back from wherever she was in her mind."

Ash'n growled low. "I understand. Is there anything you need for her?"

"No. Let me get her washed up and dressed, then Ronan can visit."

"As you wish."

As Natasha walked back to Teeka, she said, "I think you'd enjoy a hot shower. Let me help you down." She lowered the med bed so Teeka could reach the floor. Natasha wrapped the sheet around Teeka's naked body and put her hands on the youngling's waist. "Do you feel steady enough to walk on your own or would you like some help?"

"I think I can do it."

Keeping a light hand on Teeka's back for support, Natasha led her to the sanitary facilities. Turning on the shower, she said, "If you need help washing your hair, I'm happy to help. If you prefer, I can leave and wait outside the door or I can stay in the room while you shower. Whatever makes you the most comfortable is fine with me." She looked into Teeka's eyes. "No matter what you decide, I will ensure no one else enters this room without your permission. You are in control of your environment."

Teeka's lips trembled. "I'm afraid to be alone, but—"

Natasha said, "I can turn around and not watch. Whatever you need, Teeka, just tell me."

"Could you turn around, but stay and talk with me?"

"Absolutely." Natasha swiveled 180 degrees and plopped her butt on the high sink counter. "What do you want to talk about?" She heard Teeka drop the sheet and step into the shower.

"What planet are humans from?"

"Earth."

"Is it pretty?"

"Some areas are beautiful. Others not so much. We have all types of terrain, from deserts to tropical forests to snow-covered year-round."

"Sounds nice. Why did you leave?"

"That's a long story. The shortest version...the Svesti contacted my country's leaders and they chose me to visit Costonia."

"Were you scared?"

"Yes, but also a little excited. You see, humans didn't know for certain about other sentient life in space. I wanted to learn more about what's out here."

Teeka was quiet for a bit while she washed. Then she said, "On Earth, do you have males that—" Her voice broke.

"Unfortunately, yes, we have some men that hurt younglings and females. But we have lots of good males like Ronan and Largon who would never consider it."

"So you've treated other females like me?"

"For the type of abuse you've endured? Yes."

"That must be why you're so good at helping."

"Truthfully, I didn't spend as much time with them as I have you."

"Why not?"

"On Earth, we have all types of medical professionals. I'm a doctor, so I would treat the physical injuries and move on to the next patient. There just wasn't enough time to really connect with everyone. If we were on Earth, a nurse would be with you now, not a doctor. They spend more time with patients than doctors do. But even they are overworked at times."

Teeka turned off the water. When the drying tube cycle ended, Natasha said, "If you wait a moment, I'll grab something for you to wear."

"Okay."

Natasha handed a gown and slippers through the door without looking.

"Here you go." Teeka took the items from her.

Natasha smiled when Teeka came out. "Oh, your white hair is gorgeous. Let me find a brush."

Teeka returned to the med bed after brushing her hair. Just as she got settled, another knock sounded at the door.

"Are you feeling up to a visit from Ronan?"

Teeka nodded.

Natasha opened the door for Ronan, noting he had cleaned up and changed. As he walked past her, his tail brushed her leg and his scent filled her nostrils. *I really love the way he smells.*

"I'll leave you two to visit," she said.

Both Ronan and Teeka said, "You can stay." Natasha looked at them curiously.

Teeka said, "I trust you."

"And I need your professional opinion," said Ronan.

"Okay." Natasha moved closer and listened to them greet each other. Ronan asked how Teeka was feeling but did not ask her about specifics. He held the youngling's hand and said, "If you wish to talk to me about anything, I will listen."

Teeka's eyes watered and she ducked her head. Her white hair shone like a halo. Ronan told Teeka the others were safe and running Svesti warriors ragged with their energy. She observed the tension leave Teeka's body the longer he relayed stories about the others. Listening to Teeka giggle, she felt hope that the youngling's resilience would help her deal with her trauma sooner rather than later.

"Natasha, when can Teeka be released from med bay?"

Lips pursed, she said, "Honestly, she can leave any time she feels ready. However, I do not want her to be completely alone."

"Would Lady Ava be sufficient company?" Ronan asked.

"If she's willing, absolutely."

Ronan said, "Teeka, it's your choice. You can bunk with the other younglings, stay with Lady Ava, or remain here. I want to do what's best for you."

Teeka silently contemplated the choices.

"Can I visit the others so they can see I'm alive before staying with Lady Ava?"

"Of course," Ronan said at the same time as Natasha.

Securing Teeka's permission, Ronan carried her to the quarters where the other female younglings were. Natasha smiled her thanks to Rachel and Lin when she saw their freshly scrubbed faces. The young females hugged Teeka and showed off their new pajamas. *Girls are girls no matter their species.*

When Teeka began to look tired, Natasha caught Ronan's attention and jerked her head at the door. They went to the young males' quarters where the same process occurred with the males showing off their games instead of their clothes. Natasha nodded at Crulex, Emmy, and Talia. *Everyone is pitching in.*

Crutaw approached Teeka, his eyes welling with tears. "I wish I had been stronger and saved you, Teeka."

Emotionally, Teeka said, "You kept the others safe. That's what I wanted you to do." The teenagers hugged awkwardly.

Teeka told both sets of children that she was staying with Ava so she could have quiet to rest. Ronan set her down so she could walk the short distance to Ava's quarters. Ava opened her door with a wide grin.

"Come on in, girl, and let's get comfortable." Ava gave Ronan and Natasha an understanding look. "I've got her from here. If she needs either one of you, I'll comm." She turned around to follow Teeka, then said, "Oh, I left a meal for you both in your quarters, Natasha."

"Thanks, Ava. I think you're just what she needs right now." *Ava's a natural caretaker, just like Talia.*

Natasha turned to Ronan. "Hungry?"

Ronan smiled. "Yes."

Fortunately, her quarters were across the hall. Once the door closed behind them, she spun to face him.

"Were you hurt anywhere else?" Her hands restlessly moved on his chest.

"No, *caliana*, I'm fine. What about you?" His hands smoothed from the small of her back to her nape. He released her ponytail to let her hair fall free.

"A few bruises, but nothing major." She dropped her head forward as he massaged her neck and scalp. "Please tell me the animals that abused Teeka are dead." *He smells so good.*

Growling, he said, "Yes. They will hurt no one again." He rubbed his cheek along hers. *Damn, that feels nice.*

"Good. Let's eat."

He kissed her cheek. "As you wish."

Ava left them sandwiches along with some cheeses and fruits. Natasha and Ronan devoured them quickly, sharing information about their escapades during the rescue.

As Natasha put their remnants in the recycler, Ronan stepped behind her and slowly pushed her hair from her shoulder. He leaned down to kiss her bare skin, his lips warm. Shivers traveled down her spine at the light contact.

"When I saw you in danger, my heart stopped in my chest." His hot breath on her neck sent a ripple of tingles throughout her body. Her nipples puckered and her clit pulsed. She tilted her head to give him better access, her fingers entwining with his on her stomach when his arms embraced her.

"I was afraid for you, too."

Her hands followed his as they smoothed upwards to cup her breasts. A small moan fell from her lips as he gently squeezed and released.

"*Caliana*, I wish to give you pleasure. Will you allow me to do so?"

Turning her head so she could look him in his molten silver eyes, she said, "You know I will be leaving with the Svesti." *I need to be honest with him.*

Ronan licked her lips. "And I have to stay to protect the hybrids. I know all that, Natasha, but I want you regardless. I've never met a female like you."

"Because I'm human?"

His hair brushed her face when he shook his head. "No. Because you're fierce and caring, unafraid to speak your mind, and so *grakkin'* beautiful." His fingers traced the lines of her jaw. "You fascinate me." Pressing his hardness against her ass, he said, "You arouse me with nothing more than your presence." *I think my panties just overheated.*

"Then, yes, take me to bed, Ronan." She squealed when he suddenly lifted her and strode to her bedroom. She wrapped her arms around his neck and licked the underside of his jaw. *Damn, I could get used to this.*

Chapter 21

RONAN RELISHED THE weight of Natasha in his arms, her soft form resting against his body, her lips busy on his chin and neck. The feel of her tongue tasting him had his cock hardening even more as her scent grew heavier in the air.

Laying her gently on her bed, he smiled at the sight of her long, blonde hair spreading over the blanket. He crawled onto the bed to straddle her legs and rested his weight on his elbows. His hands dove into her tresses to hold her steady for his kiss. For long moments, their tongues dueled for supremacy before hers submitted to his. *She tastes so good.*

He took his time caressing and kissing her face and neck. Her indrawn breath when he nibbled her earlobe caused her breasts to rise against him. Groaning, he sat back and pushed her shirt up from her waist. Her breasts felt warm and heavy against his palms as he thumbed her puckered nipples hidden beneath her bra. Her hands burrowed under his shirt, her flattened palms pressing against his abdomen and pecs. Abruptly straightening, he drew his shirt over his head. His cock twitched at her low moan.

His lips surrounded one engorged nipple through her bra. Suckling gently, he squeezed her breast while teasing the other with his fingers. Her hands clenched in his hair and she pulled him closer. Licking a wet path across the tops of her mounds, he gave her other breast dedicated attention. Fumbling slightly, he figured out how to open the lacy undergarment to bare her to his gaze.

Ronan slipped his hands under the waistband of her pants and drew them down her long legs removing her underwear simultaneously. Dark blonde hair, neatly trimmed, hid her feminine treasures from him. He kissed his way up her legs, licking and sucking her soft flesh. Slowly, he spread her legs and her scent rose heavily in the air. Looking up at her, he licked her slit from bottom to top. Her hips twitched when his tongue met a nub at the apex of her sex.

Concentrating his efforts on the swollen bud, he licked all around it in circles before enclosing it in his mouth. Her hands clasped his horns at their base sending erotic shivers down his spine. His tongue played with the nub discovering what made her quiver and moan. Delicate fingers played with his horns as he built her pleasure. Hips restless, she pushed against his mouth.

"More, Ronan," she gasped.

His tongue entered her and her hips jerked. His thumb played with her nub as he thrust his tongue deeper, licking her juices from their source. He groaned against her flesh when she squeezed his horns tightly as her climax overtook her. Her body shook uncontrollably and her breathing hitched as she rode out her pleasure on his mouth and tongue. *She tastes divine.*

Her limbs askew, Natasha tried to catch her breath. Ronan raised his head and smiled in satisfaction at her flushed skin and trembling body. He quickly undressed and returned to lay next to her, his hardness pressing against her hip. His hands and tail stroked her soft flesh. Her satiated appearance made him grin.

She rolled toward him tossing her leg over his. Her wet core brushed against his shaft. Her blunt fingernails played with his nipples and his hips rocked toward her. A groan left his lips as her hands drifted lower to explore his cock.

Dipping her head, she kissed his chest and licked her way lower on his body. Her fingers trailed hot lines of sensation on his cock and balls.

"Mmm, you have ridges," she said. "Are they sensitive?"

His cock bobbed at her attention and he nodded to answer her question. She slid lower and nipped at his abdomen. She rubbed the head of his shaft, wetting it with his pre-cum. Lifting her fingers to her lips, she looked him in the eyes when she sucked her fingers.

"So alluring, *caliana*."

His eyes wanted to drift shut at the pleasure, but he didn't want to miss watching her. Her pink tongue licked his head, then along his length. The wet heat of her mouth surrounded him and he momentarily lost the battle to keep his eyes open. *So grakkin' good*. Her mouth and hands moved on his cock immersing him in sensation. Tendrils of bliss spread throughout his body as she sucked and licked as much of his hardness as she could reach. His hips bucked when she rolled his base node under her forefinger.

His tail slid between her legs and played with her clit. Her cheeks hollowed around him and he groaned. She pouted when he pulled away.

"I want to be inside you," he said as he rolled her onto her back. Slowly, he entered her, watching her body swallow his cock. *Grakkin' tight.* When he bottomed out, he stilled, giving her time to adjust to his size. Her legs wrapped around his hips, her heels resting behind his knees.

"Move. I need you to move," she groaned.

He withdrew most of his length, then thrust into her. Her eyelids fluttered and she moaned. His rhythm began slowly and smoothly. His pace increased when her hips rose to meet his. Sweat formed on his brows and rivulets ran down his back. He swiveled his groin so his base node would rub against her clit on his downstrokes. Panting, they rode each other frantically reaching for the final peak. Their combined scent aroused him even further.

Fire flickered up and down his spine until the heat gathered and focused between them. His balls drew up and his hands gripped her hips tightly. She threw her head back, screaming his name when her orgasm overtook her. Her cunt squeezed his cock tightly and he shot his seed deep within her, groaning her name. Rippling spasms milked him until he collapsed on top of her. He rolled them to their sides, still buried within her. Tenderly caressing her with his hands and tail, their breathing slowed. *What a perfect ending to a stressful day.*

Ronan woke to Natasha's fingers tracing his clan marking. His tail stroked her ass while his hands followed her feminine contours. Small bumps rose on her pale skin and she shivered.

"Three times wasn't enough for you?" she teased.

"I don't think I could ever have you enough, *caliana*."

Her lips curved upwards. "Good answer."

He kissed her languidly, enjoying her warm body pressed against his. *I wish I could wake up like this every day.*

Reluctantly, she drew back. "We should eat and go check on everyone."

Sighing, he said, "You're correct. I do wish to see how Largon and the younglings fared during the night."

"Sometimes it sucks being a responsible adult." She tilted her head and her long hair brushed against his chest. "This is the first time in a long time I wish I could just stay in bed." Her fingers caressed his face.

"Maybe a shower together before we eat?" Ronan widened his eyes innocently.

"I can see right through you." Natasha playfully squeezed his cheek. "Last one there makes morning meal." She hopped off the bed quickly.

Their laughter rung off the walls as he chased her into the sanitary facilities. Just as she was about to enter the shower, his tail wrapped around her waist and pulled her backward. He kissed her, then stepped into the shower.

"I win." He grinned when she realized what he had done. Her eyes narrowed.

"Cheater," she huffed.

He held out a hand. "Join me and I'll make it up to you."

After he washed her thoroughly, paying close attention to her breasts and sex, they dressed and ate a quick meal. As they walked to the med bay, he found fewer warriors growling at his appearance than the day before. When he mentioned his observation to Natasha, she shrugged.

"Word travels fast here."

Largon was sitting up when they arrived and looking much better. Natasha walked away to speak to another healer. Ronan clasped Largon's forearm—relieved at the strength in Largon's grip during the greeting.

"You seem much improved, my friend."

Largon said, "I feel good. The younglings?"

"All safe. The only injured were you and Teeka." Ronan's chest rumbled.

His eyes shadowed, Largon said, "I wish I could have saved her from that."

"We all do. They're dead and won't be hurting anyone else."

Glancing around, Largon said, "You asked the Svesti for help?"

Ronan's hair fell into his eyes when he nodded. "Natasha suggested it and I needed more warriors. The Zuvgran were planning on moving all of you today." His brows drew together. "They put a tracker in Teeka."

Largon's expression matched Ronan's. "That's unusual."

"Commander Durek suggested the Zuvgran may be looking for you and me specifically."

"That could be a problem." Largon tilted his head in Natasha's direction. "How goes it with your healer?"

Ronan couldn't stop the smile on his face. "She is well."

"Is she staying with us?"

"No. We know it's not realistic to expect our relationship to continue long term, but we've decided to enjoy it while we can."

Largon was silent. Before Ronan could question him, Natasha returned.

"Healer Markham says Largon can leave med bay. We can show him his quarters and meet up with the others if he's feeling up to it."

"I would like to see the younglings."

"Let me find you some clothes." She returned moments later. "Markham said the women synthesized an outfit for you and dropped it off. There are more clothes waiting in your quarters." She handed a pile to Largon.

"Thank you," Largon said as she pulled a curtain around the med bed for privacy.

"You're welcome. I'll wait out here. Ronan can help you if you need it."

Largon growled low. Natasha's giggle brought a smile to Ronan's face. Largon swiveled his body so his legs hung over the side of the med bed. He dressed without assistance, scooting off the bed to stand in his bare feet. Ronan handed Largon his boots from where he retrieved them near the foot of the bed. *It's good to see him upright.*

At Largon's nod, Ronan opened the curtain. Natasha looked up from where she was speaking with Rivezt.

"Did Ash'n ask you for a blood sample?" she asked as she joined them.

"Yes," said Largon. "He took one earlier."

"It sounds like we're fairly close to a vaccine that will work on all the species. Once we're sure, we'll inoculate everyone here and synthesize more for your other refuges."

"This is good news."

"Did you eat yet?"

"Yes. I would really like to see the younglings." Largon's impatience came through in his tone. *Don't upset her, my friend.*

"I understand. I hear they're in the aquiponics area now. Let's go." Ignoring Largon's tone, Natasha led the way through the ship.

Ronan was taken aback by the lushness of plants and trees in the aquiponics area. Largon inhaled deeply and smiled. *We spend so much time in shuttles and hiding, we don't get to experience nature like this much anymore.*

As they walked toward the center of the space, the sounds of joyful laughter and conversation filled the air around them. They stopped and observed for a few moments. One group of younglings with a couple human females and Svesti males sat in a circle on the blue grass with one youngling tapping each on the head naming fowl types. Teeka and Crutaw were sitting on a bench speaking quietly.

His brow crinkling, Ronan asked, "Why are they talking about birds?"

Natasha giggled. "They're playing a game called Duck, Duck, Goose. The standing child is 'it.' If whomever is it taps your head and says 'goose,' you chase them around the circle and try to tag them before they can reach where you were sitting.

Yostal tapped Crulex yelling "goose" at the top of his lungs and giggled as Crulex ran after him. Crulex exaggerated falling and missing a tap to Yostal's back. Yostal plunked himself down where Crulex had been sitting with happiness written all over his flushed blue cheeks. All the children cheered for Yostal.

Largon said, "They look like they're having fun."

"They do, don't they?" Natasha said with a grin. She left them behind and went to talk to Talia who was holding a youngling in her arms.

"Herrah asked us to think about requesting Svesti help in finding a safe location for all of us. She wants more for them than hiding. I wasn't sure at first, but now seeing them like this, I think she may be right. They deserve more than we're giving them," Ronan said quietly.

Largon's shoulders stiffened, then relaxed. "If the Zuvgran are aware of our activities and are looking to trap us, it might be time for us to step away from the rescue missions and instead protect them in a place they can grow happily as themselves. I just don't know where that might be."

"Do you think the Svesti would help?"

"If you asked me last week, I would've thought no. But seeing how they act with the younglings, I think they just might be willing."

"Can we stop the rescue missions altogether? I'm not sure how I feel about that."

"I don't know, Ronan, but if we're caught, then we leave all of them in danger. We have to weigh everyone's needs. Maybe we can do fewer missions? I'm not sure. If the Zuvgran have an idea of who we are, then the risk to the ones we've already rescued becomes too great."

"There is no easy answer, is there?"

"Unfortunately, no, there isn't."

Chapter 22

NATASHA'S CHEEKS HURT from grinning at the sight of the Svesti warriors playing with the children. Even Merix Hunnek, the older male in charge of aquiponics, interacted with the younglings. *I hope the treaty works and they find women who want to have families with them.*

"It's amazing, isn't it?" Talia said as she rocked the Mostiffian-Zuvgran hybrid in her arms. "They're huge, deadly warriors, but they genuinely enjoy spending time with the kids."

"Have you seen any pushback because the children are half-Zuvgran?"

"No. It doesn't seem to be an issue for them at all. Crulex said younglings can't choose their parents."

"I admit that I worried about how the Svesti might react to them."

"Me, too. Even Ronan and Largon don't seem to be a problem because they rescue younglings to give them a better life. The Svesti respect that." Talia shrugged. "I'm sure we will encounter some that are not as enlightened, but I've heard nothing negative."

"You ladies really came through for us—feeding, clothing, and watching the children. I know Ronan and Largon appreciate it."

Talia's brown eyes lit up. "It was fun. We've been dealing with so many frightening issues. It feels good to do something productive and nice for those who need it." She sighed. "So, are you going to tell me how you ended up with Ronan?"

"Truthfully, I'd rather not. Everyone's getting along so well. I'd like to keep it that way." *I can see your mate losing his temper if he knew Ronan kidnapped me.*

"I was afraid of that." Talia bumped her hip against Natasha. "Just don't lie to Vared. I don't know how hard he'll push for answers, but to keep his respect, you need to be honest, even if it's only to tell him it's none of his business."

"Sounds reasonable." Natasha glanced sideways at her friend. "So, fated mates, huh? How's that working for you?"

"It's great. In a way, it's reassuring to know we're meant for each other and it's supposed to work out. On the other hand, it's a little freaky to realize the infinitesimal odds of actually meeting the one person in the universe who's your other half." Talia wore a shit-eating grin. "And there are other benefits in a fated mate bond."

"Oh? Like what?" *Emmy and Lin didn't mention anything.*

"I'm not telling because if you don't end up with one, you'll be insanely jealous even if you don't believe me."

"I'm very curious now. You need to give me the inside scoop."

"Nope." Talia shook her head, laughing. "Trust me. It's better as a surprise."

Natasha said, "Commander Durek would like to meet us in the War Room."

Ronan and Largon looked at each other, then both stood. They followed her out of the aquiponics area.

"The younglings appear to be doing well," said Largon. "Teeka is doing much better than I expected. I was concerned she would hide away from everyone." They all looked at the female on the bench watching the younglings.

"Yes, although it's early yet. Teeka will likely have issues she will have to learn to cope with as time passes." Natasha's brow wrinkled. "Oh, Brauvix may ask to speak to one or both of you. Teeka's experience really shook him. I told him that either of you would be good to talk to process his emotions as you have more experience dealing with the aftereffects of her type of rescue."

"Of course," said Ronan. "We will check on him later."

"Do we know why the Commander wishes to meet?" Largon asked as they entered the lift.

"No. Perhaps a more thorough debrief?"

Upon entering the War Room, Natasha noted Durek, Tolvex, Ash'n, and Tesix were already there. Natasha nodded when Ash'n held up a water pouch. He passed three down to them. She opened hers and took a sip as she took a seat.

"Good. Everyone is here," Durek said. "Tolvex, encrypted comm to the king, please."

Holographic images of King Traxen Sovex, Narilla Rivezt, and Canaan Durek appeared above the table. Commander Durek made the introductions and gave a brief overview of what had happened. *Durek must get his lavender eyes from his mother. If his dad is anything to go by, Durek is going to age well. Lucky Talia.*

"Rivezt?" said the commander.

"We completed the simulations for the vaccine and we were able to develop one that works for all the species Natasha requested. By increasing the dosage of some components, we can keep it to a single vaccine, rather than a separate one for Zuvgran or hybrids. While it appears Svesti are immune, I would like to inoculate our warriors to reduce the chance of them being carriers. In a solar, we'll have to recheck the younglings to determine whether a second inoculation will be necessary." Ash'n glanced up from his tablet. "The information from Earth proved invaluable in developing something so quickly. It is fortunate Natasha recognized the disease and it is well researched by Earth's healers."

"Do we need to adjust the dosage for patient weights?" Natasha asked.

"We can limit it to three different dosages, depending on the size and age of the being."

Largon said, "For those we protect and our allies, we need approximately eight hundred vaccines. If we include the others already in colonies, four thousand would be enough. I'll need about a day to determine the sizes of everyone to ensure we have the proper dosage amounts."

King Sovex asked, "Once you have the vaccines, how long until you inoculate your people?"

"With my ship, approximately three weeks," said Ronan. "Our refuges are spread out on a number of planets and the colonies even further."

"I'm curious, why do you not send the younglings to the colonies?" Canaan Durek asked.

"The colonies are not self-sufficient enough to handle a large influx of younglings. Adults can work to build the colonies, so they're easier to relocate." Largon paused. "And it's safer for everyone overall. The colony has negligible defenses, so if the Zuvgran find one, any younglings there would be in even greater danger."

"The Commander told us it is possible your activities have been noticed and the Zuvgran are actively searching for you." King Sovex's eyes narrowed.

"Yes."

"Have you considered a single refuge for the younglings?"

"We would like to do so. However, we have not yet found a safe enough place for such a large group," Largon said.

"Hmm, I'm curious. How are the younglings on the *Invictus* doing?"

Durek dipped his chin at Tolvex who pulled up a security feed from the aquiponics area. Smiles formed on everyone's faces as they watched the younglings play.

"As you can see, they are enjoying themselves," Largon said. "Thank you." Tolvex discontinued the security feed.

"Lady Natasha also feels we should send the vaccination information to the Zuvgran," the commander said.

A heavy silence descended as the group pondered his words and Ronan's tail wrapped around her ankle. *This is going over like a lead balloon.*

"As a healer, ethically and morally, I agree with Lady Natasha," Lady Narilla said reluctantly.

"If it were any other species, I wouldn't hesitate," said Durek's father.

King Sovex sighed and rubbed his eyes with his hand. "As much as I hate to admit it, Lady Natasha is correct." His braids rubbed his shoulders when he shook his head. "However, tactically, I believe we should wait to do so."

Natasha gathered a breath to argue, but before she could speak, the king continued.

"With the possibility of the Zuvgran searching for d'Olorg and d'Ayen, it is best to inoculate those they protect first. Maybe even evacuate them to another location simultaneously before we give the information to the Zuvgran." *Well, hell. I don't think I can argue against that logic.*

"Do you have any ideas on where we could take them?" asked Largon.

"Possibly. Commander, can you accommodate six hundred more on the *Invictus* until you arrive at Costonia? They would be safe here as we investigate other options."

Durek looked at Tolvex, who said, "If we moved the majority of shuttles out of Shuttle Bay Alpha, we could set up temporary living quarters there. It would be crowded. Sanitary facilities would be the biggest issue."

"How do you two feel about evacuating your people to the *Invictus?*" the king asked.

Ronan exchanged a look with Largon, then said, "We would like to discuss it and give you an answer tomorrow. We have much to consider."

"Commander, are you still in orbit above Talonka Six?"

"Yes, sire. We have some medics still on the surface. We also wanted to be in position to aid d'Olorg and d'Ayen with vaccines for younglings on the planet."

"When you have your discussions, please make a list of resources you may need from us if you accept our offer to relocate the younglings to Costonia temporarily."

Ronan dipped his chin at the king. "We appreciate all of your assistance."

"I would like to speak more about your heritage, d'Olorg. The fact that you are a Svesti-Zuvgran hybrid peaks my interest," said Lady Narilla. Ronan's tail stiffened on Natasha's ankle before relaxing again.

"Lady Narilla is the main medical advisor to King Sovex," Natasha said quietly to Ronan.

Ronan said, "Perhaps tomorrow."

Natasha went to the med bay after the meeting, while Ronan and Largon went to plan their next moves. *Is it selfish of me to want them to decide to relocate everyone to Costonia temporarily? I'd have more time with Ronan before we have to end. I want more nights like last night.*

In the med bay, she told Ash'n she wanted to receive medical uploads for the other species of hybrids. He gave her one for Zuvgran physiology and set aside the others to upload later. He reminded her that receiving too much information via uploads at any given time could cause debilitating headaches.

Natasha forced down her impatience and helped synthesize the measles vaccine. She reviewed the data and dosage recommendations, pleased at how easily it all came together, especially in comparison to the last vaccine they developed to defeat the Zuvgran virus that destroyed human female and Svesti male fertility.

"Do you think Ronan and Largon will agree to bring the younglings to Costonia?" Ash'n asked.

"I don't know what they'll decide. The king is asking for a great deal of trust from them. They take their responsibilities to the younglings seriously." Natasha bit her lower lip. "I know on Talonka Six they live in caverns. I don't think they play outside at all."

"I'm hoping the king will decide to allow them to live on Costonia permanently."

Natasha's eyes shot up. "Really? Why?"

"How better to keep them protected than on our home world surrounded by Svesti? The Zuvgran wouldn't attack

Costonia. Our defenses are too good." Ash'n drummed his claws on a table. "My grandmother made a comment recently about how long it has been since we've heard youngling laughter." His fingers stilled. "Seeing the younglings play and bring joy to those around them reinforced the importance of her observation to me. Even our dour Crulex is happy around the younglings." His blue eyes shone with humor.

"You don't think they'll be discriminated against because they're half-Zuvgran?"

"There will always be some who don't understand, Natasha. At least on Costonia, they'll be free. Some might even be adopted. If the treaty with Earth gets signed, there will be humans relocating to Costonia. One of Lady Talia's ideas will bring abused females and their younglings to Costonia to heal. Those younglings have suffered, too. Perhaps they can all heal together."

Natasha rubbed her forehead. "There's a lot to think about. It would be nice to know the hybrids could grow up happy and free and have choices for their own lives in the future. But, playing devil's advocate here, what do the Svesti get out of it?"

"Besides a generation of younglings? A reminder, Natasha." His face turned solemn.

"Of what?"

"Of why we protect others from the Zuvgran and their atrocities. The Svesti have focused on the larger picture—the worlds affected, but Ronan and Largon have focused on the individuals. I think it's time both groups worked together."

"You have a point."

"Besides, if they stay on Costonia, you can decide how long you want to keep Ronan around." His eyes crinkled at her open-mouthed expression. "I have a nose, Natasha."

"I don't know what to say." *I can't believe he just said that.*

"Is he treating you well?"

"Yes."

"Then enjoy yourself. With his mixed heritage, he may not be able to form a fated mate bond, but I'm sure true mating would still be an option if you wanted."

"Whoa. That's a big leap from I like the male to fated mates, Ash'n. We haven't known each other that long." *Don't rush me.*

"One of the things I learned from my relationship with Lin is that it's not the length of time that matters, but the depth and intensity of emotions that play a larger role. How well you communicate and how honest you are with each other is far more important to a relationship's success."

Natasha stared at him. "Are you going to be one of those 'I've found someone so I want everyone else to find someone' people? If so, you're going to become annoying very quickly."

Ash'n arched an eyebrow. "Everyone should feel this good, Natasha."

Chapter 23

AT RONAN'S REQUEST, Tesix escorted Ronan and Largon to his shuttle. Tesix said he would return in an hour to escort them back.

"Why here, Ronan?"

"I thought we could talk privately and also contact the refuges with the latest updates. We might want to ask their opinions about the Svesti offer."

"What do you think?"

"It's a good offer. My biggest concern is not knowing where we'll ultimately end up or when." Ronan looked up from his comm. "Did Crutaw give you back your comm? Healer Rivezt sent me the dosages for each range of weights."

"Yes." Largon pulled it from his pocket. "Send it to me." He paused as he reviewed the information. "Let's go through our lists and get a general sense of how many vaccines we'll need of each dosage first."

Working together, they noted how many of each dosage they would require for each refuge, as well as the colonies. They mapped out potential routes to reach the myriad of locations using one ship, then again with two ships. Factoring in the time to administer the vaccines, they decided they couldn't continue planning until they talked to the refuges and knew whether or not they wanted to be evacuated.

When they reached Herrah, she shared that most of the younglings felt better and no one new was ill. Largon informed her of all that happened in the last few days.

"They are treating the younglings you rescued well?" she asked.

"Very well. They look happier than I've ever seen them," Ronan said.

As Ronan expected, she wanted to relocate, even temporarily, to Costonia.

"It would be crowded on their space cruiser until we could reach their planet," Largon cautioned.

"We can deal with that. If we can find a place where we could truly live, it would be worth it." Herrah's arms gestured excitedly. "They need to be in school, playing outdoors, and dreaming of a future that doesn't include fear of discovery."

"We'll let you know what we decide," said Largon.

"It doesn't have to be all or none, does it? If some refuges prefer to stay where they are, those of us who'd rather move will still be able to do so, yes?"

"We hadn't considered that, but I don't see why not," said Largon.

"Good."

Next, they spoke with Talos, who also agreed on Costonia as a good option. By the end of it all, the refuges with younglings were more than willing to take a chance on the Svesti helping them. However, the colonies remained more cautious. While they would ask the colonists to vote on which course of action they would like to pursue, the leaders believed they would prefer to stay where they were.

"If we start here," Ronan said as he pointed to a map he pulled up on the console, "one ship can travel to the colonies with the vaccines. The *Invictus* can visit each planet with refuges and help evacuate everyone. They don't even have to be inoculated first. We can do it on the space cruiser."

"That would leave Talonka Six as one of the last places evacuated. Since it has the most younglings, we could keep the crowding down and give them extra time to recuperate from the illness."

"The first ship can travel back this way." Ronan drew a path on the map. "Coming in from the other side of Costonia's system. It would have to go through the asteroid field on the far side of Millus, but it's doable. Both ships could meet back up before Costonia."

Silver eyes met green eyes as they stared at each other.

"We're doing this, aren't we?" said Largon.

"I think so. I hadn't realized so many didn't feel they had the right to ask for a better situation." Ronan's lips firmed and his tail whipped behind him. "That's on us."

"I'm not sure we could have found anything sooner, Ronan."

"But we weren't even looking."

"We can only do what we can do. Getting angry at yourself serves no purpose."

Ronan's tail slowed. "You are correct, as usual."

Largon glanced sideways at Ronan as he tapped on his comm. "You'll be able to spend more time with your healer."

"Yes. I'm not sure if that will make it easier or harder to say goodbye when it's time." *We've just started and I have to think of the ending.*

"You'll have more options once everyone is settled. If we're no longer conducting regular rescues, you can explore other paths. Maybe even one that will keep you close to your healer."

"What will you do?"

"Stay with the younglings. Until I took you in, I hadn't realized how satisfying it is to help a youngling grow and develop into the being they were meant to be." Largon's eyes became unfocused. "There is a great deal of joy in raising younglings." His eyes sharpened. "There are also a lot of bumps and bruises."

"Is that why you backed off on the travel?"

"Yes. You were more than capable and willing. It gave me more time to spend with them."

"I don't know what would've happened to me if you hadn't found and raised me. You were the father I no longer had."

"You were the son I never had." Largon paused. "Did you bring the items from the safe on Straxis?"

Ronan's brows drew together at the abrupt change in topic.

"Yes. I put it all in a lockbox. It's in my bag in Natasha's quarters."

"I'll get it from you later." Largon seemed to age suddenly as he rose tiredly from his seat. "It must be close to when Tesix said he would return."

Ronan followed Largon off the shuttle. *There's something he's not telling me. If he were unwell, I'm sure the healers would have caught it. I wonder what's bothering him.*

From his position on the other side of the aquiponics area, the Svesti male watched the hybrids shrieking with laughter and running around in no discernable pattern. Human females and Svesti males encouraged them, even Merix Hunnek, the old male who took care of aquiponics.

This is what our future looks like. Svesti hybrids everywhere. Instead of all sharing the same gray skin, like the Zuvgran hybrids, Svesti hybrids will be smaller and weaker—probably in a myriad of skin colors like humans. Who knows if they'll have the natural defenses of the Svesti? Some of them might not have claws or fangs or, Goddess forbid, tails. They'll be strange and freakish—like the humans.

The Svesti-Zuvgran hybrid and his Zuvgran friend joined the happy crowd. The male snorted in disgust. *And now we're working with Zuvgran?* He ignored a persistent inner voice that reminded him his uncle had allied with the Zuvgran to obtain the virus that killed human fertility.

He internally noted who interacted with the humans and hybrids so he could relay the information to his uncle when the *Invictus* returned to Costonia. Even though he now had something to report, his orders were to remain silent until they reached the home world. Despite his best efforts, he failed to frighten the human females with his attacks. Although he switched out an upload, poisoned two females, subjected another to a broken ladder and dangerous gas, exploded an oven door, and even installed a tripwire that shot needles, the females seemed happy and whole. *I would believe they are protected by the Goddess, but I know that cannot be. The Goddess wishes us to remain pure.*

Leaving the area, he muttered under his breath, "Always Svesti. You'll see."

Later, Ronan's tail wrapped around Natasha's waist when he saw her in the med bay. *Grakkin' thing has a mind of its own.* He began to withdraw his tail, but her hand absently patted it as she finished counting and storing injections. *I love the feel of her hands on me, even if it's just my tail and her attention is elsewhere.*

"I'll be finished in a moment. Did you guys make a decision?"

"We contacted everyone. It looks like the colonies wish to remain where they are, but anywhere that has younglings wants to take the chance that the Svesti can find them a permanent, safe location."

She turned to face him, her hand on his chest. His tail drew her closer so her lower body pressed against him. She raised her face to look at him.

"That's good, right?"

"Yes. I'm a little concerned we don't have a final destination in mind or how long it will take, but I seem to be in the minority." He bent forward to sniff her hair.

"I like the way you smell, too." Her lips curved upward and her brown eyes drifted shut.

"When you have a chance, I need to get something from your quarters to give to Largon." His nose nuzzled behind her ear. His cock hardened and prodded her stomach. *I love her scent and her smooth, warm skin.*

"Is there anything else you need in my quarters?" Her voice had a sultry tone to it, igniting licks of fire under his skin. Her fingers curled into his shirt.

"I would have to see what's available," he teased.

"Let's go check it out."

He lifted his head and dropped a light kiss on her lips. He drew back and willed his cock to behave.

"After you, *caliana*."

As they walked the corridors, he noticed how many Svesti greeted Natasha. They seemed pleasant and respectful, but Ronan still had to suppress his growls as each new male approached.

"Knock it off, Ronan." She slapped his shoulder.

"What?"

"Your he-man attitude. I can hear your chest rumbling every time a man gets near me. So can they."

"I can't help how I feel." *Good. Then they know you are mine.*

"No one has said or done anything improper." She stopped walking and crossed her arms while she glared at him.

"I'm aware of that, which is why there hasn't been bloodshed." He halted and faced her. *When she looks fiery like this, all I want to do is kiss her senseless.*

She stomped her foot, then strode quickly along the hall, muttering under her breath.

"What is it with men and feeling territorial?" Even with his Svesti hearing, he couldn't make out the rest of her tirade. He admired her graceful hands gesturing angrily and the sway of her hips. *Too bad she's wearing a lab coat. It hides her curves.*

He looked up when she slapped the door controls of her quarters. She tapped, then said, "Put your hand here."

Ronan followed her instructions. The controls beeped.

"There. Now you have access to my quarters and don't need me." She stepped inside.

Following her, he crowded against her as the door closed behind him. He rubbed at the tension in her shoulders. Her body relaxed against him.

"I need you because you're you, Natasha. Not for access to places." Moving her braid out of the way, he kissed her nape. His tail caressed the outside of her thigh, while his hands scooted under her lab coat and shirt to find bare skin.

Her head dropped back against his pec and she moaned. "I should stay upset with you."

"If you like." His tongue licked her earlobe. "As long as I can keep touching you, I will happily suffer your anger."

A reluctant laugh fell from her lips. "What is it about you? It's like my defenses are non-existent."

He drew back and spun her by her shoulders to face him. His hand cupped her cheek.

"Do you feel you need defenses with me?"

"Maybe defenses isn't the right word. It's just happening so fast between us. I feel like I need to protect my emotions more so I don't get hurt." Her brown eyes pleaded for his understanding.

Resting his forehead on hers, he said, "I understand. For me, though, my emotions tell me to trust in this—us—and savor every bit of it because we may not have more of it."

"I think knowing it's short term makes it more important to protect my heart."

He raised his head. "Do you wish to stop all of this? Be friends, but nothing more?" *Please say no.*

"No, I don't think I can." *Thank the Goddess.* "It will hurt either way. At least we can have some time together now."

Chapter 24

WRAPPED AROUND HIS waist, Natasha's fingers registered Ronan's sudden release of air when she said she didn't want to go back to only being friends. *I'm glad I'm not the only one who wants this to be...more.*

His hands moved to the collar of her unbuttoned lab coat and pushed it over her shoulders. The lab coat floated to the floor when she dropped her arms. Her hands tunneled under his shirt, untucking it from his pants. His hands moved to her waist and drew her shirt up. She raised her arms so he could undress her. Then her hands did the same for him. Warm, bare skin flexed under her palms as she caressed the strong lines of his back.

"Ever since I watched you put this on this morning, I've been wanting to take it off," he said as he traced the lacy lines of her blue bra. A single finger tapped a nipple and she sucked in a breath. He pulled the lace down under her breast and bent to lick and suck her stiff nub. Hands kneaded her breasts and his fingers plucked at her other nipple.

"As beautiful as you look in it, nothing can compare to you naked." His words against her flesh sent tingles throughout her body. Her head fell back and one of her hands clasped a horn. He shuddered against her. *I love how he reacts when I touch his horns.*

Through heavy-lidded eyes, she watched him lavish attention on her breasts. Delighted shivers darted throughout her when his soft beard rubbed against her sensitive flesh. The contrast of his gray skin against her paleness highlighted the differences in their bodies. His scent surrounded her warming her from the inside out.

His hands began working at the fastening to her pants. She squirmed as his knuckles brushed her abdomen. When her pants loosened, she shimmied out of them as well as her panties.

She gasped when he knelt before her and used his strong arms to lift her against the wall. His shoulders stretched her wide and his tongue circled her clit. Her head hit the wall and her hips bucked toward his hot, wet mouth. She clutched both horns in her hands.

His tongue and lips constantly moved against her. His tail slid up her side to tickle the underside of her breast. She pushed her chest forward and wriggled at the differing sensations. His beard rubbed against her core as he tongued her clit. Icy fire streaked through her veins as her pleasure built. She tried to use his horns as leverage to reach the angle she wanted, but he held her fast.

"Damn it, Ronan. I need more." His tongue left her clit to slide into her sex. She swore he smiled against her when she let out a long, drawn-out moan when his tongue thrust into her and licked her insides voraciously.

Natasha squeezed his horns so tightly she felt the light striation pattern on her palms. In the background, she heard his pants unfasten. Taking his mouth from her, he stood, lifted her higher, and shook his leg to let his pants fall to the floor. He bent his knees and lined up his hard cock at her pussy. She groaned when she felt his cock against her swollen flesh.

"Are you ready for me?"

"Either make me come now or fuck me hard, Ronan," she rasped.

"As you wish." With one steady motion, he pushed into her and pinned her between his hard flesh and the wall. He withdrew and snapped his hips forward, impaling her. His base node slapped at her clit and his ridges made her pussy whimper with happiness.

"Yes," she screamed. "More, just like that."

Her breasts jostled and his tail played with her nipples as he fucked her up against the wall. Sweat built on their bodies as he kept a steady, forceful rhythm. Her arms wrapped around his neck and she kissed him, occasionally breaking away to gasp for breath when he hit that spot inside her just right. Her legs wrapped around his waist and clung to him.

Their combined scent rose in the air. Natasha heard a low, keening sound and realized it was coming from her. Ronan's grunts became deeper. The icy fire in her veins continued to build until it exploded in a mass of convulsions as she reached her climax. Her pussy rippled around his cock, the ridges prolonging her pleasure. Ronan slammed into her one final time and held still as he jetted his hot cum inside her.

Gasping, they clung to each other as her pussy continued to milk him. Aftershocks shook them both. Her head dropped to his shoulder and she breathed him in.

"Holy shit." Her unsteady legs fell from his waist and hung limply. Her pussy pulsed with the movement.

"You are incredible, *caliana*." He kissed her deeply. His cock twitched and her pussy pulsed around him again. He sucked in a breath. "You need to stop doing that or I'll never be able to move."

"I can't help it." She laughed softly.

He nuzzled her neck, his beard creating goosebumps on her flesh.

"Do we need to be anywhere soon?"

Tiredly, she shook her head.

"Let's rest for a bit, then."

"Good plan."

The dining area was louder during evening meal with the younglings taking up a corner of the room. Teeka was quiet, but not in a brooding way. Natasha sat sandwiched between Ronan and Teeka, with Largon across from them, enjoying the happy chatter around them. Ronan gave him a lockbox when they sat down, but Largon only set it aside. He was quiet, too. *Except he seems like he might be brooding. Wonder what's up with that?*

Numerous males stopped and left more games for the younglings. She even saw a few stuffed animals. *Well, I think they're animals. I've never seen anything like them before.* One was similar to a purple elephant with a shorter trunk and six legs ending in black claws. *The kids like them. That's all that matters.*

She finished her *clepella*, a dish similar to ratatouille. *I wonder if I have room for dessert.* She glanced sideways at Ronan and suppressed a smile. *I am expending more energy than usual.*

"I'm curious. Once the younglings are settled permanently, what will you do?" Natasha asked quietly.

"I'm not sure," said Ronan. "Probably whatever is needed. Defense, security, supply runs, whatever. It's what I've always done."

"Isn't there anything you ever wished to try if you had the time? Painting, construction, anything?"

He tilted his head at her. "It's silly."

"I'm sure it isn't."

"When I was a child, I used to collect rocks."

"You're interested in geology?"

"No. The rocks brought back memories of what I was doing and who I was with when I found them. I used to envision making them into meaningful items to keep those memories alive."

She bit her lip. "Like jewelry?"

"Yes, or trinket boxes, vases, or even decorations." His cheeks reddened. "A childhood fantasy that sounds silly now as an adult.."

Natasha held his hand and rubbed her thumb over his fingers. "No. If it's something that still interests you, you should explore it. I like the idea of you creating beautiful things to keep happy memories alive." She looked at his hand in hers. *I can see him patiently shaping a stone or metal with these talented hands.*

"There is much I would have to learn. Metalsmithing, woodworking, pottery, things like that."

"Then learn it. Find a medium or two that make you happy. Life is too short to forego all our dreams."

"What about you? What would you do if you weren't a healer?"

"I'd sew, which I do in my spare time as a hobby anyway. But instead of clothing, I think I'd like to make quilts. Useful and decorative."

His fangs gleamed as he grinned at her. "So you have a creative side, too."

"I guess. Sewing brings me joy, not just the act itself, but also because it brings back happy memories of my childhood." She shrugged.

"I like knowing this about you." He leaned toward her.

Yostal popped his head between them. "Are you coming back to our quarters? We didn't see you much today."

Ronan drew back and picked up the youngling to place him on his lap. "I can visit for a little while. Have you been having fun on the *Invictus*?" He sent Natasha an apologetic look. *How could I be upset I didn't get a kiss when he's so good with them?*

Yostal bobbed his head enthusiastically. "Everyone is so nice and the food is really good."

"Yes, the food is very good. Did you eat all your dinner before you had dessert?"

Yostal gnawed on one of his thin blue fingers. "Will I be in trouble if I say no?" His three eyes widened innocently. *This kid has the puppy dog look down pat.*

"No, you won't be in trouble." Ronan tickled Yostal's tummy. "Did you eat your dinner?"

Giggling, Yostal squirmed trying to evade Ronan's fingers. "Yes, but I ate part of my dessert halfway through. I did finish all of it, though."

"That's good. You need the healthy food to grow big and strong."

Yostal planted a sloppy kiss on Ronan's cheek. "You're the best, Ronan."

Ronan rested his forehead on Yostal's smaller one. "Coming from you, that is high praise indeed. I thank you, my friend."

"Those younglings wear you out quickly," Natasha said as she soaped a cloth and washed the front of Ronan's chest. While she was tired, she was determined to spend some time exploring his body. Soaking together in the huge bathtub in her sanitary facilities was a perfect place to map his contours and relax. His wound from the Zuvgran horn was mostly healed—just a thin pink line marring his suede-like skin.

"They do have lots of energy." Ronan's eyes were glued to her breasts bobbing in and out of the water as she lifted his arm to clean it.

"It's obvious they adore you and Largon." Her nipple brushed his forearm as she maneuvered him where she wanted him. She kept her smile to herself when he licked his lips.

"Mmm. Do I get a turn?"

Her wet hair splattered rivulets of water when she shook her head. "Not yet. I haven't had a chance to investigate what similarities and differences you have from a Svesti male."

His intense growl caused the bathwater to wave away from his chest. "Have you investigated many male Svesti bodies?"

"Only in a professional capacity." She bit her lip. "I'm relying on my uploads for the important items." She washed his other arm, lacing her fingers through his to caress them before moving on.

"And those items are?" He settled back as her hands drifted lower beneath the water. She washed his stomach, counting his abs and allowing her fingers to trace his warm, wet flesh.

"I know you have ridges on this wonderful cock of yours." She tried to close her hand around him, but his thickness, especially on the ridge closest to his torso was too much for her. "I'm assuming that's a Zuvgran characteristic." She ran her hand along his hardening length, absorbing the feel of the five ridges that circled his cock. *Damn, no wonder it feels so good inside me.*

He groaned and widened his thighs. "You assume correctly."

With her other hand, she lightly danced her fingers along the top of his cock near its base.

"I believe I felt a base node multiple times. That's a Svesti characteristic."

"You are a quick study, Doctor Petrov. Yes, I have a base node." His hips moved restlessly as her fingers trailed to the tip of his cock.

"However, I don't feel any head nodes. Am I missing something? I could take a closer look." She rose her eyes to meet his and outlined her lips with her tongue.

"You are a dangerous female." Ronan sucked in a breath when the hand fisting his cock moved to cup and roll his balls.

"Well?" *I love making this big strong male weak for me.* Her thighs clenched.

"No head nodes." His breathing quickened as she exerted more pressure on his balls.

"Mmm. If I had to choose between head nodes and ridges, I do believe I'd choose ridges every time." *I want to taste him.*

Ronan groaned. "Lucky for me then."

"You're going to get even luckier. Sit up on the ledge." She drew back and waited for him to move.

He reached for her. "Sit with me, Natasha."

"Uh, uh. On the ledge. Trust me." Her arousal grew as his muscular body rose from the water and he leaned back against the wall with his thighs open to her.

"Now I need to investigate more, Mr. d'Olorg. Stay still and this won't hurt at all." She smiled at his fists clenching next to his thighs.

Natasha propelled herself forward and rose to her knees. Leaning forward, she rested her hands on his legs and examined his cock with voracious eyes. A darker gray than the rest of his body, his member was stiff and twitched when the tip of her tongue dipped into its slit. *Mmm, he tastes like he smells—coffee, almond, and spearmint with a musky undertone.*

Taking her time, her tongue trailed a wet path along his cock. She initially thought his ridges made concentric circles that widened the closer they were to his torso. Her mouth discovered he had a single ridge that actually circled his cock in a continuous line that grew thicker near his base. One hand cupped his balls rolling each in her palm separately. *Can't fit them both in my hand at one time.*

Using her forefinger of her other hand, she drew a fingernail lightly up the underside of his cock feeling it bob under her tongue. Licking a path to his tip, she lifted her eyes to his before enclosing the head of his cock in her mouth.

"*Grak, caliana.* That feels wonderful." His eyes turned molten silver as he gazed at her sucking on him. The heat in his expression caused her to squirm before turning her attention to taking as much of him into her mouth as she could. She wrapped both hands around his shaft moving them in time with her mouth.

The sounds of his groans were loud over the splashing water. Hollowing her cheeks, she sucked hard loving the involuntary jerk of his hips. She moaned around him when she felt his tail slip between her legs and play with her clit.

Ronan's hands cupped her head, his claws pricking gently on her scalp. He let her set the rhythm which she appreciated. She jerked against him when his tail entered her pussy and began thrusting. *Oh, shit. Who knew that would feel so good?* Moaning deeper, she sucked harder and faster. His tail matched her movements.

Dropping a hand to cup his balls again, she felt them tighten. She pressed a finger against where a human prostate would be and found a gland. Rolling it with her fingertip, she felt his thighs tense. *Aha. Svesti males like this, too.*

"I'm going to come, Natasha." He tried to pull away, but she refused to release him. His tail thrust frantically inside her and she came a moment after he did. After swallowing as much of his seed as she could, she let him slip from her mouth and licked along his length again as her orgasm rippled through her. She dropped her head on his thigh and closed her eyes. His fingers brushed her hair from her face.

"Thank you, *caliana*." His voice sounded hoarse.

"Mmm," she said with a yawn. "Thank you. I enjoyed that."

"Did you need to conduct some more comparison studies?"

"Too tired right now. Maybe later."

"Let's get dried off and go to bed." He slid down into the water to lift her.

"S'long as you do all the work." The last thing she remembered was him holding her in the drying tube.

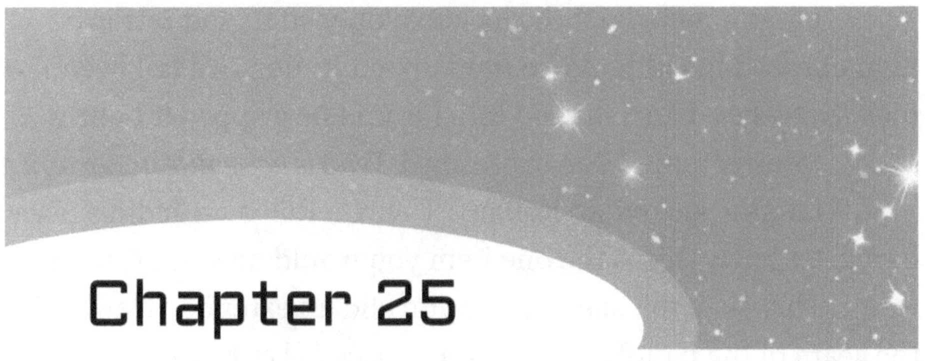

Chapter 25

T HE NEXT MORNING, Ronan and Natasha entered the War Room behind Largon with all the same people present as the day prior. They sat quietly while they waited for Tolvex to initiate the comm to Costonia.

"Have you made a decision?" King Sovex asked after exchanging pleasantries.

"Yes," said Ronan.

Largon interrupted before Ronan could continue. "There is something all of you should know before we proceed. It may affect your willingness to help," he said to King Sovex. *What the grak is he doing?*

Largon turned to Ronan, sadness in his eyes. "I apologize for not sharing this with you sooner. At first, you were too young. Then as you grew older, I couldn't bring myself to tell you. But with the Svesti involved, I feel it's time." He sucked in a breath. "I did not tell you last night because I'm not sure I can do this more than once." Largon's face appeared to age twenty solars as he spoke. *What is he talking about?*

Largon pulled out the lockbox, opened it, and retrieved an item encased in cloth. As he unwrapped it, Ronan's tail began to flick. Natasha's hand slipped into his and he gripped it tightly.

"Marris' rattle," Ronan breathed. *Why is her rattle important?*

Largon looked at Ronan. "I chose this as a hiding place because I knew this is the one item you would never part with."

The room fell silent as Largon slid an extended claw along the seam of the handle and two data discs fell out. He popped the handle back together and reverently folded the protective cloth around Ronan's most treasured keepsake. He picked up a disc and handed it to Tolvex.

"You should play the recording on this."

A few moments later, Ronan gasped as if he received a direct hit to his solar plexus. His eyes darted to the people in the video. His parents and Marris looked to be in their family home, but their faces and bodies were thin and ravaged with pain.

Jorn d'Olorg, Ronan's father, spoke with Marris screaming in the background. His eyes were wild and his speech pattern erratic.

"I don't know why you didn't come, Largon, but we escaped anyway. If I couldn't trust you to rescue us, then I can't trust you with my son." He gripped his hair near his horns. "The Emperor is going to release a virus on Costonia. You have to stop it. Just listen."

Marris' screams were constant—pain and tears could be heard in his mother's voice as she tried to calm his sister. Ronan's heart twisted in agony.

"This is what it's going to sound like all over Costonia. Females tormented unbearably. And it's your fault for not rescuing us."

Ronan glanced at Largon, noting his stoic expression and the sheen of tears in his eyes. *It's not your fault, my friend.*

Jorn rambled incoherently and paced irregularly with his tail flicking for several minutes. *This is not the male I remember.*

Marris' screams ceased. Jorn's head snapped around.

"Saletta? Did she fall asleep?"

"Jorn, come rest with her. She needs her father now," Ronan's mother said in a thick voice.

They watched as Jorn walked to the females. Saletta rose and gestured for him to take her place on the bed. With her body obviously racked with pain, she leaned over and kissed Jorn's cheek, then pressed her hand against his neck.

He stiffened and said, "Saletta? You betray me, too?"

"No one betrayed you, my love. It's just time to rest. Hold your daughter." Tears ran down her cheeks as she caressed his face until his breathing stopped. She tenderly ran a finger down Marris' cheek, then turned and walked toward the camera. She clasped her abdomen, her shoulders hunched and tense.

Gingerly she sat, lines of pain drawing her face tight. Her once-golden hue was sallow and her long dark hair hung limp and straggly. Small teeth marks marred her lips and tear tracks shone on her cheeks. Her eyes held a depth of remorse Ronan had never seen before.

"Largon, take no heed of his words," she said resolutely. "They broke him. His mind was his own no longer."

She drew in a shaky breath. "He did not recognize you as one of our last guards, but I did. I know you provided us with the extra food and water. Just as I know you had to wait for a good opportunity to affect our escape. I thank you for the extra data discs, the power failure, and the flitter waiting for us. At least we can die at home where we shared so much love."

She glanced down at her hands, then lifted one to the screen. She turned a ring around her finger.

"My cousin married a princess and she and I became good friends. I'm not sure my cousin knew, but she never had less than three items on her person at any given time which she could use to protect herself. Even some of her shoes had weapons in them. Her favorites, though, were her jewelry." Saletta pressed on the ring and a sharp needle protruded. "She gave me this ring when I first started traveling for my research. There's a deadly poison within." She shook her head tiredly and closed the ring. "It's odd how no one ever thinks to check a female's rings." Ronan heard both the Commander and his father growl low.

"I'll leave this recording in the safe, along with another data disc with all the information I could download about the virus. Our captors took great pleasure in forcing me and Marris into the lab so Jorn could witness our suffering. Jorn did not develop the virus—that was another scientist. But Jorn's research on Svesti reproduction made the delivery of the virus possible. He worked tirelessly whenever he could to try to find a way to counteract the virus. I don't know how far he had gotten. His mind declined rapidly after the infection started to ravage Marris and me."

Her shoulders straightened and she gazed directly at the camera. "I hope you discover this and can find it within yourself to raise our son as your own, Largon. You are a good male and even better friend to the d'Olorg family. If you have the right opportunity to get Jorn's work to the Svesti, please do so. It may or may not help my people, but at least I can die knowing I did my best. If possible, please bury us near the shade tree where Jorn asked me to mate with him."

Her eyes softened. "Ronan, my sweet male, I don't know if you'll ever see this. In some ways, I hope you won't. I would rather your memories of your family be of the love and laughter we shared. Not this." She gestured to the bed.

"I could not bear to have Marris suffer more, which is why I chose to use the poison. It is the hardest, most painful thing I've ever done. Before today, leaving you behind alone was at the top of the list. There was nothing left for Marris and me but agonizing pain, and your father wouldn't have survived our loss on his own. I could not risk him finding you and filling your beautiful mind and heart with bitterness. You deserve better. Trust Largon to teach you what you need to know." She sniffed.

"I debated whether to hide my actions from you, but you deserve the truth. I hope someday you will understand my choice to end all our suffering, instead of dragging it out longer. It is my choice and does not reflect on you. You have a large extended family on Costonia. I hope you get the chance to meet them. They may judge me for my actions, but they won't judge you." A small smile formed on her lips.

"Live a long, happy life, my son. Know that your family loved you and that you deserve love. Carry that with you always. While I may fear for you because of your heritage, I will not ever regret having you. You brought your father and me more joy than you realize. I wish I could be there to love and guide you as you grow into the male you are meant to be. If the Goddess allows it, I will watch over you as best I can until we can be together again."

Saletta raised three fingers on her hand, kissed her fingertips, then turned to press them against the camera. "Do not grieve long for us. Our suffering is ending soon at a time and place of my choosing. I love you, Ronan."

No one spoke as the recording ended and Ronan mimicked his mother's ending gesture.

"I love you, Mother." His voice was husky with emotion. Natasha squeezed his fingers and his tail wrapped around her ankle. Out of the corner of his eye, he saw tears falling silently down her face.

Silence reigned for several minutes.

"Saletta was probably the strongest person I've ever met," said Largon, his voice rough. He met Ronan's eyes. "She was correct. I infiltrated the lab as a guard and did what I could to make it easier for them while I arranged an escape. Early on, I realized your father didn't recognize me. With his mental state, I didn't trust him to be able to keep the escape or my presence a secret. When I slipped your mother the data discs, all I could tell her was, 'be ready for any opportunity.' Several days later, I shut the power down remotely after leaving the flitter somewhere close."

"Was this when you left me at a refuge a few months after they were taken?" *I remember being terrified you were abandoning me for good like my family did.*

"Yes, after I received confirmation on where they were being held. I didn't know how long it would take, if I would be caught, and I certainly couldn't take you with me." Largon sighed heavily. "It was almost a week after their escape before I made it back to Praxis to check if they'd left me a clue as to their whereabouts." He closed his eyes. "I found the three of them in that bed. She'd left a note that simply said 'safe.' I retrieved the discs, then buried your family where your mother requested." He opened his eyes and stared at Ronan with remorse on his face. "I'm sorry. If I had been faster to get there, I might've been able to save them."

"Doubtful," said Lady Narilla sadly. "It was almost four months after infection of the first females on Costonia before we tried removing their reproductive organs. No one would've have known what to do to save Saletta or Marris."

"The princess your mother mentioned, Ronan, was my wife," said Canaan. "And Vared's mother."

"She was also my sister," said King Sovex. "I think she would've been pleased that her gift to Saletta offered options she might not otherwise have had, even if its usage was not what was originally intended."

Ronan wasn't sure how he felt. "I'd like to think about this some more before discussing it." Natasha's thumb stroked his repeatedly. He inhaled, letting her scent settle him.

Largon slid the second disc to Tolvex. "This was the other disc she left. Much of it made no sense to me, but my background is not science." He looked around the room. "Does what you've seen and heard change your minds about helping us?" Everyone answered no.

"In that case, the colonies would appreciate the vaccine but prefer to remain where they are. All the refuges with younglings would like to be evacuated," Ronan said.

"Here are the numbers and dosages needed," Largon said as he tapped his comm.

Tolvex showed a space map in the center of the room. Ronan pointed. "If the *Invictus* gets us here, my shuttle can take the vaccines to the colonies and meet it again here." He pointed to Millus. "In the interim, the *Invictus* can go with Largon to evacuate the refuges, leaving Talonka Six as one of the last ones before meeting us. We believe it would be faster to inoculate the younglings after they've been evacuated."

"You're going to the colonies?" Natasha said quietly.

"Yes."

"I think I should go with you. I can ensure the colonists understand how to administer the vaccine."

"That won't be necessary."

Natasha's hand released his. She crossed her arms.

"I didn't ask if it was necessary." *Grak. She's getting angry.*

"I thought it might be better if you stayed on Talonka Six until the *Invictus* returns. They are still dealing with the illness."

Ash'n said, "If we're leaving Talonka Six as one of the last evacuation sites, I'd like to send a healer and some medics down to help until we return. I also agree that Natasha's presence at the colonies might be best. She has the most experience with this disease and will be able to brief the colonists succinctly about how to treat it and what to look for regarding complications."

"I'm not sure I'm comfortable sending Lady Natasha," said the commander.

"There has been no known movement of Zuvgran anywhere near the colonies," Largon said. "It's one of the reasons those locations were chosen."

"Will we be able to do twice daily check-ins with the *Invictus* similar to when I was Talonka Six?" Natasha asked.

"Yes," said Ronan. *Of course, she's going to get her way again. She's very good at that.*

Chapter 26

FTER THE MEETING, Natasha told Ronan she was going to the med bay and would meet him later. She would much rather spend the time with him helping him deal with the information about his family's deaths, but the way he reacted to her suggestion she go with him to the colonies confused and angered her. *Why wouldn't he want to spend more time together? Did I miss something in the meeting?*

In the med bay, Ash'n conducted the last three medical uploads she needed. *At least I now have good information to use.*

"Thanks for backing me up in the meeting," she said.

"I know you'd like more time with Ronan, but I really do believe you're the best choice to go to the colonies. You have knowledge of the disease that none of us have."

"It means more that you did it because of my qualifications, not my personal life."

She helped Ash'n divide the doses using the list Largon provided into specialized light-blocking crates that would also keep them frozen at the proper temperature. They set aside the ones for the colonies to be taken to Ronan's ship.

"I'm including extras of each dosage amount, just in case," Ash'n said.

"Good thinking." She paused. "How many people are you thinking to send to Talonka Six?"

"Sinoaz and six medics. All of them have already had the pertinent medical and language uploads."

"That's good. They could use the help."

Lin came in as they were finishing up. Ash'n leaned down to kiss her. *Geez. Come up for air, guys.*

Lin's cheeks flushed. "Did you two need any help?"

"No, *bataavi*, we're good here."

"Actually, do we have any of that *yuffa* solution left? I think it might help with itch relief for some of the younglings on the planet," Natasha said.

"Good idea." Ash'n opened a storage compartment and pulled out several containers. "I'll put this with some bandages so we don't forget it."

Lin hooked her arm through Natasha's. "You're coming with me for midday meal. We women haven't had a chance to catch up since you came back."

"I should check on the younglings."

"The males are taking care of them. Besides, we'll be at a table near them." *Maybe some time with the girls will clear my head.*

"Okay, lead the way."

Ava plopped down on the chair next to Natasha with a *leringa* pie.

"Here. Have a piece before everyone figures out there's pie." Ava cut a slice and placed it on Natasha's empty plate.

"Mmm. Thanks. I've missed your cooking," said Natasha between bites. "Synthesizer food all the time gets old, especially since they don't have any of your recipes."

"What had everyone looking so serious after the meeting this morning? You all looked shell shocked," Talia asked, concern in her voice.

"Some personal stuff for Ronan and Largon. I'm not sure how much I'm allowed to share. It was very emotional for both of them and for the rest of us," Natasha said with a frown.

Ava wagged her eyebrows. "So? You and Ronan? Are the rumors I'm hearing true?"

"What rumors?"

"That he is bunking in your quarters, not Largon's," said Emmy.

"Yeah, that part is true." *I'm not sure how much to share.*

"Well, spill it. We want to hear all about your romance," said Talia.

"I also want to hear about the rescue of the little ones," Rachel said.

"The rescue went really well overall. They used hidden tunnels and they were able to get everyone out safely. We didn't know they put a tracker in Teeka, so we got taken off guard when the Zuvgran attacked as they were coming out of that tunnel with her."

"Where did all the blood on you come from?" asked Emmy.

Natasha chewed her lip. "One tried to choke me from behind. I used one of Rachel's moves to get free. Then I stabbed him in the neck with a dagger Ronan insisted I wear."

Rachel narrowed her eyes at her. "You're okay? It's not easy killing someone."

"No, it's not." Natasha blew out a breath. "But it was him or me and I plan on sticking around awhile."

"Good. If you ever feel you need to talk about it, find me."

"I will, Rachel. Thanks."

"Okay, gory stuff done. Let's talk about the ugly stuff." When everyone looked at Emmy like she had two heads, she said, "You know—bumping uglies? Geez. Tough crowd."

"Are you sure you're an adult?" Lin teased.

"Legal and everything, baby." Emmy mimed tapping ashes off a cigar and tugging on a mustache. The women laughed.

"We knew when we started it could only be a short-term thing."

"Been there, done that." Emmy faked a look of confusion. "Don't have a T-shirt for it."

"That's a surprise. You have a T-shirt for everything else," Rachel said drily.

Emmy pulled the hem of her T-shirt to lie flat and pointed at her chest. Everyone laughed when they realized it said, "Byte me."

"Wow, Emmy, you're in rare form. Must be the fated mate bond." Ava's lips curled upward.

"I'm happy. I want everyone else to be happy, too. This is a new feeling for me."

Natasha reached over and squeezed Emmy's hand. "I like it, even if you'll drive us crazy. It's a good look on you."

Emmy became serious. "So does the short-term thing work for you?"

"I don't know. It's been so fast, but I really care for him...a lot. I thought we agreed to try to spend as much time together as possible before we were forced to part ways. But today, he tried to talk me out of going with him to the colonies to distribute the vaccine. I'm not sure what he's thinking." Natasha's fingers played with the end of her braid. *Shit. I haven't done that in years. It screams lack of confidence.*

"You need to talk to him," said Lin softly. "You know you do."

"But what do I say?"

"Tell him what you're thinking and feeling—whatever it is. Find out what he's thinking and feeling. Find a middle ground that works for both of you if you can."

"Lin's right. Speaking from recent experience, even a short-term relationship will be rocky without honest communication." Emmy shrugged, then her face brightened. "But the makeup sex, especially with those nodes, is so much fun."

"Nodes?" said Ava with an arched brow.

Emmy brown curls bobbed when she nodded. "On their dicks. One near the base and three on the head." She scrunched her nose. "You know, I never asked if the number of nodes is consistent or if it varies."

Suppressing a laugh, Talia said, "I believe it's the same for all their males."

"Well, Ronan's half-Svesti, so maybe he's got nodes. Do Zuvgran pack extra, too?" Emmy looked at Natasha.

Natasha's cheeks heated and she dropped her hand into her hands. "Ridges," she muttered.

Lin whispered, "Did she say ridges?"

"I think she did," said Rachel.

"Holy crap. Ridges and nodes? Definitely talk to him," said Emmy.

Natasha's head came up. "Could you keep it down? This is embarrassing enough."

"Why? You're a doctor. You're just telling us the differences in physiology."

"Emmy, please."

Emmy ducked her head. "I'm sorry. I didn't mean to upset you."

"I know, but I'm not as comfortable as you are exchanging personal information about someone else, especially in public."

"Is that a dig about my hacking?" Emmy's eyes fell and her fingers drummed on the table.

Natasha grabbed her hand. "No, it isn't. It means I care about Ronan and gossiping about his equipment feels wrong."

Emmy raised her eyes. "I really am sorry, Nat. I sometimes forget others have different boundaries than I do."

Natasha smiled at her. "I know. But friends sometimes cross boundaries without meaning to. I'm sure I'll have my turn in the future."

Emmy sighed. "Okay, to satisfy my curiosity, but recognizing boundaries, would it be safe to say your new boyfriend has more to him than human males?"

Natasha laughed and shook her head. "Yes, Emmy, you would be safe in saying that."

"Cool. Lucky you. Lucky us."

Later that day, Natasha joined Ronan, Sinoaz, and the six medics on Ronan's shuttle to go to Talonka Six. She silently nodded in approval of the medics Ash'n chose. She knew they were competent, observant, and compassionate from her time working with them at the mine.

Ronan comm'd Talos while they were in the air to ask him and his group to be ready to go to the *Invictus* after they finished at the larger cavern. Talos' yellow eyes gleamed happily as he told them the younglings were ready for another adventure.

When Ronan landed the shuttle in what she had been coming to think of as their cavern, she saw the maglev near the decontamination unit. *That's odd. I don't remember leaving it there.* When she asked Ronan about it and he said that he'd asked Herrah to make sure the maglev made it back before they arrived so the Svesti wouldn't have to carry their bags. *That makes sense.*

The Svesti loaded their medical and personal bags, as well as the vaccines and medical supplies, onto the maglev. Natasha was pleased to see the *yuffa* solution there.

When they reached the cavern, Natasha noted that the coughing seemed less, both in amount and harshness. She saw some of the previously ill younglings sitting in chairs next to cots, playing with others quietly. *Much better. What a relief. My guilt about being gone so long can stop.*

Herrah greeted them happily. Ronan made the introductions and the Svesti got to work inoculating the younglings. At Sinoaz's request, she had one of the adults escort the healer and a medic with some vaccines to where the others were in quarantine. Natasha checked on the patients who had been suffering the worst and all of them were doing much better.

"Is there anything you need, Herrah, before we leave the Svesti with you? The *Invictus* should return in four days to evacuate everyone here," Ronan said.

"No. We should be fine. That will give us time to pack and get ready."

"Largon should be on the *Invictus* to help. Natasha and I won't be rejoining all of you until a week and a half after you get there. We're going to the colonies to drop off vaccines."

"We'll be fine, Ronan. We're looking forward to something new and exciting." Herrah's four arms widened. "Give me a hug before you go, now that I don't have to worry about infecting you." Natasha watched as they embraced, the sight of four gray hands patting Ronan's back tickling her funny bone. *Claws, horns, tails, fangs, even different numbers of digits don't seem to be strange to me, but extra limbs do. That's so weird.*

Vepiv, one of the medics, opened a box and smiled. Natasha drifted toward him. She laughed when she saw the contents.

"Ava sent cookies?"

"Yes, Lady Natasha, it looks like she did."

"Well, you'd better hand them out. They're sure to spread a little happiness."

Vepiv grinned. "As you command." Amused, she watched him pocket two for himself. *Ava should open a bakery on Costonia. She'd be rich within a week.*

Natasha received a four-armed hug from Herrah before they left to return to the shuttle. *Feels weird, but nice.*

Their boots echoed in the cool tunnel. *This is the first time you've been alone with him since the meeting. Just talk to him.*

"What's wrong? I feel like you're pushing me away and I don't know why," said Natasha.

"It's for your own good." Ronan's tail snapped wildly behind him.

"That tells me nothing, Ronan. I need you to explain."

"You're too good to align yourself with me."

"What the hell does that mean?" *Calm down, listen to what he has to say before you put your foot in your mouth.*

He halted and faced her with his arms crossed. Pain lined his features. "You're going to make me say it, aren't you?"

"Say what? I don't understand."

"I'm the son of murderers," he spit out. "I always suspected my father's research contributed to all those Svesti deaths, but my mother..." His voice trailed off.

Shocked, she stared at him, open-mouthed. "Is that what you took away from the recording?"

"We watched my mother kill my family." Moisture coated his silver eyes.

She stepped closer and placed her hand on his cheek. Tunneling one arm under his elbow, she attempted to hug his stiff body.

"That's not what I saw."

His arms dropped, then wrapped around her to hold her close. His tail captured her ankle. He buried his face in her neck, one horn nudging her braid, and his body shook.

"What did you see?" His words were thick with emotion.

"I saw a woman in agonizing pain, both physical and emotional, who was watching her family suffer with no way out except death."

"Could you have done what she did?"

Natasha drew back to look him in his eyes, her thumb stroking his cheek. "I don't know. I'm not sure anyone can say with any certainty what they would do in her situation." She inhaled deeply.

"I remember discussing euthanasia in one of my medical ethics courses. It's still hotly debated on Earth as to whether or not it should be legal to allow a merciful death to those who are suffering without any recourse available to them. Some argue that it's murder or suicide no matter what, while others believe a person should be able to die with dignity." She held his gaze. "I think it's a very personal, heartrending decision either way and it's not my place to judge another's choices in that type of situation." She tucked his hair behind his ear tenderly.

"Instead of focusing on her final actions, maybe try to understand what your mother experienced and why she made the choices she did. She was in excruciating pain—aware that horrible deaths awaited her and her baby girl. She couldn't count on your father. Maybe he could've healed them with the proper help, maybe not. Her focus then became protecting the one healthy member of her family from the hurt and confusion he could've inflicted on you. Despite all that, she took advantage of Largon's opportunity to escape with her family...to die free."

"Regardless of what you decide about her choices, there are two things you need to remember."

"What?"

"Your parents loved you and you are not your parents. You are your own person." His body tensed then relaxed and his embrace felt less desperate.

"You really are too good for me, *caliana*. Smart, beautiful, compassionate, and a caring heart. Much more than I deserve."

Natasha met Ronan halfway when he bent to kiss her. To her, their mouths interacting felt less physical, more emotional. She took in his pain and sent understanding and support back to him. The longer their tongues tangled, pain turned to gratitude, then arousal.

Long moments later, they broke off the kiss, chests heaving. His unique scent surrounded her.

"Let's get Talos' contingent and head back to the *Invictus*, *caliana*. I wish to be alone with you."

Chapter 27

RONAN PILOTED THE shuttle to the smaller caverns where he left Talos and the other younglings from Pellotia. While he remained alert enough to keep them safe, part of his mind still churned over the revelations of the day.

At the meeting, his emotions were in turmoil after watching his mother end the lives of his father and sister. The echoes of Marris' screams replayed in his head like a broken recording, stabbing at his heart over and over. When Natasha spoke of going to the colonies, he knew he had to let her go for her own good. Her couldn't stop his thoughts—both his parents were murderers. Perhaps not by inclination, but in deeds. He could not spend over a week alone with Natasha on his shuttle and not reach out to her. So when she ended up coming, he decided he must keep her at arm's length.

Then Brauvix approached, his eyes tired and bruised, and Ronan felt panic that he couldn't help Brauvix with his emotional fallout when his own was an ever-growing avalanche. Fortunately, Largon pulled Brauvix aside and spoke with the male.

Ronan felt as if he were splintering into smaller fragments. He realized he never truly reconciled the two halves of his heritage in his heart. Despite saying and knowing he was a hybrid, in his heart he wanted to be a 'good Svesti' like his mother rather than an 'abnormal Zuvgran' like his father or Largon. To suddenly have the good stripped from his mother left him floundering. And he also knew in the deepest recesses of his heart, he felt his father had been weak. He should've escaped Praxis with his mother before ever attempting to have children. He didn't keep his family safe.

Ronan couldn't believe Natasha had pushed him to talk rather than walk away from him. She offered comfort and an objective point of view. She melted his avalanche of thoughts into a single flowing river of calm. And that kiss. It felt as if she had collected all his fragments and returned them to him whole. A bit damaged, but still whole.

He brought his attention completely back to the present as they approached the landing site. Natasha let out a sound of excitement.

"I've only seen a picture of a Pellotian-Zuvgran hybrid, never in person." Her forehead wrinkled as they approached. "Is there something wrong with their wings?"

Ronan looked to where Talos and the younglings waited with their bags inside the cavern just beyond where he parked the shuttle. *I guess they are excited to leave.*

"The Zuvgran routinely mutilated the wings of Pellotians and hybrids. They'd never allow them to fly and feel free. From what I understand, it causes them lifelong pain."

"Fucking bastards. I wonder if there's anything the Svesti can do, even to reduce or eliminate their pain." Her brown eyes turned fiery. *Grak. Her passion is compelling. No wonder I can't resist her.*

Ronan opened the ramp door and everyone piled into the shuttle. He made the introductions, then told them to strap in.

Annika took a seat in the cockpit behind Natasha. Ronan lifted off and piloted them toward the *Invictus*.

"So, Ronan, what is the plan?" she asked.

"We'll join the Svesti space cruiser, *Invictus*, where all of you will stay until it reaches Costonia. There are already twenty-three other younglings onboard and the *Invictus*, with Largon's help, will evacuate the others. Natasha and I have to leave in a couple of days, but we'll rejoin you in a week or so and accompany you onto the planet. We'll be staying there for awhile. I don't know how long or where we'll go after that. The Svesti king has offered to find a suitable place for all of us to be together safely."

Annika crossed her arms and stared at him. "Will we be safe among the Svesti?"

"Yes," said Natasha. "There are also some human women there, my friends, who will help. If you have any concerns or you feel someone is treating any of you poorly, you can talk to them and they'll take care of it."

"It will get crowded for about a week as the *Invictus* evacuates the other refuges," Ronan said. "But I think you will enjoy the food and the aquiponics area."

"We'll see." Annika leaned back with a distrustful expression.

"Annika," Ronan said gently. "I know you have helped Talos lead your group and kept them safe. Part of the reason we are doing this is so you can relax and enjoy a childhood like you deserve. We'll still depend on you, but you will have the opportunity to let the adults do the majority of the worrying now."

"I'm not sure I know how to be a child."

"Then we'll be happy to help you learn."

When they arrived in the shuttle bay, the younglings stayed quiet as they disembarked.

"Hello, everyone, I'm Healer Rivezt and this is my mate, Lady Lin. We're glad to have you here."

"Let's follow the healer to the med bay so they can check your health," said Largon. "Then we'll show you where you'll be staying so you can drop off your belongings. After that, we'll get some food and you can meet the first group."

"Where will we be staying?" asked Annika as they walked the corridors.

"Well, you lucked out, youngling. Since you're only the second group evacuated and there aren't that many of you, you'll be able to stay in quarters with the first group. The rest will be dorming in a shuttle bay for the duration of the trip."

Flitos asked, "Will Talos be staying with us?"

"No, he'll be staying with me, but we're very close to where you are," Largon said.

At the back of the group, Ronan reached out and held Natasha's hand. His tail rose to settle in the small of her back as he listened to the observations and questions of the younglings.

In the med bay, Flitos volunteered to go first and let the healer examine him. Rivezt tapped his tablet.

"Well?" Flitos said impatiently. Ronan choked back a laugh at the youngling's imperious tone.

"Well, young Flitos, overall you are in good health. I need you to eat a nutritional supplement pack once a day in addition to your regular meals so we can get your reserve levels of nutrients where they should be. It should only be necessary for a week or two." Flitos looked concerned at the healer's words.

Rivezt continued, "I wouldn't worry about the supplements, Flitos. Even the warriors on *Invictus* have to eat them sometimes to stay healthy. The damage to your wings, do you remember when it happened?" He inoculated the youngling as he talked.

"No. They've always been like this."

"Do they cause you pain?"

"My shoulders are always achy, but I'm used to it." Ronan's chest rumbled.

"With your permission, I'd like to take a closer look at them tomorrow after you've had a good night's sleep. I might be able to correct some of the damage and relieve a bit of the pain."

"Really?"

"I'm not saying you will be able to fly, youngling, but if we can get rid of the pain, it would be an improvement, wouldn't it?"

Flitos bobbed his head and clicked his beak twice. "I'll be here."

"There's one more thing. I'd like your permission to inject you with a tracker."

Flitos shook his head and his ruff fluffed. "No."

"Hear me out, please. The *Invictus* is a very large ship with some dangerous areas for younglings, and Costonia is a very large planet. We want to be able to find you quickly if you get lost. That is its sole purpose—to help us keep you safe."

"Talos took out my Zuvgran tracker."

"And I'm glad he did. That tracker was meant to keep you afraid and a slave, Flitos. I promise you, by the Goddess, that is not what this one means."

"If it helps, Flitos, I have one," said Natasha patting her upper arm.

"As do I," Ronan said.

"Mine is here," Rivezt tapped his upper arm as well.

"Do you get lost often?" Annika asked. Everyone laughed.

"No, but when I have, it helped my fellow Svesti rescue me."

"I still don't know," Flitos said.

"Okay. Think about it. Talk to others, if you like. If you change your mind, you know how to find me."

"You're not going to force it on me?"

"Absolutely not. You're old enough to make the decision." Rivezt looked at Natasha with an odd expression. "I won't take away your right to say no." Natasha narrowed her eyes at Rivezt, then nodded with a smile. *What was that about?*

The exams for the remainder of the younglings went quickly. The healer only implanted trackers on the ones under five solars. All the older ones wanted to think about it more.

When Rivezt examined Talos, Ronan heard him say quietly, "Your wings cause you a great deal of pain, don't they?"

Talos nodded. Natasha and Lin kept the younglings occupied on the other side of the room.

"I'm going to do some research to see what we might be able to do to relieve the pain and possibly regain some movement. I can't promise much, but I would like to help."

"I appreciate it, Healer."

"I can give you something now to take away the worst of the pain for several hours."

"No. I've lived with it this long. I can wait for a solution that doesn't require me to routinely take meds."

"As you wish."

They went by the living quarters, dropped off their belongings, then went to the dining area. The younglings clustered close to each other when they saw the hundreds of Svesti warriors. They began to relax as they went through the food line and started to chatter excitedly once seated with the other younglings from Straxis. It wasn't long before they seemed comfortable with their new situation. *It looks like the two groups are meshing well. I hope it goes as smoothly with the other groups. How soon before I can be alone with Natasha?*

After his shower and braiding his hair, King Traxen Sovex dressed in comfortable clothing before exiting his bedroom via a hidden passageway. Twenty feet later, he came to a valadium door with a single lock. Once he was through, he relocked the door and walked to a similar door about the same distance away.

This door had three locks, one of which was coded to his DNA. It automatically locked behind him as he entered the main tunnel. If one didn't know the door was there, they would never see it. Only his Spymaster knew this door existed, but as much as Traxen trusted the male, he would never give another the means to enter his personal space unfettered.

Soundlessly, he strode through the dimly lit passageways until he reached a room at the center. Opening another door lock coded with his DNA, he noted the Spymaster seated in a darkened corner of the room. He went to the sidebar and poured himself some Estalan liquor.

"You do realize I already know what you look like," Traxen said as he arranged himself in a comfortable chair.

"My apologies, sire. Occupational hazard." The Spymaster rose and took a seat across from Traxen, taking a sip of his own drink.

Traxen looked at the male dressed comfortably in black. Upon first glance, there was nothing remarkable about him. Average height, dark hair, dark eyes, caramel bronze skin, no visible scars, or body tics—nothing to make him stand out in a crowd. But if you were observant, you might see the intelligence and calculation behind his watchful eyes and the fact that his tail rarely made a movement that wasn't pre-planned. In public, the Spymaster was an expert in disguises and personalities. Sometimes Traxen wondered if the male remembered the beginning of his life.

"Again, no need for the title. Have you learned any more about the traitors and how organized they may be?"

"Whomever they are, they are cautious. I've heard the phrase 'Always Svesti' in hushed tones, but nothing of regular meetings or the hierarchy so far. I'm still working a couple different angles to gain clarity, but as yet, nothing definitive."

"*Crek*. I expect the *Invictus* to return in about two weeks. I hoped to have this resolved before they arrived."

"There is another disturbing rumor. One that involves overthrowing the crown and installing a new ruling family."

"Someone always wants the throne."

"This sounds more plausible than usual. Furtive whispers cutting off when someone new crosses their paths. My gut says the two issues are related."

"Someone who wants racial purity wishes to rule as well?"

"Or someone who wishes to rule is using those who believe in racial purity as a base."

Traxen swirled the expensive liquor in his glass, silently admiring the deep amber tones of the fluid tinged with pink. He sipped and wondered how the Estalans infused the alcohol with the smoky flavor.

"Do you have any suspects for the upcoming attempted coup?"

"Several using the list you gave me from the Council meeting a couple months ago."

"Who tops your list?"

"Two mid-level Council members from Houses Nuxar and Troliv, Marek Tolvex of House Vramel, and Pluvi Frulix of House Srotix." The Spymaster tapped an extended claw on his glass. "Signs point to Tolvex, but they feel off."

"Someone setting him up?"

"Possibly. Tolvex doesn't have the brains to pull off a coup nor lead a group insistent on racial purity. He's also too abrasive to garner that type of support."

"I'd have to agree with you. He says what he means, even if it's ill-advised or ignorant. If one were so inclined, one could admire him for that."

"All four of them recently left Costonia for parts unknown. That concerns me."

Traxen grinned. "You do dislike not knowing."

The Spymaster tipped his glass at Traxen. "Truth."

They sat in silence and enjoyed their libations.

"I've also heard another rumor," said the Spymaster.

"Which is?"

"You are settling Zuvgran hybrids on Costonia."

"It's in its early stages, but yes. I haven't even extended the offer to them yet. Approximately six hundred hybrids. Canaan and I talked about it and think the land between our two holdings would be best. Both Houses will share in the expense."

"Where that old monstrosity was built by some forefather of yours sits?"

Traxen chuckled. "Yes, there is water and good land. They will be close enough to the city, but distant enough from the congestion to allow them some peace from our less forgiving citizens. We will be demolishing that monstrosity and building several orphanages and a market area."

"Whomever is planning to overthrow you will use this against you."

"I'm aware, but it's the right thing to do. The younglings did not choose their parents or heritage, but a sympathetic Zuvgran and a Svesti-Zuvgran hybrid saved them. They deserve a chance at a normal life."

"A Svesti-Zuvgran hybrid?" The Spymaster's eyes widened. Traxen hid his smile. *It is rare to see the Spymaster surprised.*

"Yes, the son of my late sister's friend, Saletta Yemez."

"I thought Saletta died on Himita Prime."

"As did we. However, a Zuvgran scientist saved her and she subsequently fell in love with him. As I understand it, as a geneticist, her mate found a way for her to bear his young."

"Does Saletta still live?"

"Unfortunately, no, she died about thirty solars ago."

"There's a bigger story here."

"Your instincts are correct. I will not be sharing that story this evening. However, I will tell you this. A Zuvgran male accompanies them. He's run an underground for disaffected Zuvgran and hybrids for forty solars. Perhaps he'll have information my Spymaster might find useful."

A thoughtful expression settled on the male's face. "If he already has sympathetic contacts on Zuvgran-controlled planets, we might garner better intelligence."

"My thoughts exactly."

Chapter 28

NATASHA COULD SENSE Ronan's impatience to be alone while they settled Talos' group of younglings on the Invictus. Unlike how he withdrew from her earlier in the day, now his tail or his hand was constantly touching her. He seemed to find reasons to lean close to her. She loved it, but he made it difficult for her to concentrate.

Finally, after taking everyone to the aquiponics area, Natasha found an opportunity to speak with Talia, who was measuring the newcomers for clothing.

"Will all of you be okay if I take Ronan with me for the evening? We need to talk."

With a knowing smile, Talia said, "Of course. Do what you need to do."

Natasha caught Ronan's eye and jerked her head toward the exit. He met up with her as she was leaving the group.

"Leaving so soon?"

"Talia said she would ensure the younglings were taken care of. I think we need to talk some more."

His hand lightly touched her back as he matched her stride.

"As you wish."

In her quarters, she said, "Do you want something to drink?"

"Water is fine."

Handing him a water pouch and taking one for herself, she sat on the couch. He dropped down next to her. Both took sips of water.

"We haven't had a chance to really talk after the cavern. How are you feeling?"

"Much better." He looked down at the pouch, then at her. "You gave me much to think on."

"Are you still feeling that I shouldn't go with you to the colonies? If so, I will respect that and see if I can get someone else up to speed to take my place." *Damn, that hurt to offer.*

"No. You're the best person for the job...and for me. I should've spoken with you first." His fingers gently removed the elastic from her braid and loosened her hair. "Forgive me?"

She grabbed his hand and looked him in the eye. "Promise me one thing."

"Anything, *caliana.*"

"Never try to make a decision for me about our relationship again. If you want to stop because of your own feelings, that's one thing. But you tried to unilaterally end it without taking my feelings into account. You disrespected me."

He rested his forehead on hers. "You are correct. I'm sorry, Natasha. My only excuse is my emotions were all over the place and all I wanted to do was protect you from making a mistake with me."

"Bullshit. You were protecting yourself because you didn't trust me to trust you."

His other hand tunneled into her hair, gripped it, and tugged her head back far enough to look into her eyes.

"Thoughts of protecting myself never crossed my mind, Natasha. Now you are disrespecting me—assigning imaginary motives to my actions." His chest rumbled. "I will own my mistakes, but not ones I did not make."

Her lips curved upward and his eyes turned confused.

"Good. Don't let me walk all over you. Tell me if I've upset you or correct me if I'm wrong." His fingers loosened and she leaned forward to kiss him lightly on the lips. "I'm sorry."

He wrapped his arms around her and kissed her deeply. Their tongues danced while their hands and fingers explored each other. Their bodies shifted and she fell back on the seat cushions, his weight pressing into her. She squirmed against his hardness to settle him between her thighs and pressed upwards. He lightly thrust against her. *Yes. That feels so good.*

Hot hands caressed her, one pausing to cup a breast before squeezing gently. She broke off the kiss and gasped as his fingers played with her hard nipple through her clothing. His lips moved along her jawline, sending tingles down her spine.

"Too much clothing," she said breathlessly.

"Let's take care of that." He sat up and pulled off his shirt. *Oh, that chest.*

Her fingers tripped over his pecs and brushed his nipples. His abs tightened when he sucked in a breath at her touch. Drifting lower, she reached behind him for the fastening to his pants. They fell, but his cock stayed hidden from her view. She burrowed under the material and caressed his length with eager hands.

"Now you, Natasha." He stood and lifted her to a seated position. He pulled her shirt off and extended a claw to slice through the front of her bra. *That's hot.*

Retracting his claw, he grasped her waistband and tugged on her leggings. She wiggled her hips to help and he groaned as he bared her wetness to his gaze. He removed her shoes and socks, kissing her feet lightly, while he shimmied out of his pants and boots. She fell back sideways on the couch as he worked his mouth and tongue up the insides of her legs slowly. Wriggling restlessly when he nipped her flesh lightly with his fangs before licking, she tugged on her engorged nipples.

Ronan knelt on the couch and spread her legs wider, placing them over his broad shoulders. Eyes closing briefly, he inhaled, then looked up the length of her body. She licked her lips as she met his molten silver gaze, passion emanating from its depths.

"You smell delicious." He lowered his mouth to lick her clit. Her back bowed with rapture at the sensation of his hot wet tongue against her most sensitive flesh. She wrapped her fingers around his horns and squeezed as his tongue worked its magic. Tingles of heat from all over her body rushed to her core. Happily drowning in his scent, she moaned as he inserted a finger into her pussy and leisurely pumped.

"Feels so good, Ronan. More."

He added another finger while the tip of his tongue stiffened and lightly circled her clit over and over. His beard softly scraped against her delicate skin creating more heat. Wet sounds filled the air along with her moans and his groans of enjoyment. When he added a third finger and curled them inside her, her body convulsed in spasms of white joy. His mouth and fingers continued to torment her in the best possible ways before her body finally fell limp and her hands fell from his horns.

He rose and lifted one of her legs over the back of the couch and held the other up against his chest. Face wet with the evidence of her arousal, he fisted his cock and pressed the tip against her entrance.

"Look at how swollen and red you are, inviting me to *grak* you, *caliana*." Slowly he entered her, the lines of his face tight.

Natasha whimpered as his ridges rasped the inside of her pussy which clenched and released in response to his intimate invasion. *So full. So good.* When he bottomed out, she groaned.

Ronan began to move, slowly thrusting in and out in a steady rhythm. Natasha put her arms over her head and placed her palms against the inside of the couch arm. She used the leverage to keep from sliding as his hips pumped and to push back against him. A long, low moan left her lips as he reached deeper inside her.

Sweat rivulets fell from her face and her skin felt damp as they moved faster. His balls slapped her ass and her pussy rippled over his ridges, grasping and sucking at his hardness. Her heavy breasts bounced as he thrust harder.

"You're so *grakkin'* beautiful, Natasha." His tail lightly slapped at her nipples and she gasped as the heat traveled to her clit. His base node rubbed her swollen nub on each downstroke.

"I'm coming, Ronan. Come with me." Natasha's voice sounded hoarse with exertion.

Waves of pleasure shot through her body as her orgasm erupted. Her pussy spasmed uncontrollably and her body shook under the onslaught of sensation. Through the sound of rushing blood in her ears, she heard him shout her name as he buried himself deep within her. Her legs fell to cradle him. His hard body dropped against her though he kept most of his weight on his elbows. She wrapped her arms around him, stroking his back. Panting heavily, they caressed each other and kissed as their bodies calmed.

"Does this qualify as makeup sex?" Ronan asked. "If so, I like it."

"You heard that?" Heat rushed to her face. *I'm going to kill Emmy.*

"I inherited the Svesti enhanced hearing. It was a very interesting conversation." His eyes sparkled with amusement.

"The girls can be a bit much sometimes." *Crap. What did I say?*

"I like how much they care about you, *caliana*. It's also enlightening to hear what goes on in a female's mind."

"Did I say anything to upset you?"

"Not at all. I thought you were very circumspect. I did have one other question, though."

"What?"

"Human males do not have ridges or nodes?"

She laughed. "Nope. Not even close."

Over the next two days as the *Invictus* traveled to where they would depart on Ronan's shuttle, Natasha's attention was split. She spent time in the med bay, discussing options with Ash'n and Healer Markham on how best to heal the damage to Pellotian-Zuvgran hybrids as well as Talos' wings. Ash'n felt they could help the younglings on the Invictus as they each had a single cut on each shoulder. For Talos, he wanted to involve the Master Healers on Costonia as his damage appeared much more extensive. Flitos volunteered to go first. Natasha assisted during the procedure. Hours later, she fought back tears when Flitos moved his wings. The sheer joy on the youngling's face as he experienced the first moments of his life pain-free was exhilarating and humbling to see.

She also spent time with the younglings, getting to know each one as an individual. Even over the short span of time, she saw them losing some of their fear and becoming more confident. She and the other women shared their observations and made plans to best encourage each youngling.

Ronan got her nights and mornings. The sex was amazing, but she also loved discovering more about him and his thoughts. She listened when he shared how his heritage affected him. She had no answers, but was more than willing to be supportive. She held him when he relayed his emotional conversation with

Largon about the recording. and how relieved Largon was when Ronan told him he didn't blame him for his family's deaths or suffering. Natasha wished she could have been a fly on the wall when Ronan informed the male that he considered Largon the father of his heart.

Ronan reciprocated as she told him that she always felt like she didn't belong with her parents. They had been so concerned with status and what others thought that her own feelings and beliefs came second. They pushed at her to do better than her peers, not so that she would be the best, but so they could boast about her success. Her *Babushka* always made her feel loved, just as she was, which is why her death had left a huge hole in Natasha's life. Ronan thoughtfully questioned if she believed she was naturally driven to do her best or if it was a learned behavior in an attempt to have her parents notice her. She didn't know, but wanted to consider that when she had more time, if only to understand herself better.

Not everything was serious. The male loved to tease her and see her relaxed. Even though they'd only known each other a short time, she felt he understood her better than anyone other than her *Babushka*. She definitely knew and understood him better than any other man she had dated, including the four-year relationship she had during medical school.

Now she stood in the shuttle bay, having already said goodbye to the women and younglings, watching it being loaded with supplies and vaccines. Ronan's tail wrapped around her ankle as they spoke with Tolvex.

"I'm sending you three frequencies. We're requesting you scan for them continuously on your trip and if you receive a signal on any of them, please contact us immediately," said Tolvex, his teal eyes solemn.

"Trackers?" said Ronan.

"Yes. Two for beings and one for a ship. We've lost contact with them."

"Wurvez and Jevax?" asked Natasha.

Tolvex's tail snapped. "How did you know?"

"I know I haven't been around a lot, but I haven't seen either of them in weeks. Besides, given their personalities, they wouldn't be avoiding the younglings. They'd be getting into trouble with them."

Tolvex snorted. "Fair point. Yes, they left on a secret mission and we don't know what happened to them."

Ronan said, "We'll be happy to scan for them."

"Thank you."

"Tell Emmy I said stay out of trouble," said Natasha.

Tolvex' fangs gleamed against his caramel bronze skin. "I will, but I doubt it will make a difference."

"True." Hearing footsteps, she turned to see Largon, Durek, and Talia approaching.

"We wanted to see you off," said Talia.

"Remember to check in with us twice a day," said Durek. He glanced at Tolvex who dipped his head.

Natasha nodded. "We will." She hugged Talia. "Take care of everyone. We'll be back soon."

Largon clasped Ronan's forearm. "Stay safe. We'll expect you to rejoin us at Millus."

"We'll be there." Ronan put his hand on the small of Natasha's back. "It's time."

"Oh," said Talia. "Ava said she sent a box of food for you."

"That's great. Tell her thanks," Natasha said as she boarded the shuttle.

They took their seats in the cockpit and Ronan coordinated their departure. As they left the *Invictus*, Natasha lips curved into a satisfied smile. *With the exception of our colony stops, we have nine days alone together.*

Chapter 29

RONAN ENGAGED THE the cloaking and dampener when the shuttle cleared the Invictus. He set the auto-pilot and turned to see Natasha's licentious grin.

"We won't reach the first colony until tomorrow." He unfastened his restraints and watched her do the same.

"Whatever will we do to occupy ourselves?" She swiveled to face him, resting her head on her hands. She left her hair loose as he liked and he obviously approved.

Ronan pretended to think. "Perhaps see what Ava sent. You were right, she's an excellent cook."

"Hmm, we could. Or we could work up an appetite first."

"Did you have something specific in mind?" His nostrils flared as her scent grew heavy and his cock hardened.

"I've had this fantasy."

"Oh?"

"It involves a cockpit, nakedness, and a cock."

"Sounds interesting. Whose nakedness?"

"Both of us." *I'm ready if you are.*

"That's doable. We're already in a cockpit and the last time I checked I have a cock. I think we should explore your fantasy more."

"I'm glad." She stood and unbuttoned her shirt, then tossed it onto a seat.

"Is there anything special I should do to help this fantasy along?" His eyes watched as she removed her pants, shoes, and socks, leaving her in her nanosuit. *I love her curves.*

"Get naked and sit."

Ronan hastened to do her bidding, removing his clothing at record speed and tossing everything behind him, while Natasha shimmied out of her nanosuit. He sat as instructed and gestured at himself.

"Is this satisfactory, *caliana*?" He admired the sway of her breasts and hips as she approached him.

"I have a feeling I'm going to be very satisfied," she purred as she placed her hands on the armrests and leaned over him.

"I will endeavor to ensure that you are." *Kiss me. Touch me.*

She straddled his knees and nuzzled his neck, her long hair brushing his shoulder and chest. He tipped his head back to give her better access and her lips and tongue blazed a trail along his jawline. When she reached his mouth, her blunt teeth closed around his lower lip and she bit it gently and tugged. A surprised hiss left him. *That felt good.*

Her lips curved against his skin as she continued to lick, suck, and intermittently nip at his flesh. Leaving her hands on the armrests, she worked her way along his shoulders and chest. She spent long moments teasing his nipples, biting with a small twist of her teeth, then her tongue soothed the sting with gentle laps. His erect cock stuck straight up reaching for her. He shifted in his chair trying to get comfortable. *She's tormenting me and it feels wonderful.*

Her hair fell over his thighs as she continued her trail of fire over his abdomen. Hot wetness surrounded his base node and his hips bucked. *Sweet Goddess, she's dangerous.*

Her tongue licked a path to where his pre-cum was flowing. His tail moved between her thighs and pushed inside her.

She lifted her head. "Did I tell you to use your tail?" He stilled.

"It has a mind of its own." *It likes being inside you almost as much as my cock does.*

"Do not make me come yet. I plan to use your cock for that."

"As you command." *I love her confidence. It's so grakkin' sexy.*

Her mouth returned to the head of his cock, licking and sucking with no relief. His tail thrust slowly, increasing her wetness. Her hips undulated against him. Leaving her hot core, his tail spread her wetness up toward her clit to circle it slowly, then dipped into her again before seeking entrance at her rosebud. Her ass pushed back against his tail giving silent permission. He gently worked it into her as she sucked harder on his cock. *So grakkin' tight.*

She raised her head and moved forward on his thighs.

"Help me," she said as she raised her hips clenching her ass on his tail.

His hands grasped her ass cheeks and he lifted her onto his cock. She lowered herself slowly until he was buried within her hot, wet cunt.

"So fucking full, Ronan. It feels so good."

Her head fell back and her hair brushed his thighs and tail. She used the armrests as leverage and lifted and dropped herself on his cock. Her hardened nipples rubbed against his chest. His cock could feel his tail moving inside her. *Grak. So much sensation.*

Their combined scent filled his nostrils. He extended his claws and they lightly pricked her ass. She moaned as she took him deeper and faster. His eyes hungrily traveled over her beautiful body—her heaving breasts bouncing, her neck extended, her mouth wide with pleasure, and her cunt clasping and sucking at his cock. *Her beauty is unmatched.*

"You're amazing, *caliana*. Use me for your pleasure. Let me see you come all over me. Drown me with your desire."

She moaned and panted heavily at his words. Her cunt squeezed around the ridges of his cock sending lightning up and down his spine. His hips and tail matched her increasing rhythm. Her head snapped forward and her passion-filled eyes met his.

"Come with me, Ronan. Now."

She slammed herself down on him, shifted her hips to rub her clit against his base node, and her body shuddered. Her pussy squeezed his cock and her ass clenched his tail so tightly he couldn't move within her. Her silken inner walls milked his orgasm from him, his seed leaving him in a hot rush. His fangs elongated, surprising him, then his body tensed and he roared as his climax seemed never-ending as she rippled around him. Aftershocks shook her cunt and traveled along his cock. They panted as their damp skin cooled.

She pressed her mouth to his and slipped her tongue in to play with his lazily. He retracted his claws and ran his hands along her supple spine, hugging her body close to his. His tail gently slid from her as her muscles relaxed.

"Mmm. Fantasy fulfilled," she said against his lips.

"Please let me know if you have other fantasies, *caliana*. I quite enjoy them."

They both laughed tiredly as she cuddled in his lap.

At the first colony, Ronan introduced Natasha to the leaders and their healer. She explained how to operate the special injection device which thawed a vaccine dose to the proper temperature before it could be administered. Although, they could thaw doses in a separate unit, she stressed that a dose was no longer effective eight hours after thawing. Proudly, he listened as she gave them a briefing on how measles normally manifests, how to treat it, and potential complications. She answered all questions patiently and competently. He could see that she made a good impression with this colony.

They continued to travel to each of the remaining colonies, only staying long enough to ensure everyone understood and leave ample supplies behind. Every new place they landed, she took a moment to appreciate the fact that she was on another planet. Her enjoyment wasn't affected by terrain or weather, just the wonder of actually stepping foot on a planet other than Earth.

Her attitude was one of the many traits he was coming to love about her.

In between colonies, they had sex all over the shuttle. Sometimes slowly and sweetly, other times they came together in a primal, carnal fashion. They talked a lot and he realized how lonely he had been over the years with no one who understood him. He loved her moods, even when she was cranky, because she always found some new way to delight him—the way she played with her hair, bit her lip, or furrowed her brow when she researched something.

Early during their trip, she asked him to teach her more about piloting the shuttle. Ronan enjoyed teaching her. She had a quick, orderly mind and good reflexes. The flash of self-pride when she achieved a new level of ability made him as proud as if he had done it himself.

With the last colony successfully behind them, they had two more days of travel before they hit the asteroid field near Millus. Natasha had laid in their course and set the autopilot with Ronan overseeing her actions—her face expectant when she looked at him.

"Good job, Natasha. You did very well."

She grinned. "That felt good to do it by myself, professor."

"I think you deserve a reward."

"Oh?"

"I have my own fantasies." He loved how her scent grew heavy with arousal so quickly.

"Do I need to do anything to help your fantasy along?" She fluttered her eyelashes at him.

"Lock the console and let me see that beautiful body."

She tapped the proper sequence on the console, then stood and slowly stripped for him. He palmed his growing erection as she flirtatiously turned her back to him and let down her hair. She slid her shirt from her shoulders, letting it catch on her elbows as she released the front catch of her bra. The clothing fell to the floor when she straightened her arms. Still facing away from him, she kicked off her shoes and shimmied her pants down her hips slowly before turning to face him clad only in barely-there panties.

Glistening wetness between her thighs soaked the panties. He growled as she walked toward him.

"No. Face the console and place your hands on it. Stick out that gorgeous ass of yours and let me admire it."

She inhaled sharply, her nipples hardening under his hot gaze. Following his instructions, she made a pretty picture, but he wanted more.

"Spread your legs wider, Natasha. I want to see you open for me." He stood and stripped quickly as she moved her feet further apart.

Ronan stroked softly from her nape to the small indentation above her ass.

"No, still not right."

Breathing heavily, she said, "Is there something I can do to make it right?"

He reached beneath her and pinched an erect nipple. She squirmed at the unexpected touch.

"Spread your arms as if you're flying, *caliana*. Put your weight on the console."

Natasha did as he said, moaning when her breasts came in contact with the cool plastic that covered the console. Her new position raised her ass higher.

"Oh, yes, you look lovely like that. A naked goddess streaking through space." He licked his lips as wetness dripped down her inner thighs. *I love how willing she is to play.*

He brushed her hair back from her ear and growled low. "I'm going to make you fly, my wonderful female."

"Please..."

He moved, knelt behind her, and pulled her panties to the side. He buried his face between her thighs and licked voraciously at the wetness seeping from her core. Rubbing his beard between her legs, her scent filled his senses, and he attacked her clit with a hungry tongue. She wriggled and moaned, trying to push harder against him. He drove her higher and higher and when her legs began to shake, he slowed his movements, ripped off her panties, and backed away.

"No," she wailed. "Ronan, I was so close."

Rising to his feet, he reached out and wrapped a handful of her hair around his arm and fisted it. Tugging slightly, he kicked her legs even further apart and lined his cock up to enter her from behind.

"Are you ready for me? I'm going to *grak* you hard."

She pushed her ass backwards. "Do it. Fuck me as hard as you want."

He bent his body over her back to breathe in her ear. "No, I'm going to fuck you as hard as you want." He straightened and entered her in one fast thrust, pushing her up against the console and lifting her onto her toes.

"Yes," she screamed. "More."

Pounding into her deep and fast, he kept hold of her hair so her back stayed arched. She met him thrust for thrust, groaning when his base node hit her rosebud. His tail circled underneath to play with her slippery clit.

He slapped her ass and she shrieked. More wetness poured from her making squelching noises as he worked to go as deep into her hot, clutching core as he could. His fangs elongated and he released her hair to grasp her hips in his hands. He pulled her back as he thrust forward.

"You are mine, *caliana*. No other male will ever see you this way." Unbidden, words poured from his mouth. "No one else can make you feel like this. A confident, primal female taking what she needs from her male. Tell me." He slammed into her harder.

"Yours. I'm yours, Ronan." Her body began to shudder as the heat built in his spine.

"Yes, Natasha, you are mine."

She gasped. "And you are mine. That cock belongs to me."

A groan erupted from the depths of his chest. "Yes, yours, *caliana*. I'll always be yours."

Her body writhed against his as her climax overtook her, which triggered his own. His back bowed with the force of his orgasm, shooting his seed into her depths as far as he could. Her cunt quivered and shook around his cock causing him to moan and his legs to weaken. He fell forward and wrapped his arms around her, cupping her breasts.

Sucking in gulps of air, he tried to slow his breathing as he dropped kisses along her temple and ear.

"My dear professor, I believe this was my favorite flying lesson yet." His chest rumbled with laughter, shaking both their bodies.

"I swear, female, one day you're going to kill me with that wonderful cunt."

She huffed. "But what a way to go."

Chapter 30

NATASHA'S NIPPLES WERE sore from rubbing on the console and her body felt well-used. She loved it. *Damn, when he goes all caveman, it really turns me on.*

She curled into him when he lifted and carried her to their quarters. Laying her on the bed, he left to get a warm washcloth to clean her up. Satiated, she enjoyed the attention. Her muscles felt loose and a nap sounded like a really good idea. She was just drifting off when he returned to cuddle with her under the sheet.

"Natasha, are you asleep?"

"Mmm, almost."

"Never mind. It can wait."

She lifted her head to look at him. "What?"

"I wanted to tell you something important, but I'm not sure how you'll take it."

Wide awake now, she watched his eyes. "You're not married, are you?"

"What? No, I'm not mated. At least, not yet." *Engaged? Promised?*

"Ronan, you're confusing me and making me worry along lines I've never thought would be an issue with you. Just tell me what's on your mind."

"My fangs have been elongating."

She stared at him. "Your fangs have been elongating. Okay, you're going to have to give me more to work with so I understand."

He took a deep breath. "I want to true mate with you."

True mate. Biological need to bite. Lifetime commitment. Oh, shit.

"I know we said we'd enjoy what time we had, but I want forever with you." Hopeful silver eyes watched her face carefully.

"Ronan, you're talking about a major commitment. I'm not sure I'm ready for that discussion."

His face fell. "I understand. I just wanted you to know." *I feel like I just kicked a puppy.*

"What we have is special. There's just so much uncertainty about both our futures. I admit I'm a little afraid to make that leap when we don't know what will happen on Costonia."

"It's okay, *caliana*. I do understand. You know how I feel and if you ever feel the same, I'm willing."

She kissed him tenderly. "I do care about you, Ronan, more than I've ever cared about another male. And I'm honored. I'm just not ready."

He brushed his fingers through her hair. "Hush. Sleep now."

Natasha settled back onto his chest and caressed his abdomen. She closed her eyes and focused on their breathing. *I'm afraid I can picture forever with you. I just don't know how to make it work.*

When Natasha awoke, she was alone. She padded naked to the sanitary facilities and relieved herself. Turning on the sonic shower, she admitted to herself she really missed water showers. Washing quickly, she brushed her teeth and hair before dressing in a T-shirt and panties. *I hope it's not awkward with Ronan this morning.*

She found him in the dining area making their morning meal. They'd long since demolished all of the goodies Ava sent, so they were down to synthesizer food. It wasn't bad, there just wasn't a large variety of choices on Ronan's shuttle.

When she attempted to bring up the true mating conversation, he stopped her.

"*Caliana*, if and when you are ever ready, we can speak of it more. But I don't want you to feel pressured to talk about it or worry about my feelings. I am grateful for whatever time we have together. I know, better than most, how circumstances can change suddenly."

Hugging and kissing him, she said, "You are the best, Ronan. I don't deserve you."

"Eat. More training for you today."

"Yes, sir."

The next day, they flew into the asteroid field. As a precaution, Ronan told her to wear her nanosuit under her clothing. Since they would be rejoining the *Invictus* soon, she agreed so she wouldn't have to hear the commander grumble about her not wearing it.

Ronan took the controls from her as they got closer, but explained everything he did. To have maximum power available to the thrusters, he turned off the cloaking and dampener.

It took them several hours to traverse the field with Ronan competently avoiding various sized asteroids with a gentle touch on the thrusters. As they left the field, Natasha felt her shoulders relax. *I'm glad Ronan guided us through. I'm not ready for something like that.*

Suddenly, the shuttle rocked.

"What the hell was that?" She looked at all the readouts trying to find an alarm or warning to tell her the cause.

"Zuvgran fighters. There." Ronan pointed. He tapped the console and the shuttle changed direction.

"What do we do?" *Fuck, fuck, fuck. Where the hell did they come from?*

"We try to avoid them for now and comm the *Invictus*. There are no significant defenses on this shuttle, just some shields."

The *Invictus* answered their comm. "Commander, we're in trouble," said Natasha.

"Status."

"Two Zuvgran fighters are attacking us. Ronan is attempting to avoid them, but we have no defenses other than shields."

"Position."

Ronan pointed and Natasha relayed the information to Durek. Durek ordered, "Maximum speed to those coordinates. Maintain cloaking." Turning back to Natasha, he said, "We'll be there as fast as we can."

In the background she heard someone say, "Commander, we're still a day away."

The shuttle took another hit and began listing to one side.

"*Grak*," Ronan spit out. "We're going to have to try to land on Millus."

Durek said, "Acknowledged." Turning to someone on the bridge, he said, "Track them and do not lose them."

An alert caught Natasha's attention. "We're getting a weak hit on one of those frequencies."

"Which one?" Durek leaned forward.

"The one ending in six, six, two. It's getting stronger the closer we get to the planet."

Natasha glanced at Ronan. "Is there anything I can do?"

"Make sure you're strapped in securely, *caliana*, and keep the *Invictus* informed as long as you can."

Natasha relayed information and watched Ronan struggle to get the shuttle in a good position to enter the atmosphere.

"Can you land us somewhere near water? We have to survive until the *Invictus* can get here."

"*Caliana*, we need somewhere to hide from those fighters. We can always take water from the shuttle with us."

"There," she pointed a few minutes later. "It looks like some kind of large structure."

"Old fighting pit. That might work."

"Did you hear that, *Invictus*?"

"Affirmative, we also have Natasha's tracker."

"Tell them Largon has the frequency for mine. I'll activate when I know we'll be stationary for a while."

"Acknowledged. We are coming for you."

The transmission cut out as they took another hit from a fighter. The shuttle wavered sideways before Ronan could straighten it out again.

"Natasha, as soon as we land, arm yourself and get your medical bag. If we have time, we'll grab some nutrition bars and water and a couple other things."

"Got it."

"If, for some reason, I don't make it, find a place to hide that's easily defensible and do your best to stay alive until the *Invictus* can retrieve you."

"None of that shit, Ronan. We do this together. You are not allowed to fucking die on me." Natasha hid her shaking hands by tugging on her restraints.

Ronan's fangs gleamed when he grinned darkly at her. "As you command, Natasha. No dying today."

The ground approached faster than Natasha liked. Ronan gave full power to the last remaining thruster to turn them and create a dust cloud behind them.

"Brace yourself," he yelled.

Natasha bent forward and covered her head. The shuttle hit the ground hard and slid forward aimlessly. Something fell from the ceiling, hit her on the head, and then...nothing.

Someone groaning woke Natasha. *Why does my head hurt? And who's groaning?*

She attempted to open her eyes but closed them quickly when she felt nauseous. Then she realized the pained noises came from her. She focused on her breathing and tried to remember what had happened. *Why can't I move?*

She patted herself and felt the restraints. *Shuttle. Zuvgran. Crash. Ronan!*

Breathing shallowly, she forced her eyes open a little at a time. Dust swirled outside the cracked viewscreen. The console looked damaged and unlit. Slowly she turned her head in Ronan's direction to see him slumped forward, blood on his temple.

She undid her restraints, testing her limbs. Everything appeared to be in working order but shaky. Blood dripped into her right eye and she gingerly touched her scalp. *Ouch. Head wound. Possible concussion. How long was I out?*

Cautiously, she stood, holding onto the console for support. She dropped to her knees in front of Ronan. She checked him for other injuries, especially around his neck, but everything appeared fine. Looking at his temple wound closer, it looked like a piece of the viewscreen flew into him when it broke. She called his name.

Not wanting to move him before he was conscious if she could wait, she tried to figure out what to do. *What did he say before we crashed? Oh, arm myself.*

She opened the compartment with the weapons and pulled out some knives and sheaths, as well as a couple blasters. Strapping a knife to each thigh, she stuck a small dagger in her boot. Dizzy, she worked her way back to Ronan with the other weapons she pulled out and tried to wake him again.

This time the groaning emanated from his chest. *Oh, thank god.*

"Ronan, can you hear me?"

"Natasha?"

"Can you open your eyes?" His eyes opened slowly and appeared unfocused.

"How many fingers do you see?"

"Huh?"

"Ronan, focus. How many fingers?"

"Two."

"Good. Slowly try to sit up and stop immediately if you feel any significant pain."

In uncoordinated movements, he followed her instructions, hissing when he tried to move his left arm.

"Let me see." She checked his arm gently. "I think you sprained your elbow."

"Okay." His eyes started to clear and he looked at her head in alarm. "You're bleeding."

"So are you. That happens in a shuttle crash or so I hear."

"Shuttle crash?" He paused. "*Grak.* The Zuvgran. We have to move. How long was I out?"

"I don't know. I was knocked unconscious, too. I grabbed some weapons." She gestured to the pile on the console.

He stood, wavering a little before gaining his balance. Strapping on weapons, he said, "Is your medical bag close?"

"Dining area."

Glancing at the dead console, he said, "*Grak.* No sensors to give us an idea of where the Zuvgran are. Okay, dining area for your bag and a limited amount of supplies, then we need to get out of here." *I'm so glad he's here to take charge. I'm in way over my head.*

They held onto each other for support and made their way to the dining area. She pulled the strap of her medical bag over her head and across her torso to free up her hands. Ronan grabbed two knapsacks and filled each with water pouches and some nutrition bars. He handed her the lighter one which she put on while he strapped on his.

When she turned toward the ramp, he caught her hand and shook his head. Putting a finger to his lips, he drew her into the cargo bay. He led her through to the secret area and pointed for her to sit on a cot. Confused, she followed his instructions. He opened a compartment, pulled out a medical scanner, and ran it over her body. He sighed in relief and put the scanner down to pull out supplies to clean her head wound.

Gently, he cleaned her wound, then ran a healing wand over it. She started to speak, but closed her mouth when he shook his head. *What the hell is going on?*

When he finished, she gestured for him to sit next to her. Then, she did the same for him. The scanner confirmed a sprained elbow. She pulled forceps out and removed the viewscreen fragment from his head. Fortunately, it didn't resume bleeding, so she cleaned and healed it. Finding an inflatable splint, she pulled it over his elbow and inflated it to keep his joint immobile at a ninety-degree angle.

He pulled out a tablet from another compartment. Silently, he tapped on it and frowned at what he saw. He turned it toward her. She could see four land vehicles getting larger. He tapped again and another scene showed a Zuvgran fighter circling in the air. *The tablet must tap into security cameras that don't rely on the shuttle's main power. Oh, fuck. They're coming for us.*

His shoulders drooped. He leaned close and whispered in her ear.

"They'll be here soon. Normally this area has a dampening field around it for trackers and heat to hide it, but it uses the shuttle's main power source. It won't take them long to find us."

"Would it be better to surrender peacefully?" she whispered back.

"I have no idea. I don't even know why Zuvgran are here. They were forced from Millus centuries ago and there have been no indications that they returned."

Natasha mulled it over for a little bit. "Wait. We got a hit on one of the trackers. Wurvez and Jevax might be here. Do you think we'll end up near them? It would be easier to escape with their help and a rescue attempt would go faster if all of us were together."

"True. But I don't know what they'll do to you in the meantime, *caliana*. You saw what they did to Teeka. I don't think I can handle having you hurt because I made the wrong decision."

"I don't like the idea of being assaulted and raped either. But I'm afraid if they have to work too hard to find us, they'll hurt both of us even worse."

She watched the internal debate in his eyes and knew by the defeated look that he would try it her way.

"Pretend to be disoriented when I open the ramp door. Do not struggle or fight. Let them disarm us." He held her tightly. "Sweet Goddess, please protect Natasha."

Her eyes filled with unshed tears. "We'll be okay. Hopefully, they'll keep us together."

He tapped his bracelet and his appearance changed to Svesti. He stood and held out his hand to her. She placed her hand in his, rose, and followed him to the ramp. At the door, she squeezed his hand, drew in a deep breath, and nodded. He hit the manual controls for the ramp and they stumbled down to the dusty planet holding onto each other. At the bottom of the ramp, they fell to their knees.

Vehicles roared to a halt, kicking up dust. Natasha and Ronan coughed. Multiple Zuvgran warriors surrounded them. She faked a dazed look and lack of comprehension when they ordered them to drop all the belongings in Zuvgran. The harsh guttural sounds of the language were easily recognizable.

"Help, we need help," she cried out in Galactic Standard. "Our ship crashed."

"Take them to the lab," one Zuvgran ordered. "The female's species is unfamiliar. The scientist might have a use for her."

"If not, we do." Harsh laughter sounded around them. *Oh, shit. Scientist or gang bang. Not a whole lot of good choices here.*

Natasha tried to keep her fear manageable. Ronan stiffened beside her. *Don't do it. Not yet. We're seriously outnumbered.*

They were stripped of their knapsacks and weapons, but the warriors failed to find the dagger in her boot. The Zuvgran placed restraints on both of them before dragging them to one of the vehicles.

The vehicles took them to the ruins of a fighting pit. They parked in an underground structure, then marched through dimly lit tunnels for awhile before they reached more modern, extremely bright tunnels. They passed a number of closed doors before they were led further underground to a series of cells. Some had force fields, some had bars, while others enclosed rooms with one-way mirrors.

Natasha covertly looked in all the cells, but most were unoccupied. Then she saw inside one of the enclosed rooms. There was a blue alien girl in a see-through white gown crouched in the corner. Pieces of a bed lay strewn around the room. A bloody Svesti was huddled naked in the corner furthest from the girl with what looked to be a piece of the bed sticking out of his upper thigh. *Wurvez! What have they done to you?*

The Zuvgran accompanying them laughed. "He still foolishly tries to maintain his honor. I hear the boss has a new torture planned for him soon." Natasha tried to keep from reacting to the scene in Wurvez' cell and the guard's menacing words, but her heart raced so fast she thought she was going to pass out. Surprisingly, it was Ronan's low growl that centered her emotions.

They shoved Ronan and her into a similar enclosed cell. One guard held a blaster to Ronan's head while the other removed her restraints. Her guard pointed to the bed. She tentatively went to the bed and sat on the edge with her hands folded. Eyes watchful, she internally sighed in relief when her guard pointed a blaster at her head while Ronan's guard took off his restraints. Both guards backed away towards the door, while she and Ronan remained motionless. As soon as they were gone, she hopped up and ran into Ronan's arms.

Chapter 31

RONAN'S HEART BEAT thunderously in his chest as he held Natasha. Having her in Zuvgran captivity frightened him more than he could articulate. Seeing the condition of the Svesti nearby didn't inspire confidence that he and Natasha were going to come out of this situation unscathed. And when the Zuvgran held a blaster to her head, his rage almost exploded out of him. *How dare they threaten her life?*

He maneuvered them to sit comfortably on the bed. When she began to speak, he nuzzled near her ear and whispered, "Cameras may have audio. Be careful what you say."

She paused before continuing in a normal voice. "Did you see that other cell? What do they do here?"

"I do not know. Nothing good, it seems."

"How's your head? Your elbow?"

"Both are fine. And your head?"

"No headache or nausea, so I think I'll be okay. I wish they left us our water, though."

"I can check the sink and see if there's drinkable water."

"No. Just hold me." She whispered, "I have a small dagger in my boot that they didn't find."

"You wonderfully resourceful female," he whispered back. "We'll hide it later. Given how the young Jalaxian was dressed, they may make us change our clothing."

"This keeps getting better and better," she said drily.

"How is it you can make me want to laugh under conditions like these?"

"Talent, I guess."

"Let's rest while we can and hope the *Invictus* gets here soon."

He laid her onto the bed facing the wall and spooned her from behind so his back faced nearest the cell door. Activating his tracker, he kissed her temple lightly. *They'll have to go through me to get to her.*

Hours later, Ronan woke when he heard footsteps outside their cell. He slowly turned over to face the door, keeping his eyelids lowered most of the way. The door opened and a tray of food slid across the floor. When the door shut with no one remaining behind, he relaxed.

Natasha said quietly, "Who was it?"

"Someone delivering food."

"Is it safe to eat anything they give us?"

"I don't know. My nose might sniff out common poisons, but unless a drug has a definitive scent to it, I might miss it."

"Water is more important for our survival right now." She paused. "Do we know what time of day it is?"

"Based on when we they captured us and how long I think we've been here, I think close to evening meal."

"Okay." She sat up and brushed her hair from her eyes.

He rose as well and moved to give her more room. "Did you get any rest?"

"Yes. I think between the crash, concussion, and stress of being captured, my body had no choice. It helped that you were holding me. It makes me feel safe." Her cheeks turned pink at her admission.

"I will always do my best to keep you safe." His thumb stroked her cheek where it was the pinkest. "This is a good color on you."

"You're too funny." She looked around. "Bathroom? Uh, sanitary facilities?"

He pointed to the far corner. "Next to the sink."

Disgust showed on her face. "A hole in the floor? You've got to be kidding me."

"No. I can stand in front of you to try to block anyone seeing you."

Figuring out the logistics took a few minutes, one of which was Natasha asking him to use his claw to cut a couple swatches from her shirt for her to use. From where he stood hiding her from view, Ronan could smell the embarrassment in her scent as she relieved herself. She rinsed her hands and the used swatch in the sink, leaving the swatch to dry. Then she wiped her hands on her pants and shrugged. *Even in adversity, she maintains her dignity.*

He picked up the tray and brought it to the bed since there was no other place to sit. It was simple fare consisting of cheese and hard rolls. There were two water pouches on the tray. He smelled and tested everything and deemed it safe for her to eat. When they were done, he placed the tray by the door and sat on the bed, leaning against the wall. His tail and arm wrapped around Natasha as they cuddled quietly.

"It's the waiting that's going to make us crazy, isn't it?"

"This must be torturous for you, Natasha, having nothing to do," he teased.

"It wouldn't be so bad if I had a tablet to work on. Or if there weren't cameras watching our every move."

They stopped talking when they heard howls of pain coming from the other cell. The anguished sounds continued non-stop for several minutes, then an agonizing scream followed by abrupt silence. Ronan looked down to see Natasha biting her lower lip and tears streaming down her face. He tucked her head against his shoulder and stroked her head and back. Her body shook as she silently sobbed and soaked his shirt. *Oh, caliana, I hope your friend survives. Goddess, I hope we all survive.*

The guards left them alone until morning, which had Ronan on edge. Hard rolls, cheese, and water arrived for them again. He made sure Natasha ate and they hid her dagger under the mattress. Not long afterwards, the guards returned.

Four of them came this time, all armed. They ordered Ronan and Natasha to stand against the wall. Then they restrained him with the manacles—one around each ankle and wrist.

"Move the wrong way, Svesti, and the next thing will be a pain collar."

Ronan growled. Natasha inched closer to him.

"You." The guard gestured with his blaster. "Sit on the bed."

Hesitantly, Natasha moved back to the bed and sat on the edge.

The guards moved to allow a scientist to enter. He was holding a vaccine dosage in his hand.

"What is this?" the scientist demanded.

"A vaccine for measles," Natasha said quietly.

"Are you trying to infect us?"

"No. We developed it for others, but it will help Zuvgran, too."

"I don't believe you."

Ronan could see Natasha getting angry. *This is not good.*

"Listen, mister. I don't care if you believe me. It's the truth. I recognized the disease that's spreading on Crestillia. The Svesti helped me develop a vaccine. We were trying to distribute it to some friends before the Svesti gave the information to your Emperor to use to inoculate your race. Unfortunately, that might not happen because your goons shot us down." *Stay calm, caliana.*

"I should inject you to see what happens."

Natasha shrugged. "Go ahead. I've been inoculated since I was a child. It won't help or hurt me."

"And your companion?"

"Svesti are immune to measles."

"Tell me more of this measles."

As on the colonies, Natasha gave a succinct, but thorough accounting of the disease, symptoms, complications, and treatments. Ronan could see the scientist's interest growing the longer she spoke.

"Come with me, human."

"Where are we going?"

"To my lab."

"For what purpose?"

"Whatever purpose I choose." The scientist began losing patience. "You may show above-level intelligence for a female of an inferior race, but you are still a prisoner. If you do not comply, you will be given a pain collar. Then you will be more than willing to do whatever we say."

Ronan shook his head slightly when she looked at him, willing her to avoid the pain collar. She stood.

"Fine. Can you at least release my companion?"

"He will remain as he is until you return. Whether or not he will be released will depend on your compliance."

Ronan met her eyes and hoped she saw encouragement in them. He'd stay in the restraints all day if it kept her safe from harm.

"Okay. Lead on."

The guards escorted Natasha and the scientist out of the room. One hung back to punch Ronan in the stomach. Ronan breathed through his mouth to control the pain.

"Just a preview of what you can expect, Svesti." Ronan narrowed his eyes at the Zuvgran male. *You will be the first to die.*

Time passed slowly as Ronan anxiously awaited Natasha's return. Not knowing what was happening to her kept a continuous growl sounding low in his chest and his claws extended.

Eventually the door opened and Natasha walked through. She looked angry, but unhurt. Ronan's heart settled into a normal rhythm.

One guard kept a blaster aimed at her head while another released him from the restraints. He rubbed his wrists to encourage blood flow. His sprained elbow ached. Once both guards stood at the door, the one holding Natasha shoved her at Ronan. He caught her before she could fall. The guards' laughter became muted as the door closed behind them.

Ronan ran his hands over Natasha's body gently.

"Did they hurt you?"

"Not really. Just pissed off. The scientist took some of my eggs, then injected me with a virus. He took more eggs and seemed angry when they were fine." She wore a self-satisfied expression. "There's more to explain, but not here."

"I was imagining all sorts of horrible things."

She rested her head on his chest. "I know. I was doing the same. I thought they might be torturing you when I wasn't here."

"We're together now." He moved them to the bed and settled her on his lap. His tail and hands stroked her body, reassuring himself she was fine.

"Did you learn anything useful?" He whispered into her hair.

"The facility seems large, but the only occupied cells are ours and the other one. The lab is located in a corridor behind the cells across from us."

"The other captives?"

She shuddered. "Wurvez looked unconscious facing toward the wall. His back was a mess, but the injuries did not look fresh. I couldn't see what they might have done to him last night. The female hasn't moved since when we came in."

"Are you in danger from whatever the scientist injected you with?"

Her lips curled against his throat. "I doubt it. It's confidential, but Talia was kidnapped and injected with a virus that kills human female fertility and Svesti male fertility. After she was rescued, we developed a vaccine to protect both races. The *Invictus* destroyed that lab, so the Zuvgran don't know that the virus worked at all. They don't know that we know about it or that our vaccine renders the virus inert."

"So you were already protected before he injected you?"

"Yes. Wurvez too. So are you. I had Ash'n give it to you when he inoculated you for measles." She stilled. "I should've gotten your permission. I'm sorry. I just wanted you protected and we weren't allowed to tell you about it."

"You're forgiven, *caliana.* I'm just glad you're safe."

"Ronan?" Natasha drew back to look at his face. "When we are rescued and in a safe place, I want to true mate with you."

His eyes searched hers. "But you said you weren't ready. That it was too fast."

"I know. But being here made me realize I love you. The thought of you being hurt kills me. The thought of being without you at all makes my heart weep. I don't know how we'll work it all out later and I don't care, so long as we are together."

Leaning down, he kissed her tenderly. "Once we're safe, *caliana*, if you feel the same way, I would be honored to true mate with you."

She sighed happily. "I won't be changing my mind."

The remainder of the day passed slowly. Twice more, food and water slid across the floor for them, but no one came in. Occasionally, guards would taunt them over the speakers, but Ronan and Natasha ignored them. As far as he was concerned, so long as they didn't try to touch or take Natasha, they could say what they liked.

"Why have they left us alone?" Natasha whispered as they spooned on the bed.

"I'm not sure. I think maybe because of you."

"What do you mean?"

"You're a human female and they need you as a test subject. But you also have knowledge of a disease they don't. That makes you valuable enough to keep unharmed for now. When the scientist doesn't feel the need to keep you unharmed anymore, I expect they will begin torturing me."

"Hopefully, they won't get the chance. They must be close by now."

"They still need to plan, but they'll come."

Ronan estimated it was the early hours of the morning when sounds of fighting woke him. Instantly alert, he shook Natasha's shoulder. She stiffened, then sat up next to him. He grabbed the dagger from its hiding place and hid it near his waist.

The door to their cell opened.

"They're here," said Tesix.

Ronan and Natasha stood and rushed to the door. Tesix removed a blaster from his weapons harness and handed it to Ronan. Ronan gave the dagger to Natasha, just in case. As they entered the hall, Durek led the others towards them.

"Are you okay?"

"Yes, Commander," Ronan answered. "One of your males is in the next cell badly injured. There is a Jalaxian female with him."

"The other male?"

"We haven't seen Jevax at all," Natasha said.

Durek turned to the group. "Tolvex, Rivezt, with me. The rest of you stand guard." He blasted the door controls for Wurvez' cell. Ronan held Natasha back as she tried to follow.

"No, *caliana.*"

"I'm a doctor."

"So is Rivezt."

Durek yelled, "Lady Natasha, come help the female. Someone find a stretcher."

Natasha wriggled out of Ronan's grasp and ran to the young female. She wrapped a blanket around her and helped her out of the room into the hall.

"They won't hurt him, will they? He is an honorable male," the Jalaxian asked.

"They're his brothers. They're here to rescue him," Natasha said.

Ronan wrapped his arm around Natasha's shoulders, guiding the females to a safer position as Largon ran into the cell pushing a stretcher.

"Wait here," Ronan said. He ran back to their cell and grabbed their blanket. Running back to Wurvez' cell, he tossed it to Tolvex, who nodded gravely at him.

"Move everyone out," said Durek. "Make sure there are no others to be rescued, then destroy this place once we have the data."

Svesti surrounded the stretcher and the females. Ronan kept close to Natasha. He saw the Jalaxian looking fearfully at Largon.

"He's not going to hurt you, young female. He's with us." Ronan tapped his bracelet and appeared as himself. The Jalaxian stared at him with wide eyes. "No one will hurt you with us."

Natasha drifted closer to the stretcher, but Tolvex shook his head, his braids snapping sharply.

"Rivezt will care for him, Lady Natasha. No one else." Tolvex' deep voice sounded anguished.

Natasha huffed in annoyance. *She just can't help herself—wanting to heal everyone around her as if no one else has the ability.*

Ronan glanced at the stretcher. Only Wurvez' head was visible—his body concealed by a blanket. *I hope he makes it.*

They passed multiple dead Zuvgran on their route. When they finally reached the end of the tunnels, Durek led them to one of the five waiting battle shuttles. Svesti warriors broke off to board other shuttles. *Grak. He wasn't taking any chances.*

Ronan helped Natasha and the Jalaxian strap in before doing so himself. The shuttle took off from the planet and the ride to the *Invictus* was made in silence except for Durek. The commander rattled off orders and received status reports while standing near Wurvez' stretcher.

Leaning back, Ronan laid his arm around Natasha's shoulders and his tail encircled her ankle. His body relaxed. *She's safe.*

Chapter 32

BACK ON THE *Invictus*, Natasha felt the worst of her tension leave her body. She hid it as best she could from Ronan, but she'd been terrified the entire time they were on Millus. *That's one planet I wish I could say I hadn't stepped foot on.*

They rushed to the med bay, where Ash'n took Wurvez to the private area where Teeka had been. Her eyes narrowed when she heard Ash'n order that no one was permitted entry except for Durek and Tolvex. *They're being very protective of Wurvez. He must be in really bad shape.*

Natasha picked up a scanner to check out the Jalaxian, whose name was Molla. Healer Markham took it from her.

"Hey, I was using that."

"You must be checked out yourself, Lady Natasha. I will look after both of you, as well as d'Olorg."

"I'm quite capable of working."

"You were in a shuttle crash and held in captivity. You will not be working until Healer Rivezt gives his approval."

"You can't do that," Natasha protested.

"It's already done, Lady Natasha. Go, eat some food, and get some rest. Healer's orders," Markham said with a stern expression.

Ronan, who had been speaking with Largon, approached.

"Is something wrong?"

"Markham won't let me treat Molla."

"Good." Ronan stood still as Markham scanned him, then used a healing wand on his wrists, ankles, and elbow.

"Same instructions as Lady Natasha. Food and rest," Markham proclaimed.

Natasha silently fumed as Ronan forced her from the med bay. Her ire grew as they walked the darkened corridors to her quarters. Once inside, she turned to face him.

"There was no reason I shouldn't treat Molla, or you, for that matter."

"Natasha..."

"No, I don't understand why you didn't back me up with Markham."

Ronan tunneled his hands into her hair and stepped close to her.

"*Caliana*, breathe. You are not useless. You do not have to be the one to heal everyone around you to prove your worth or be noticed. It is okay to let others help." He paused. "Even if you never healed another being again, I will still love you—just as you are."

Her eyes darted around, not meeting his gaze for long moments. Then her body sagged and she looked into his concerned, silver eyes.

"Is that what I'm doing?"

"I think so. You've been feeling out of control since the crash and healing others makes you feel in control." *Damn, I think he may be right.*

"Why do you want to be with someone as messed up as me?"

"You're not messed up, Natasha. We've been through a traumatizing few days. You just weren't ready to truly recognize how it affected your actions."

"You are a smart male, Ronan d'Olorg. Thank you." She leaned forward and kissed him as she hadn't been able to in days with cameras watching.

She stepped back and took his hand. After leading him to the bedroom, she began to undress him. Caressing the warm skin as she exposed it, she explored his contours with her mouth. Humming happily, she became distracted by his nipple. Taking her time, she licked and sucked. His cock hardened and she ground her lower body against it.

"Lift your arms," he said as he tugged her shirt over her head. Unfastening her pants, his hot hands slid under the material to cup and squeeze her ass before pushing the pants down. He pressed on the fastener for her nanosuit and slid a finger slowly downward to part it from neck to crotch.

Pushing the nanosuit down, his hands caressed her bare shoulders. He leaned forward to brush his beard along the tops of her breasts, keeping his horns away from her skin. She shivered and her head fell back. Soft, warm kisses dotted her flesh as he moved to her nipples. A fang dragged over a hard nub and she moaned. Then wet heat surrounded it and the suction sent riptides of pleasure to her clit. She clutched at his back, reveling in the bunching of his muscles as he worshipped her breasts.

Sometime later, they were on the bed, naked and rubbing against each other. The sensual fog dimmed her memory of undressing and moving, and she didn't care in the least. She just wanted more of him. Her fingers encircled his tail and followed it to the base of his spine where it was thicker. Squeezing lightly, she smiled when his hips jerked. *Another sensitive place.*

"True mate with me, Ronan." He stilled and gazed into her eyes.

"Are you sure, *caliana*? We don't know what the future holds."

"Absolutely. If you have to leave Costonia, I'll go with you. All I need is you."

Joy shone from his adoring face. "I am honored, Natasha."

He dropped light kisses all over her face. His hands followed her torso to her hips, while his tongue licked a wet wave of heat down her abdomen. Maneuvering himself lower, he gently spread her legs and kissed the apex of her thighs.

His mouth and tongue lavished attention on her clit, while his tail slipped inside her pussy to thrust gently. Squirming, she chased his clever tongue. Her hands clasped his horns and tugged him closer. His groans against her sent delicious chills along her nerve endings. When he gently grazed her clit with a fang, she screamed his name and bucked uncontrollably. Her pussy clenched on his tail, holding it immobile as she rode the tsunami of pleasure. His tongue never stopped moving and his scruff teased her skin.

Breath uneven, her body lay still except for her heaving chest. She looked down at him, loving the heat in his eyes and the satisfaction on his wet face. His tail withdrew from her inner walls and he kissed her hip. Then he meandered his way back up her body with his hands, mouth, and tongue.

"I will love and adore you, Natasha, every day of our lives. You never have to be anyone but who you are with me." His words were interspersed between his reverent ministrations to her flesh. "I will be your anchor when you need one. I will help you fly when you reach for the stars. There is nothing we can't face together." He hovered over her lips. "There is no other female for me, *caliana*. Without you, I am nothing." Tenderly, his mouth covered hers and his hard cock entered her pussy slowly.

She broke off the kiss and looked him in the eyes, hoping all the love she felt for him showed. "You are the only male for me, Ronan. Tomorrow means nothing if you aren't there to share it with me." Her hands caressed his jaw and she pulled him close again. "True mate with me and make me yours forever."

His mouth crashed down on hers and their tongues clashed wildly as their passion spun out of control. Her fingernails scored his back as he pumped his hips in a hard, fast rhythm. His tail played with a nipple and she rubbed against it wanting more. She bent her knees to push against his hips harder.

"Deeper, Ronan," she cried. "So close."

His hand snuck under her to wrap around her shoulders from the back. He pulled her tighter against him. Sweat dripped from both their bodies and their moans grew louder. His base node slapped her clit over and over while his hard cock filled her voracious pussy.

Her orgasm began at her toes and swiftly worked upwards along her body. Her pussy spasmodically clenched and she screamed his name. She bit down hard on his shoulder.

Ronan roared her name and thrust deeper. His back bowed and he nuzzled her shoulder before his fangs pierced her flesh. A sharp pain, then more orgasmic pleasure liquefied her veins as his cock vibrated. Her vision turned white, and she felt as if her body exploded into millions of pieces before reforming. When she returned to herself, he was licking her shoulder and breathing heavily.

Panting, she said, "Holy shit, Ronan, that was incredible."

He lifted his weight onto his elbows and brushed her hair from her damp face.

"My cock vibrated. It's never done that before."

Her hands smoothed along his back.

"I'm pretty sure that's what I felt." Her eyes traced his beloved face, then she looked lower to see if she'd broken the skin when she bit him. "Uh, Ronan?"

"Mmm?"

"Your clan marking." At her words, he pulled back and looked down at his chest.

"Is it gold now?"

"Yes."

His finger touched below her collarbone.

"You have one."

"What?" Sitting up abruptly, she turned her chin and saw what he saw.

"Fated mates?" Ronan's face shone with wonder. "I didn't think that would ever be possible for me."

"Fated mates. Wow." Natasha let that information settle inside her. *That feels right.*

"The Goddess has blessed us."

Natasha started laughing so hard tears ran down her face.

"*Caliana,* are you okay?" His eyes grew concerned and he sat up.

"Talia," she gasped. When she finally had herself under control, Natasha said, "Talia told me there were other benefits to being fated mates but refused to elaborate. She said I would be jealous if I never experienced it." She gave him a quick, happy kiss. "I'm betting vibrating cocks is what she meant."

Humor lit his eyes. "I hope it's a benefit. It definitely adds a certain something to making love to you." He pulled her body against his. She swore her flesh sighed in contentment. He played with her hair while her fingers danced over his body.

"Ronan, I love you."

"I love you too, Natasha."

"But there's one thing I forgot to make clear before we mated." His body stiffened.

"What's that?"

"If we're going to be using your shuttle to travel a lot, you have to install a water shower. I hate the sonic shower." Her lips curled up as a surprised belly laugh erupted from him. *Yum. Look at those abs contracting.*

"As you wish, *caliana*. I'll make it happen somehow."

Much later, after a couple rounds of testing cock vibrations, Natasha snuggled against Ronan, her back to his front. As she drifted off to sleep, she sent a silent message out into the heavens.

Babushka, you always told me that someday there would be a man who loved me as I am and would help me fly. You were right. If you had anything to do with Ronan and me finding each other, thank you. If not, and you come across the Goddess, thank her for us, please. I finally found a home and it's not a city or country or even a planet. It's in his arms.

As she drifted off to sleep, she felt her hair brushed back from her face and light kisses on her brow. The scent she associated with her *Babushka* combined with flowers filled her nostrils. *It's just my imagination, isn't it?*

Recap

Races thus far

Human - Enough said.

Svesti - Warrior Race. About seven feet tall, skin in various shades of bronze, semi-retractable fangs, tails, and retractable claws. Ruled by a King. Honorable race protecting many regions of space from the Zuvgran, including near Earth. Most Svesti females died or were rendered infertile thirty Earth years prior due to a virus released by the Zuvgran. Plural is Svesti.

Crestillian - Reptilian Race.

Durelian - Mercenary Race. About seven feet tall, orange skin, three bulbous black eyes.

Ermipa - Mining Race. About four feet tall, furry, round head, oval eyes.

Estalan - Sybaritic Race. Known for its quality liquors and drugs.

Frezzian - Mercenary Race. Adverse to personal risk. Considered dishonorable.

Jalaxian - Warrior Race. About seven feet tall, blue skin, fangs, retractable claws, and tail. Considered honorable. Many work as mercenaries after the Zuvgran decimated their world fifty Earth years ago.

Mostiffian - Mammalian Race.

Nulorian - Mammalian Race.

Pellotian - Avian Race. Green skin and wings.

Praxite - Mammalian Race. Lavender skin and tails. Females have three breasts.

Romittel - Mammalian Race.

Straxian - Mammalian Race. Brown skin

Wrestikan - Mammalian Race. Four arms and red skin. Home planet was Himita Prime.

Zuvgran - Warrior Race. About seven feet tall, gray skin, fangs, claws, and horns. Ruled by an Emperor. Dishonorable race that invades planets to strip them of their resources and take the inhabitants as slaves. Considered violent. Plural is Zuvgran.

take the inhabitants as slaves. Considered violent. Plural is Zuvgran.

Planets and Space Stations thus far

Earth - Really not the center of the universe as humans might believe.

Costonia - Svesti Home World.

Crestillia - Crestillian Home World. Zuvgran-controlled.

Himita Prime - Wrestikan Home World. Zuvgran-controlled.

Millus - Unoccupied planet outside of Costonian galaxy.

Nulorn - Trading planet halfway between Pellotia and Talonka Six.

Pellotia - Pellotian Home World. Zuvgran-controlled.

Praxis - Zuvgran-controlled.

Romitte - Zuvgran-controlled. Closest planet to Lestanus system.

Straxis - Agricultural and trading world. Sixth planet in the Lestanus system.

Talonka Six - Mining world closer to Costonia than Earth. Fourth planet in the Lestanus system.

Theron - Space Station approximately one quarter of the distance from Earth to Costonia.

XB9428B - Uninhabited planet, home to a Zuvgran lab.

Svesti Houses

 **Davelk** - Ruling House of Costonia.

 **Binova** - Primarily merchants.

 **Fresida** - Primarily educators and scientists.

 **Glixon** - Primarily merchants.

 **Kreliz** - Primarily scientists.

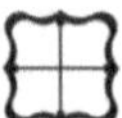 **Midnar** - Primarily agriculture.

 **Nuxar** - One of the two Houses that strictly adhere to the old ways of worship.

 **Ruxila** - Primarily agriculture.

 **Srotix** - One of the two Houses that strictly adhere to the old ways of worship.

 **Troliv** - Primarily merchants.

 **Vramel** - Primarily warriors and educators.

 **Yula** - Many Svesti healers come from House Yula.

 **Terran** - New human clan marking.

Characters

Humans

Natasha Petrov - Russian, medical doctor.

Lin Chang - Chinese, botanist.

Rachel Llewellyn - British, MI-6.

Emmy Norton - Australian, hacker.

Talia Sullivan - American, U.S. Ambassador of Interplanetary Relations.

Ava Taylor - Canadian, chef.

Svesti

King Traxen Sovex of House Davelk - King of the Svesti.

Lieutenant Triv'n Brauvix of House Kreliz - Communications officer on the *Invictus*.

Lieutenant Hozan Crulex of House Yula - Science office on the *Invictus*.

Commander Vared Durek of House Ruxila - Commander of the space cruiser, *Invictus*, the flagship of the Svesti military. First cousin to the king.

Merix Hunnek of House Nuxar - Head of aquiponics area on the *Invictus*. Rank - Major.

Grulen Jevax of House Midnar - Warrior.

Gal'n Kalix of House Binova - Security officer.

Rexus Markham of House Yula - Healer on the *Invictus*. Rank - Captain.

Nerid Mantoor of House Glixon - Warrior.

Talen Previv of House Fresida - Warrior. Head Cook on the *Invictus.*

Ash'n Rivezt of House Yula - Head healer on the *Invictus.* Rank - Captain.

Narilla Rivezt of House Yula - Council member, Main Medical Advisor, Master Healer, Ash'n's grandmother.

Nerob Sinoaz of House Troliv - Healer on the *Invictus.* Rank - Captain.

Lieutenant Devik Tolvex of House Vramel - Head security officer on the *Invictus.*

Clen'n Vepiv of House Nuxar – Warrior and medic.

Lieutenant Leriv Volax of House Kreliz - Supply Master on the *Invictus.*

Lieutenant Gat'n Wrox of House Fresida - Head engineer on *Invictus.*

Lieutenant Karid Wurvez of House Binova - Head tactical officer on the *Invictus,* second in command of the space cruiser.

Brestov Xoriv of House Fresida - Security officer.

Saletta Yemez of House Ruxila - Ronan's mother.

Zuvgran

Largon d'Ayen - Jorn d'Olorg's best friend and surrogate father to Ronan.

Jorn d'Olorg - Ronan's father.

Other

Ronan d'Olorg -Svesti-Zuvgran hybrid. Son of Jorn and Saletta.

Marris d'Olorg -Svesti-Zuvgran hybrid. Ronan's sister.

Annika - Pellotian-Zuvgran hybrid.

Brenos - Pellotian-Zuvgran hybrid.

Kito Dresine - Wrestikan. Shop owner on Nulorn.

Flitos - Pellotian-Zuvgran hybrid.

Gromm - Wrestikan-Zuvgran hybrid.

Herrah - Wrestikan-Zuvgran hybrid.

Molla - Jalaxian female.

Rina - Pellotian-Zuvgran hybrid.

Overseer Roho - Ermipa on Talonka Six, head of the Veba Mine.

Talos - Pellotian teacher.

Yostal - Mostiffian-Zuvgran hybrid.

Zela - Crestillian-Zuvgran hybrid.

Svesti Words thus far

Bataavi - Cherished one.

Bloniv - Spice similar to Earth's turmeric, but grows in tube-like clusters.

Brellia - Small, rumik-filled pastry.

Caliana - Beautiful female.

Cold season - Comparable to Earth's winter in the northern hemisphere.

Crek - Fuck.

Drelix - Spice similar to Earth's ginger, but grows in tube-like clusters.

Estrecaro - Beloved grandson.

Forliza - Flower similar to Earth's jasmine, but with purple petals.

Harvest season - Comparable to Earth's autumn/fall in the northern hemisphere.

Hot season - Comparable to Earth's summer in the northern hemisphere.

Kirani - Female feline found in the wild. Similar to Earth's lioness.

Leringa - Fruit that has a hint of spice when ingested.

Lobile - Purple tuber, cross between Earth's potato and sweet potato.

Lunar - Month.

Maxiem - A large animal that resembles a hybrid between Earth's ox and cow. Used as a source of meat, milk and beasts of burden.

Mentok - Similar to Earth's myna bird, but larger and with plumage reminiscent of an Earth's peacock. Chatters incessantly.

Milara - Small brown bird with periwinkle/white chest and underside of wings. Known for its cunning.

Naroon - Large furry animal, similar to Earth's ape, with blue fur. Gregarious and known to be silly in their family groups.

Pertiza - Creamy yellow sweet yogurt made from maxiem milk.

Picana - Little one.

Plostiv - Meat similar to Earth's chicken.

Renewal season - Comparable to Earth's spring in the northern hemisphere.

Ristern - Ermipa organ that filters dangerous gases.

Rulah - Small, furry animal similar to Earth's cat.

Rumik - Meat similar to Earth's ground beef. Comes from maxiem.

Shurlix - Similar to Earth's tomato, but yellow.

Solar - Year.

Tempika - Green berries that taste tart, but also sweet.

Trezoura - Capital city of Costonia.

Trulet - Similar to Earth's oak tree, but with dark blue leaves and orange bark.

Valadium - Steel-like ore when tempered is one of the hardest substances known in the universe.

Wimma - Blue citrus fruit similar to Earth's lime.

Woolah - Red flower that blooms on Costonia during Harvest season.

Yeddom - Orange bean-like vegetable that tastes like Earth's asparagus.

Young – Baby/infant.

Youngling – Child.

Yuffa - Plant similar to Earth's aloe, but with orange ball-like leaves.

Other

Ermipa

Ristern - Extra organ that filters out air impurities.

Pellotian

Annum - Year.

Zuvgran

Grak - Fuck.

Thank you for reading Ronan and Natasha's story. If you enjoyed this book, please leave an online review where you purchased it. This lets other readers know whether they might enjoy it, too!

If you'd like to hear about Wavy's other books, you can sign up for her newsletter or find her social media links at wavymartin.com.